STAR CAT

BOOK TWO: PINK SYMPHONY

Star Cat: Pink Symphony (Book 2)

Written by Andrew Mackay

Edited by Ashley Rose Miller

Cover design by Kveather

ISBN: 9781983072390

This is a work of fiction. Names, characters, places and incidents either are products of the author's imagination or are used fictitiously. Any resemblance to actual persons, living or dead (or somewhere in between), events, or locales is entirely coincidental.

Chapters

Chapter 1

How long had it been? Twenty minutes? Twenty days? Months? Years?

No one knew.

No one was even aware of what had happened.

The least likely member of Space Opera Beta to ascertain what had happened was Jelly Anderson. Being a cat, she had no concept of space or time - you know, the things we value and live our lives by. The crew weren't much help, either.

Tripp Healy, the assumed captain of Opera Beta, lay unconscious across the flight deck.

He was the first thing Jelly saw when she opened her eyes.

The ship wasn't moving. Everything was eerily silent by all accounts. Whatever happened when she'd forced the ship through the pink light show on Enceladus was beyond comprehension.

It was either venture into Saturn's moon or stick around to be rescued. With just seventy-two hours of oxygen? Sticking around would have prolonged the misery.

If rescue ever came, of course.

Even if it did it would have been five hundred days too late…

The Control Deck

Space Opera Beta - Level One

Jelly rolled around on the floor and stretched her legs. She felt waves of muscular atrophy disappear within seconds. A quick lick around the mouth, and she was up and at 'em.

She trundled toward the flight deck and ran her face along Tripp's heel in an attempt to catch his attention.

He didn't budge.

"Meow," she cried and looked up at him. A couple of blinks squeezed a blob of liquid out from her right eye. It splashed to the floor next to the sole of her captain's shoe.

The communications console buzzed to life. It had been humming ever since she woke up a few moments ago.

A familiar holograph appeared above her head. A book named Manuel, whizzing through its pages, acclimatized itself to the result of having gone through a wormhole - or a portal - whatever that *thing* was on Enceladus.

"Meow."

Manuel fluttered above her head and folded the outer edges of his pages toward her. "Greetings, Miss Anderson."

"Meow."

"I beg your pardon?"

Jelly yawned and revealed her fangs. For the briefest of moments it looked like she was screaming. She hopped onto the deck and nosed around the controls. Her infinity whiskers arrived at the yellow thruster lever. The same one that had blasted them through Saturn's sixth largest moon and saved their lives.

"What are you doing, Miss Anderson?" Manuel shifted across the deck for a better view of Jelly pawing away at the plastic handle.

It didn't move, still locked into *thrust* mode.

"Meow."

Jelly hadn't meant to use it. She wanted to draw Manuel's attention to the action she'd performed to rescue the ship.

"Yes, very good," Manuel said. "I'm afraid I don't know where we are."

"Meow," Jelly turned to the expansive flight deck windshield expecting to see stars, or some evidence of where they were. Instead, she was greeted by a black canvas. They may as well have been shut inside a capsule for all the good the visuals were.

Just then, a haze of pink dust seemed to dance from the right of the screen, like a blotch of paint thrown across a black bed sheet.

The event perturbed Jelly. The effect looked creepy - as if an alien had spewed across the screen.

In an attempt to gain some protection, Jelly sniffed around Tripp's face. His right cheek lay across the panel, exposing the majority of his face. His nose twitched, covered, in part, by his pink tears.

Jelly's wet nose sniffled around his, causing his closed eyelids to flutter. Her action was enough to make him cough and splutter into a state of awareness.

"What the—?" he said, opening his eyes and spluttering back to consciousness. "What's g-going on?"

"Good morning slash afternoon slash evening, Tripp," Manuel said.

Tripp groaned and pressed his hands to the console. He pushed himself upright in the pilot's seat and blinked, clearing the gunk away from his eyes. "What happened?"

Manuel took a moment to reveal not very much at all. "In short, we have absolutely no idea."

"Why did you say morning slash afternoon?"

"In short, I have absolutely no idea what the time is, either."

"Jelly?" Tripp turned to the cat looking up at him and ran his fingers over her head. "Hey, girl. Are you okay?"

"Meow."

"Thank God," Tripp jumped out of his seat, intending to run over to the communications console. He lost his footing, stumbled forward and dropped to his knees like an infant. "Oh God, I don't feel too well—"

Manuel interrupted, "It's better you take time to orient

yourself. Please don't rush."

Tripp spat a lump of phlegm to the floor. It was all he could do to not spew everywhere. It wasn't until he glanced at the gelatinous substance that he realized it was pink.

"Huh?"

The inebriating effects of having traveled through Enceladus had an adverse influence on his stomach.

"My organs feel like pâté."

"That's quite common," Manuel said. "It's something of a miracle your body wasn't flung around the flight deck when we went through whatever that pink thing was."

"Enceladus?" Tripp staggered to his feet and wiped his face. "We went through Enceladus?"

"It would appear so."

"My God," Tripp thumped the communications console switch.

Jelly hopped after him and climbed onto the comms seat. Tripp stood back and inadvertently knocked the side of the chair with his hip. It sent Jelly spinning around - the result making her look like a dizzied, carnival fool.

"Whoops," he caught the backrest and stopped the rotation, "Sorry, pet."

"Meow."

"Manuel?" Tripp waited for the screen to fire up. "Please tell me that Anderson and I aren't the only ones left alive."

"I'm afraid I cannot confirm anything. For some reason, I am unable to perform a geo-scan on Opera Beta. I can only see the contents of the flight deck which, considering we're already here, is rather useless."

"You don't say," Tripp spat, knowing anxiety was due any moment, "Why isn't the comms deck working?"

"I don't know."

"Come here, girl," Tripp scooped Jelly into his arms and examined her face. "Let me see you."

Jelly stared into Tripp's eyes as he cradled her. She

seemed at peace. Nothing out of the ordinary about her face, body or demeanor gave rise to concern.

"How are you, girl?"

"Meow," Jelly exercised her infinity claws on Tripp's sleeve.

"Ah, da-da," he protested, unhooked one of the sharp ends from the material, "Move your paw, girl."

Whizz, whizz. She moved all four claws and her new thumb around, demonstrating that she was perfectly fine. "Meow."

Tripp smiled, satisfied that she was uninjured and in proper operating order. Which was more than could be said for Manuel.

"Good," Tripp released Jelly onto the chair and made for the door. "We need to find our friends and make sure they're okay. Okay?"

"Meow," Jelly seemed to agree.

Tripp snapped his fingers over his shoulder as he reached the panel on the wall. "Manuel?"

"Yes, Tripp?"

"Do whatever you can to get the comms back on, please."

"I'll try my best, Commander."

"Commander?" Tripp stopped and let out a sarcastic sigh. "I'm the *captain*, Manuel. After Katz perished with Alpha."

"Oh," Manuel floated back, apologetically, "Is Captain Katz no longer with us?"

"Are you serious right now?" Tripp remembered everything. He couldn't believe Manuel wasn't able to. A quick, informal diagnostic was required. "Manuel? Don't mess around, tell me you remember."

"I'm sorry, Tripp. I *do* remember now—"

"—I don't believe you. Don't take this the wrong way, Manuel, but I want only quantitative responses. I need reassurance that you're fit and operational. Now, tell me about Enceladus."

Tripp suspected Manuel was buying himself some sympathy - or at least some time. "I can assure you that this isn't necessary, *Captain*."

"Are you disobeying a direct order?" Tripp asked, close to throttling the transparent image hovering in front of him. "Answer me."

"No, Captain."

"Okay. I won't ask again," Tripp said. "Tell me about Enceladus."

Manuel flipped through his pages and arrived at a picture of an oblong pastry with a meat and vegetable filling. The image fizzed and shifted around.

"It is a tortilla that covers a range of meats and vegetables, often containing a hot—"

"—What?"

"—Chili Sauce."

"That's *enchiladas*, you moron."

"Meow," Jelly added.

"Oh," Manuel busied himself by flipping through his pages. One by one, they revealed a blank slate. Several of them appeared torn and incomplete.

"Manuel, I'm sorry. You've taken a lot of damage. You need recalibrating."

"I feel I am able to autopilot," Manuel explained. "I can run a check on—"

"—No, you've demonstrated that you're *unable*," Tripp butted in, "I want you to shut down. Just temporarily until I do a sit-rep."

"But, Tripp—"

"—Don't take it personally, Manuel," Tripp beckoned Jelly over to the door with him. "Go offline. Just for an hour or so. We can't afford to have you confuse H2O with waste water."

"I'm not stupid, Tripp," Manuel slammed his covers together in a strop.

"I'm afraid for the moment you are. Please power down. I promise I'll wake you up when I figure out what's going on."

"*Fine*." Manuel blurted. He vanished from the room completely, leaving a befuddled Tripp to stare at Jelly for a reaction.

"Crazy, huh?"

"Meow."

"Out of all of us, Manuel should know better. If he's not fully operational then he should be shut down until we can fix him."

Jelly ducked her head and retracted her claws.

"Come on, girl," Tripp held his palm to the wall panel, "Let's go check on the others."

The door slid open, allowing the pair out of the control deck.

Chapter 2

Something felt *off* to Tripp as he walked across Beta's level one corridor.

The entire ship felt like it had powered down. The subtle rumblings and vibrations that he'd become accustomed weren't present.

For the first time since they'd left Earth he could hear his own footsteps clanging against the metal grille as he walked. Jelly turned a corner just behind him, anxious to find out what had happened to her *humans*.

"Let's head to Medix and find your mommy," Tripp held his forearm to his mouth. "This is Captain Healy. Does anyone read me?"

Nobody responded. The radio device on his arm seemed flatter than normal. No static or any sign of life.

"I repeat, this *is* Captain Healy transmitting on Individimedia. The radio and internal comms are down," he stopped in his tracks, "Can anyone read me?"

If Tripp felt alone during the course of their mission, it was nothing compared to how he was feeling right now. All he had was a confused autopilot and a cat for company. With the comms down the universe felt smaller than ever.

Tripp squinted at the door to Medix thirty feet ahead of him.

"I don't like this."

Clunk.

The sound of a shifting metal object thundered along the corridor from the far end. Another turn in the corridor.

A faint sniffing followed the unusual noise.

"What's that?" Tripp whispered to Jelly. She pricked up her ears and moved in front of Tripp, investigating the source of the sound.

"No, no," Tripp her aside with his boot, "Stay there."

"Meow."

"Who's there?" Tripp reached for his Rez-9 firearm on his belt.

The sniffing stopped, as did all sign of life from the turn in the corridor. Tripp unhooked his gun and pointed it forward. "I said who's there?"

"Meow," Jelly seconded Tripp's question.

"Stay back, girl. We don't know what's—"

A silhouetted figure moved in front of the screen door to Medix. A familiar profile outline - tall, voluptuous, and with shoulder-length hair.

"Who are you?" Tripp asked.

The figure lowered her head to her opened hands and sobbed. Her voice sounded familiar, although she hadn't actually spoken.

"Bonnie?"

The figure lowered her arms, revealing the outline of a Rez-9 in her right hand.

"What's h-happening to me?" The figure asked herself through her tears.

"Hey," Tripp shouted down the corridor, "What are you doing?"

His hollering caught the woman's attention. The figure turned forty-five degrees and held her Rez-9 firearm at Tripp, "Where am I? Who are you?"

He squinted, trying to figure out who - or what - was standing in front of him.

"Bonnie? Is that you?"

Jelly hissed, shaken by the strange person's presence.

The figure stepped toward Tripp, keeping her gun pointed at him. She entered a shaft of light from one of the bulbs on the ceiling.

It was *her* - a confused, upset, and pink-splattered Bonnie Whitaker. "Who are you?"

"It's *me*. Tripp Healy."

"Who?" Bonnie pushed her gun forward, threatening to blow his head off. "How do you know my name?"

"What?"

"I said how do you know my name?" Bonnie squealed through her tears, "You don't know *me*."

"You're… one of us."

Bonnie kept her gun aimed at Tripp's face. "Don't come any closer."

Tripp offered his surrender and held out his arms. "Okay."

"You *tell* me where I am and how I got here."

"We don't know, Bonnie. We went through some sort of wormhole on Enceladus. We don't know where we are—"

She blasted a warning shot at Tripp. The charge streaked past his shoulder and blew a hole in the side of the wall.

"Jeez," Tripp held his hands up in surrender, "What the hell—"

"—I swear to God I will kill you. Let me out of here."

"Let you out of here? What are you talking about?"

Bonnie screamed again, close to rupturing her vocal chords, "Where am I?"

"Wait, wait," Tripp tried. "What do you remember? Did you just wake up?"

The question resonated with Bonnie's desire for answers. Tripp could see the tactic worked when she tilted her head at Jelly.

"Yes, I did."

"Please don't shoot us," Tripp said. "We've just woken up, too. You're confused, just like we are."

"What are you talking about?"

"Space Opera Beta. You know what that is, don't you?"

"No," she yelled, "I don't remember anything."

"You're a cosmologist," Tripp said. "You're Bonnie Whitaker, and you're a part of our team."

"Liar," Bonnie aimed the gun at Tripp's head. "You're trying to trick me. I want to go home to my husband and son."

"Where are they, Bonnie?" Tripp tried to rescue himself from death and convince Bonnie he wasn't the bad guy. "Go on. I'm listening. Tell me where home is."

"I don't know."

"That's right, you *don't* know," Tripp nodded at the firearm in her hand. "And why would we give you a gun if we were keeping you here against your will?"

She looked at the Rez-9 in her hand and tried to calculate the information. "I don't know."

"Bonnie, trust me. You can't do anything hasty if you don't know all the facts. Please."

"No, no," Bonnie yelled, "You're lying. Tell me where I am."

"I told you already. You're on Space Opera Beta on a rescue mission on behalf of USARIC."

"USARIC?" Bonnie asked, none-the-wiser.

"My God, you really don't remember, do you?"

A pink tear rolled down Bonnie's cheek as she cried. "I just want to go home…"

"We all do, Bonnie."

She closed her eyes and gave up the will to live.

"Now, just put the gun down…"

Bonnie lifted her head and stared at Tripp. "There's one way I can get out."

"What?"

Bonnie lifted the barrel of the Rez-9 to her temple and threatened to shoot herself.

"No!" Tripp said, reaching his hand out. "Don't do that—"

"—I'm sorry," she hooked her index finger around the trigger.

"Meow," Jelly flapped her tail, trying to divert the woman's attention.

"Bonnie, no!"

Tripp launched forward, flinging his body in her direction. He threw out his hands and attempted to grasp the gun from hers.

ZAP!

He didn't reach her in time.

The gun flew from her hand - something had hit it before Tripp got anywhere near her.

"Agh!"

The bullet flew out from the barrel - but missed the side of her head and flew into the wall.

Strands of her hair feathered into the air from the blast as Tripp pushed her to the ground.

Bonnie looked up from underneath him to see a tall man in an exo-suit looking down at the pair. He adjusted the titanium glove on his right hand. "Bonnie? What's gotten into you?"

She screamed at the top of her lungs. "Help! Help!"

Tripp turned over and saw Jaycee smiling at him.

"Hey, Tripp."

"Jaycee," Tripp stumbled to his feet and patted the giant on the back. "You're here."

"Of course I'm here," he said, looking down at Bonnie. "She was about to blow her brains out."

"I know."

"What did you do to her?"

"I didn't do anything," Tripp collected Bonnie's Rez-9 from the floor and pointed it at her. "She's out of her mind."

"Probably blew a fuse when we entered Enceladus," Jaycee took out his K-SPARK shotgun and cocked it. "We better get her regenerated. Or whatever it is we do to them."

Bonnie remained on the floor, completely overwhelmed by her assailants. She pushed her top half up by her elbows and kicked her feet against the ground.

"Hey, Bonnie," Jaycee said. "Seems you're suffering from a touch of amnesia, there."

"Brain damage, more like,' Tripp said.

"P-Please, h-help me," she wiped a pink tear from her cheek, "I just want to go home."

"Still crying pink?" Jaycee asked, close to blasting her to smithereens. "You're hysterical. Get on your feet, Doctor."

Bonnie obeyed and staggered to her feet. She caught sight of her right leg as she adjusted her pants. The limb was made of metal with wires twisting around the joints.

"My leg. What did you do to me?"

"We didn't do anything to you," Jaycee turned to Tripp and whispered, "We need to get her to N-Vigorate."

"I know," Tripp addressed the distraught woman as carefully as possible. "Bonnie? We need to get you some help."

"What?"

"Something has happened to you. We need to shut you off for a while and let you rejuvenate."

"No," Bonnie took a step back, afraid for her life. Two men she didn't know held their weapons at her. For all she knew, she'd been abducted by aliens. Perhaps they'd perform a probe or vivisection on her. "Stay away from me."

"Where are you gonna go?" Jaycee smirked through the sight on his shotgun and stepped towards her. "You don't know where you are."

"Leave me alone."

"She doesn't wanna come, Tripp," Jaycee turned over his shoulder. "You want me to persuade her?"

Tripp hung his head and nodded. He knew all about Jaycee's ways of *persuasion.*

"Stay away from me, you big hunk of slime," Bonnie held out her arms and threatened to punch him.

Jaycee clenched his fist and gained on Bonnie as she walked backwards. "Come here, Bonnie. It's for your own good."

"Be gentle with her," Tripp called out to Jaycee and scooped Jelly into his arms. "Don't watch."

"I said stay away from me—"

THWUMP.

Jaycee thumped the back of her head and knocked her out. Tripp trained his eyes on the unconscious woman falling into the giant's arms.

"Damn, Jaycee. Remind me to never get on your bad side."

"Had to be done. At least when she wakes up she'll forget she's a damn Androgyne," he said, dragging her backwards under her arms. "The equivalent of switching them off and back on again."

N-Vigorate Chamber

Space Opera Beta - Level Three

Jelly pressed her claws to the panel on the wall and opened the door. Tripp and Jaycee carried the unconscious Bonnie into the cylindrical chamber.

"God, she's heavy," Tripp struggled with the weight of her lower-half.

"That'll be her leg," Jaycee said, carrying her under her arms.

"*You* should have taken her legs."

"Why?"

"You're stronger than me," Tripp nodded at the electric chair at the far end of the room. "Set her down there. We'll get her plugged in."

"Okay."

Jelly ran ahead of them, jumped onto the electric chair made herself comfortable.

"Oh no, Jelly," Tripp frowned as he and Jaycee carried Bonnie toward the device. "Not there, pet."

"Meow."

"*Move.*"

Jelly just stared at the pair as they approached her.

"I said move," Tripp tried to shoo her away with his boot. "Go on, get off."

Jelly climbed down and circled around the men's feet.

"Still her usual self, then?" Jaycee chuckled as he negotiated his footing around Jelly's playful insistence. "A bit surplus to requirement now, though, isn't she?"

"She saved us. Remember that," Tripp dropped Bonnie's legs onto the seat as Jaycee pushed her against the backrest. "If it wasn't for Anderson, we'd be sitting ducks. Sitting, suffocating ducks."

"Hang on a second," Jaycee looked at Jelly and squinted. "Did Anderson just open the N-Vigorate door for us?"

Tripp looked at the passed-out Bonnie, somewhat amused by Jaycee's surprise. "Yeah, I think she did."

"But, how—"

"—As I said, she's the only one who could have engaged the thrusters. We think we went through the pink wormhole thing on Enceladus."

Jaycee nodded at Jelly. "*She* did that?"

"Yeah."

"How do you figure it was her, though?"

"Well, we must have gone through Enceladus," Tripp tightened the strap on Bonnie's lap, "We're not in our solar system anymore. We must be somewhere else."

"Meow," Jelly held up her right paw and yawned.

Tripp winked at Jelly and held his right hand up at her, enacting a cute high-five, "Manuel hasn't the first clue where we are."

"Manuel is an idiot," Jaycee crouched and held his hands out to Jelly. "Who's a good girl, then?"

She ran into the giant's arms and purred. He picked her up and watched Tripp grab a fistful of Bonnie's hair. He held it up to reveal a small tattoo-like text behind her ear that read: *Manning/ Synapse.*

He sighed, quietly, and shook his head. "I'm sorry, Bonnie."

"What's up?" Jaycee asked, allowing Jelly to purr away in his arms. "Everything okay?"

Tripp took the end of a chunky cable from the console and lifted the cap away, "I just feel sorry for her, that's all."

"Why?"

Tripp slid the back of her neck open and plugged the cable in, "We all know Series Three is relatively new technology. But for a while, there, I forgot she *wasn't* human."

"You can't let those Androgyne things get to you, my friend. She's a droid. She'll be fine."

"I know that," Tripp locked the cable and released her hair around her neck, "But you'd have thought USARIC would have been more sensitive to its needs."

"Sensitive? *USARIC?*" Jaycee let out a sarcastic smirk, "Since when did a corporation care about anything other than its bottom line?"

"It'd be funny if it wasn't true," Tripp yanked the lever on the console. It fired to life, along with the rejuvenation cable. Bonnie's eyelids lifted up, revealing two pink retinas. "At least N-Vigorate is working."

Tripp peered into Bonnie's lifeless face and eyes. Lifeless, of course, to a point. Everyone except her knew she wasn't a real human being but, damn it, her visage was extremely convincing.

"Okay, that's her taken care of. She'll be fine in a few hours."

Jaycee ran his gloved fingers over Jelly's head, "Tripp. Can I ask you something?"

"Sure."

"Are you ever going to tell Bonnie?"

"Tell her what?" Tripp asked, knowing full well what his colleague was referring to.

"That's she's not human."

"God, no. No, we can never tell her. You know what happens when an Androgyne finds out it's not human."

"But she's a Series Three model. That doesn't apply to them, does it?"

"Hey, you saw how she behaved a few minutes ago. Not exactly a shining endorsement of mental well-being, is it?"

"No, but—"

"—It's not worth the risk, Jaycee," Tripp insisted. "We need to find out what's happened. The last thing we need is Bonnie, of all people—"

"—So to speak," Jaycee interrupted jovially.

"—Very funny," Tripp tried not to smile, "The last thing we need is for her to run rampant and cause more problems for us. Besides, she's human to *us*. That's all that matters."

"I can't argue with that," Jaycee said. "But if I chose to argue with it, I'd win, because I'd just kick your ass all around this room."

Tripp shook his head and smiled. "Have you ever heard the saying 'if you resort to violence then you've lost the argument', at all?"

Jaycee thumped his fists together so hard that it shook the ground, "Uh, *no*."

"I thought not."

Tripp gave up his attempt to educate Jaycee. Instead, he offered Jelly his hand. She swiped at it, playfully.

"Did you see Wool, or our two Russian *friends*, on your travels?"

"No. I woke up and found you and Bonnie. I've seen no one, yet. Other than you, Bonnie, and Jelly, here. The two Russkies should be in N-Carcerate where we left them."

Tripp rubbed Jelly's head and turned to the door, "They'd better be. Let's go and get them."

"Did Manuel run a sit-rep?"

Tripp walked toward the door in haste, "Manuel is, uh,

experiencing some technical difficulties."

"Technical difficulties?"

"Yeah. I shut him down till we figure out what's going on." Tripp pressed his palm to the panel on the wall. "How are you feeling, Jaycee? You look okay, but it'd be remiss of me as your captain not to ask."

Jaycee bounced Jelly in his arms and kissed her on the head. "I've never felt better."

"Is that pink stuff still coming from your eyes?"

"Yes, but it doesn't hurt. In fact, all my usual aches and pains are gone. How about you?"

"I'm fine."

The door slid open. Tripp took one final glance at Bonnie fast asleep in the chair. The poor *woman* - something of a prisoner in her own mind. A product, or victim, of the Manning/Synapse company - feelings be damned; destined for a lifetime of confusion.

"It's just not right, you know," Tripp whispered a bit too loudly for comfort.

"What's not right?"

"What they've done to her."

"Bonnie?" Jaycee smiled and tried to console his colleague, "Don't worry about Whitaker. She's a fighter. She'll be fine."

"I guess," Tripp walked through the door. "Promise me one thing, though, Jaycee?"

"What's that?"

"If I die, make sure they don't turn me into one of those things."

Chapter 3

Medix

Space Opera Beta - Level three

Wool ar-Ban lay unconscious across Jelly's medical bed. Fast asleep, her breathing extremely slow. Her radio sat on the desk beside her under a picture of Jamie stuck to the wall.

A pink patch of liquid fell from her closed eyelids and bleached into the fabric of the mattress.

Three beds away from her lay Haloo Ess. She'd died before Opera Beta had ventured into the wormhole on Enceladus. Jaycee had attempted to revive her.

The issue wasn't so much the revival but what had caused it. Like everyone else, Haloo had caught the bug brought back onto the ship. Her reaction was unlike that of the others. She'd developed an allergy and fell into a cardiac arrest.

The heart rate monitor continued to emit the sound of a flat line. The wires from the unit were still attached to her breastplate.

Haloo wasn't breathing. Her face looked gaunt and pale. The stench was undeniable - not quite enough of a pungent aroma to bring Wool out of her slumber, but certainly strong enough to hit Jaycee and Tripp as they entered the chamber.

"My God," Tripp clocked Haloo immediately and ran

over to her. "What happened to her?"

Jaycee released Jelly onto the floor, offering her the chance to run around and make a bee line for Wool. "She didn't make it, Tripp."

"So you just left her here?"

"What was I supposed to do? Stuff her in the incinerator?"

"No, but—" Tripp took a long, hard look at Haloo's sunken, gangrenous face, "What the hell happened to her?"

Jaycee switched the heart monitor off. "That pink stuff. Whatever it is it finished her off."

Tripp swallowed his emotion down to his gut. Jaycee and Jelly may have been the only members of the crew to see his reaction. Nevertheless, he kept his composure and pulled the blanket over Haloo's face.

Peace, in the end.

"I don't understand?" Tripp took a step back as the room fell to silence. A reminder that her heart had long since stopped. "Why her?"

"Why her?"

"What's so special about her? Why didn't the pink stuff kill all of us, too?"

"Your guess is as good as mine—"

A loud scratching and fuss from Wool's feet caught Jaycee's attention. Jelly clawed at her feet, encouraging her to wake up.

"Meoooowww… W-Wooool…"

"What are you doing, girl?" Tripp walked over to her and immediately spotted that Wool was breathing. Effectively sleeping. "Wool?"

Her eyelids fluttered and her breathing quickened.

"Wool? Are you okay?"

"W-Wool," Jelly coughed up a pink fur ball and spat it on the floor.

"Hang on a second," Jaycee joined Tripp, entertaining his surprise. "Jelly?"

The cat looked up at the man standing over her. She shifted her head as if to say "Who, me?"

"Yes, *you*," Jaycee said. "Did you just… *speak*?"

Jelly looked to Tripp for the get-out he couldn't offer her.

"You're talking *lessense*, Jaycee. Of course she didn't speak."

Tripp shook his head and turned his attention back to the sleeping Wool. "Hey, are you okay?"

Jelly jumped up onto Wool's lap and nosed around her inner-suit. She ran the side of her face along the contours of her stomach, forcing the woman out from her slumber.

"Ugh," Wool squeezed her eyes shut and lifted her head, licking at her lips, trying to assuage the morning mouth effect. "What h-happened?"

She looked at her lap to find Jelly staring up at her, longingly. "Meow."

"Oh. Hey, honey."

Wool moved her elbow forward, knocking the radio off the desk. It hit the floor in time for Jelly to have a nose around.

"How are you feeling, Wool?" Tripp asked.

She stretched her arms out and let out a huge yawn. "I feel great, actually."

"Good."

Wool cracked out the knots that had formed in her neck from her sleep. "What happened?"

"What do you remember?" Tripp asked.

Jelly hopped onto her bed and demanded Wool's attention by rubbing herself over the woman's arms.

"Umm, I remember Opera Alpha disappearing. You came back," Wool gasped as the memory of a fight flooded into her memory. "Oh my, the Russians?"

Jelly looked at the picture of Jamie and purred. She tried to run her face along it, but it was too high up. "'Jay," she croaked, blinking at the picture.

"Yes. Tor and Baldron," Tripp said. "You remember

that, too?"

"Yes, I remember everything." She rose to her feet and lifted Jelly from the desk.

"Mwah," she clawed at the picture of her former owner and rolled across the length of Wool's arms.

"What happened? Are we waiting for rescue? Did you hear from USARIC? Where are we?"

Tripp held out his hands and nodded at the cat in her arms. "Calm down, we're okay. Jelly put us through Enceladus."

"She did?"

"Yes. It was either that or stay and run out of oxygen."

"Wow," Wool smiled at Jelly and felt like crying. "You saved our lives, huh?"

Jelly lifted her chin proudly, wanting a reward from her new mommy, "Meow."

"Who's a *good* girl?" Wool rubbed her face against Jelly's and breathed in her scent.

Tripp and Jaycee smiled at the bond between the two girls.

"Are you telling me that Jelly was able to launch the thrusters? All on her own?" Wool lifted Jelly's right paw up and inspected her claw. "The infinity claws work?"

"They work fine," Tripp said.

Wool sniffed around, puzzled by the stench that drifted under her nostrils. "What's that smell?"

"Wool, listen, we need to tell you something..." Jaycee stepped back, enabling Wool to spot Haloo's covered corpse a few beds away. "Ess didn't make it."

Wool's mood soured as the revelation sank in. She instinctively dropped Jelly to her bed and walked, slowly, to Haloo's bed. "Is that her?"

"Yes, it is."

Wool stood still, wondering whether or not she should take a look. "I, uh—"

"—It's okay," Jaycee stepped behind her and massaged her shoulder, "We'll remove the body once we're sure everything is fine."

Wool got upset. A blob of pink liquid ran down her face. "What's happening to us?"

"We don't know," Tripp braved the situation and jumped into captain mode. "But we're going to find out."

"What's Manuel saying? Sure he knows where we are, right?"

"Manuel's on shutdown. He's not in proper operating order. Something happened to him when we went through the wormhole. At least, we *think* it was a wormhole."

Wool turned to Tripp and stared him out. "You don't know very much, do you?"

Tripp could have returned with a nasty retort but chose not to. "No, we don't. But we know you're okay. We need to get Manuel and Pure Genius up and running *and* in proper working order. Until we do we're open to all sorts of trouble."

Wool folded her arms for protection, "Haloo and Katz. Both dead?"

"Yes."

"How do you propose we get the system up and running? None of us know how to operate Manuel. "

"Very true," Tripp unclipped his Rez-9 firearm from his belt, "But we know a man who can."

He waved Jelly and Jaycee over to the door with him.

"You can't be serious?" Wool ran after Tripp, allowing the door to slide behind them. "*Those two*?"

"He and his friend may have tried to kill us but Tor Klyce is the only one who can operate Manuel."

Jaycee hulked his K-SPARK in both arms as he clanged down the corridor alongside his superior. "What makes you think they'll play ball?"

"Nothing."

"Nothing?" Wool asked, hesitantly. "What do you mean nothing?"

"I don't think Tor Klyce or Baldron Landaker are going to play ball. We'll have to persuade them or we're stuck here."

"Don't worry," Jaycee moved ahead of the group, determined to destroy something, "I've got just the thing to make them agree. I'll meet you at N-Carcerate."

"Where are you going?"

Jaycee stopped and looked at his glove. "Weapons and Armory. Unless they want to lose their heads, I'm sure they'll behave themselves."

"Okay, be quick," Tripp waved Wool and Jelly up the corridor, "I'll go and speak to them."

"Good. If they say anything, don't believe a word." Jaycee stormed off, his giant boots thundering across the gantry toward a room full of heavy artillery and torture devices.

"I keep forgetting just how much of a behemoth Jaycee is," Tripp said to no one in particular.

"I wouldn't want to get on his wrong side," Wool turned to Jelly. "Come on, girl. Let's go see the bad guys."

"Meowww-aaar…"

"Huh?" Wool shrugged her shoulders at Jelly's somewhat human tone, "Whatever, let's go."

USARIC Weapons & Armory

Space Opera Beta - Level Four

Jaycee's titanium fist slammed against the fourth bay. The door slid open to reveal an array of lethal-looking gadgets.

Not firearms or grenades - or dumb bombs or smart bombs - but a selection of unusual devices. Sword-shaped slabs of metal. Oblong units of *something* one wouldn't want to be on the receiving end of. Plastic sheets, gauze, and lengths of good old fashioned rope.

And then, the item Jaycee was looking for.

"Bingo."

A cylindrical disc with a ten-inch hole in the middle. It resembled a twelve-inch vinyl record, only made of metal. A fierce-looking piece of equipment weighing at least fifteen pounds.

He opened the disc apart from the side and scanned the room with a terrific impatience. "Come on, what can I test this on?"

A spent, battered dumb bomb sat on the service counter. "Ah, good. Let's see if you're working."

Jaycee placed the opened hole of the disc around the bomb and clamped it shut. The bomb's fifteen-inch width held the contraption in place. Jaycee tilted his head and blinked a couple of times. The disc surrounding the bomb *sort of* resembled Saturn and its rings, "Huh. Ironic."

He lifted his glove and hit a button on the wrist strap. "Calibrate one-one-eight, *Decapidisc*."

A light flashed on his glove. A corresponding white light sprang to life on the Decapidisc, followed be a second and third light, indicating that it had been armed.

The metal device began to vibrate along with a repetitive set of beeps.

"Five… four…" Jaycee whispered, keeping an eye on the disc. The beeps grew quicker and quicker, threatening to form one, prolonged flat line effect.

"Three… two… and…"

Beep-beep-beep… beeeeeeeeep.

"One."

SCHWIPP!

The grenade toppled around. The top half slid away from the bottom and crashed to the counter, releasing the Decapidisc. It clanged onto the surface of the desk.

The blades whirred around within the central hole and slowed down, eventually fanning out and back inside the metal.

"Good ol' *Decapidisc,*" Jaycee picked it up and planted a kiss on its shiny surface. "Now if *that* doesn't get them to comply, nothing will."

N-Carcerate

Tripp entered the cell and swung the keys in his hand, "Wakey-wakey, cretins."

Tor Klyce and Baldron Landaker lay across the bench, shackled together by an ankle chain. The chunky iron bolts streaked along the floor, clamped to the wall.

Wool could barely stand to look at the men - Tor in particular. She held her jaw and thought of the time he knocked her out.

"Kick them like the mules they are," she said. "Kick them *real* hard between the legs so they can't procreate. No grandchildren for them to tell how painful it was."

"No, Wool. We're better than that. We're not Neanderthals, unlike them," Tripp clapped his hands, "Hey, cretins. I said wake up."

Jelly snaked through Wool's legs and approached the sleeping men. She sniffed around Baldron's battered chest. He'd taken quite the kicking from Bonnie during the fight before the dumb bomb went off in Botanix.

"Jelly, no. Stay away from him. He's a bad, bad man," Wool crouched to her knees and patted her legs. "Come here, girl."

Jelly wouldn't follow her instructions. She turned to the men and let out a loud, nasty hiss.

Tor opened his eyes and instinctively kicked his chain.

"Hello, Tor," Tripp said with a venomous grin, "Glad you could join us."

"Hissss," Jelly roared in Tor's face.

"Gah," Tor climbed back along the bench and grabbed at his shackled ankle. His eyes followed the chain over to the sleeping Baldron. "What the hell? What's going on?"

"You don't remember?"

"No, no," Tor rubbed his face and grabbed the bench, frightened for his life. "No, I don't remember anything."

Wool placed her hands on her hips in anger. "Liar. Stand up."

Tripp laughed at Tor's anxiety. "Oh dear. You've upset her, now."

"What?"

"I said stand up," Wool stomped her foot to the ground and demanded satisfaction. "Do it."

"Okay, okay. I'm standing. Jeez," Tor stood up and reached eye level with the furious woman.

"You don't remember a thing?" Wool stared him dead in the eyes.

"No, no, I don't. What's happened? Where are we—"

SMACK.

Wool punched Tor in the face, sending him crashing ass-first against the bench. "Maybe *that* will jog your memory."

"Oww, she hit me," Tor held his jaw in his hand.

"Like I said. You upset her. *Comrade.*"

Heavy footsteps rumbled down the corridor from behind the N-Carcerate door.

"God damn Yanks," Tor kicked his heels along the floor with frustration, "I should have put a bullet in you when I had the chance."

"So you *do* remember?" Tripp left a deliberate pause for drama, "Of course you remember. You jeopardized my crew's safety. You sabotaged Opera Beta's mission. I ought to put a bullet in the back of your—"

"—Screw you, *American*," Tor spat a lump of phlegm at Tripp and snorted.

Jaycee pushed through the cell door and deliberately slammed it against the tough wall. The impact made Tor jump from the bench in utter horror.

"Hey, Jaycee," Tripp winked at Wool. "Glad you could join us. We were just talking about you."

Jaycee held up the two metal discs on his hands. "Really?"

"Wh-what are *those*?" Tor asked, fearing for his life.

"Oh, these?" Jaycee grunted and clanged to the two Decapidiscs together, "I'm glad you asked. Some people call them compliance units."

He lifted one of the discs and opened it out. An imprint displayed the company logo on the side in black writing: *Priestly Enterprises.*

"I prefer their actual name. Decapidisc. Sounds more frightening, don't you think?"

"Wh-what are you doing?" Tor backed up a few inches as Jaycee approached him. He shoved the half crescent mid-section around Tor's neck and clamped the disc shut, pinching the skin over his Adam's Apple in the process.

"Aww, doesn't he look cute wearing it?" Jaycee bumped fists with Tripp.

"Yeah, it suits him."

"Looks a bit like one of those things the Victorians used to wear. What were they called?"

"A ruff, I think?" Tripp thoroughly enjoyed the ceremonious torment with his colleague.

Tor fumbled around the disc and pulled the flap of skin on his neck free, "Oww." A futile effort to a man. Locked into place and humming with life, the Decapidisc would make even the most hardened perpetrator beg for their mommy. Tor was no exception.

"Wh-what is this? What are you d-doing?"

"It's called a *Decapidisc*, Tor," Jaycee lifted his right hand and showed him the white button on his glove. "We need to know you're going to play ball. If I press this button, those three lights on your new collar light up and your head comes clean off."

"Oh, sh-shi—"

"—Hey!" Tripp snapped, showing Tor that he wasn't playing games. "Don't curse on *my* ship, you pathetic excuse for a human being."

Jelly moved back and hissed at Tor once again.

No matter where the man looked, he was surrounded by people wanting his blood.

"Here, Wool," Jaycee tossed the second Decapidisc to her. "Sort Baldron out with this special necklace, yeah?"

"My pleasure."

Wool moved over to the unconscious Baldron and clamped the disc around his neck.

Tripp stepped forward and folded his arms. "Now, listen very carefully to me, Tor. Are you listening?"

"Y-Yes, I'm listening."

"Jaycee, here, wants to press the button and mount your severed head on his souvenir wall. Do you know why?"

Tor looked at Jaycee playfully teasing the white button on his glove.

"Yes," Tor whispered as a tear of pink effluence dribbled away from his eye duct. "I'm sorry. I'm so sorry."

"It's too late for any of that, now," Jaycee said.

"He's right. What's done is done," Tripp added. "You and Baldron are responsible for the death of Opera Beta's captain and my friend, Daryl Katz. You're also responsible for Haloo's death. In fact, I hold you responsible for absolutely everything that has happened to us. Do you understand what I've said?"

"Yes."

"Now, we find ourselves at a bit of an impasse. None of us know how to fix Manuel. But *you* do."

Tor finally lifted his head, his face solemn and remorseful. He knew what was about to be asked of him. "Ask me."

"Am I going to regret this?" Tripp nodded at Jaycee and his fabulous white button of death.

"No. Ask me."

" We went through Enceladus, thanks to Jelly. We don't know Beta's current state. We don't know how much oxygen we have. We don't know if anything works, apart from the back-up generator that's giving us power and light. But we don't know how much longer that will last. We don't know where we are. We take a look outside and see nothing. We look at the screens and all we see is black. We could be *anywhere*. In fact, we probably *are* anywhere and, as Beta's captain, *anywhere* just isn't good enough."

"How's Manuel?" Tor asked.

"*Not well* is probably quite apt given the circumstances. He's talking crap and can't be trusted and needs professional help,' Tripp thought of a perfect put-down mid-sentence, "which is why I thought of you to help us."

"Or else what?"

"Or else you lose your head and all of us will probably die out here. Alone. Undiscovered. It would have all been for nothing."

Tor looked at the unconscious Baldron laying across the bench, "I need some sort of guarantee."

"Guarantee?" Tripp asked. "What, that Jaycee won't push the button?"

"That, and you promise not to kill me or my comrade after we do what you need me to do."

Tripp took Tor's sincerity literally and clenched his fists, "We're not killers. Unlike you and your boyfriend. I'll rip your damn head off with my own hands. Forget the Decapidisc."

"Aww," Jaycee played up to Tripp's taunting of their captive. "Tch."

"P-Please, don't hurt me."

Tripp squared up to Tor and stared him out. "Is that what you told my captain before you blew the connecting bridge between Alpha and Beta?"

"I'm sorry. It was nothing personal, I was only following ord--"

"—Sorry? You're sorry?" Tripp screamed in the man's face, blowing the hair on his head back a few millimeters. "How about Haloo, eh? Try telling her you're sorry. She's not even around anymore to argue with you."

Tor burst into tears as Tripp closed his eyes and calmed down. The tips of their noses practically touched.

Jaycee found the argument between the two men somewhat comical. "Are you two going to kiss?"

"Shut up," Tripp spat and lifted Tor's crying face up by

his chin. "So, what's it to be, Tor? Instant death? Or a sliver of a possibility that you, and all of us, survive?"

Tor took a deep breath and glanced at Jaycee, who taunted him with the white button on his glove. Jelly's sneering didn't help matters much, either.

The decision was inevitable.

Chapter 4

South Texas, USA

A hideout somewhere on the South-Eastern Peninsula

Handax Skill unfolded a piece of black cloth and held it at arm's length. Two eye holes stretched out across the soft material. "Perfect."

He looked around the hideout, refusing to let the grim interior warehouse walls get to him. The *People Against Animal Cruelty* placards lined most of the right-hand wall. They filled him with vigor.

Leif, a petite woman in her twenties, approached the central table. She unclipped her thumbnail on her right hand and set it on the surface, "Two hours to show time."

"Display Individimedia. Put it on Dreenagh Remix's channel."

"That blood-hungry piece of crap in heels?" Leif chuckled as she swiped the ink on her forearm.

Handax ran his fingers through his bright blue hair, contemplating the plan they were about to carry out. He saw his team having second thoughts about the forthcoming event. "Yeah, let's see how she's spun the story."

Dreenagh's name appeared on Leif's arm. Seconds later, the thumbnail threw a giant holographic live feed above the table.

An empty podium outside USARIC headquarters with dozens microphones waiting to be utilized.

"We're on."

"Guys, come and take a look at this," Handax turned to the two men.

One of them stared down the barrel of a long-range rifle.

"Denny, man," Handax said. "Pay attention."

"Yeah," Denny stood up and walked over to the table. "What's good?"

"Pay attention."

Dreenagh commentated off-camera on the non-event, "As you can see, USARIC is preparing to make an official statement of affairs. In a couple hours from now we're expecting USARIC's Deputy CEO, Dimitri Vasilov, to respond to allegations of sabotage."

"Just shut up and get to the good stuff," Handax muttered as he paced around the bench. "Look at her, spinning the story. I bet she doesn't even mention the twenty-three Russian delegates who were forced out of—"

"—Tensions are high after the expulsion of twenty-three Russian delegates from the United States shortly after the last communication from Space Opera Beta. An allegation from the captain of the ship suggests that the mission had been deliberately sabotaged by Russians. Stay with me for USARIC's official reaction."

Leif ducked her head and sighed. "She's just killing time, now."

"Put her on mute," Handax said. "I can't stand her voice."

Leif held out her pinkie and index finger and threw her hand through the image, cutting off the volume. "There, that's better."

Denny placed his rifle on the table. "So, we're still on?"

"Of course we're still on." Handax turned to the fourth member of the crew. "Moses?"

The man looked up from his lap and halted his work on a opened drone. "Yeah, we're still on."

"Gather round the table. We don't have much time."

Moses placed the drone on the seat of his chair and joined the trip. "Do I get a mask, too?"

"Everyone gets one."

Handax threw a balaclava each to Leif, Moses, and Denny. "Make sure you wear them the right way round."

Denny chuckled sarcastically. "Yeah, thanks."

Handax pressed his thumb to his forearm, enabling a rotating vector image of the USARIC's complex to appear above the table.

The west side of the building flashed drawing their attention to the main entrance. A vast complex stood north-west - an area of interest to all concerned.

"The compound," Handax said. "Leif and I will be on point to infiltrate thirty seconds before Denny takes the shot."

"Yeah. What if he misses, though?" Leif asked.

Denny picked up the rifle and looked down the sight. "With firepower like this? I never miss."

"Don't point that thing at me," Leif pushed the end of the barrel away from her.

"Don't worry. It's not charged, yet."

"I don't care. Just don't point it at me."

Handax cleared his throat. "Denny?"

"What?"

"Behave."

"My bad."

"*My bad?*" Handax quipped. "What is this, twenty-twenty-five? Have you been watching those old movies again?"

"Sorry."

"Just concentrate, for heaven's sake," Handax continued. "We need everyone on point. We're about to make history."

Moses slipped on his balaclava and punched his fists together. Somehow, even in his spurious mask, his near seven-foot frame seemed all the more threatening. "They won't know what hit them."

"No, they *must* know what hit them. That's the whole idea," Leif reached into her belt and retrieved her handgun, "We better load up if we're going to hit our marks."

Handax took a deep breath. The severity of what they were about to do socked him in the gut. "How are we all feeling?"

"It needs to be done, man," Moses clocked Handax's anxiety instantly. "Hey. You're not chickening out now, are you? This was your idea."

"Yeah, I know. It's just that…"

Handax never finished his sentence, which caused consternation for the others. He knew he had to remain in control for their sake. He lifted his head, angrily.

"Guys, we can't allow these murderous, corporate scumbags to get away with what they've done—"

"—I'd say *bastards* is about right," Leif said, inspecting her handgun. "Let's hit them where it hurts."

Handax thought very carefully about his next statement. "If you could save those tortured creatures and stick it to USARIC's nefarious practices by killing just one man… would you do it?"

"Hell yeah," Denny smiled. "For that alone, sure, but also for sneaking Russians on an American vessel. Two reasons, one bullet."

Leif and Moses nodded in quiet agreement, leaving their leader feeling invigorated and confident. Handax slipped on his balaclava and reached into his belt.

"God help us all."

One Hour and Fifty-Two Minutes Later…

Hundreds of journalists crowded the entrance to USARIC's headquarters. The podium remained empty. Tensions were high - almost as much as the scores of drones that buzzed around in the air vying for the best view.

Dreenagh secured one of the best positions in cordoned-off press area. Five armed security guards lined the front of the podium, itching for the opportunity to take someone out.

"Hey, you!" Dreenagh shouted to one of the guards. "When is Vasilov coming out?"

"Stay back, please," he said. "We're expecting him soon."

Dreenagh looked up and saw her drone get knocked by another. "What the hell?"

She turned to her left and clocked her silver-haired, suited-and-booted rival, Santiago Sibald. He shot her an evil wink. "Hey, Dreenagh."

"Is that your drone attacking mine?"

"Seems so," he said. "Your useless piece of junk doesn't stand a chance."

"Denny, do you read me?" Handax's voice was stern, yet precise.

"Yeah, man. I'm all set."

Denny placed his index finger in his ear and grabbed the steering wheel. He'd set up his long-range rifle across the front seats. The barrel rested against the opened passenger window, perfectly lined-up to take a shot at USARIC's frontage.

"There's literally thousands of people in the way," Denny said into his forearm. "It's okay, though. I have a clear line of sight to the podium."

"Good."

"Are you in position?"

Handax, Leif, and Moses moved to the corner of the building. Dressed as civilians in shirts and jeans, they blended into the furious crowd extremely well.

"We're about thirty meters from breach," Handax looked at the inked countdown on his forearm. "Twenty-six seconds into the speech. Then we're on."

"Understood," Denny's voice came through earpiece.

Handax nodded at two security guards standing in front of the side entrance to the compound.

"There they are," he said to Leif and Moses.

The emotion from the crowd doubled as the doors to the entrance opened. "We demand answers!" screamed a civilian from within the virus-like baying mob.

Dreenagh slid her fingers across her forearm and moved her drone down to her face. "Hey, good people. Dreenagh Remix, here. It seems Dimitri Vasilov is making an appearance."

A dozen officials exited the building protecting an elderly man. They ushered him to the podium and kept an eye out for trouble from the crowd.

"Yes, yes. If you look at your screens now, we can see that Dimitri Vasilov is on time and about to make a statement. It had better be good. As I stand here there are thousands of civilians demanding answers."

The crowd erupted with anger. The armed guards grabbed their weapons and forced them back, threatening to attack.

"Stay back. Stay back."

A large man screamed at the top of his lungs, "USARIC scumbags."

"Stay back," a security guard threatened a man attempting to climb over the cordon. He lost his balance and fell to the ground in pain.

Dimitri caught sight of the security guard burying the nozzle of his gun against the protester's head, "My God. It's a jungle out here,"

"Get up, you chunk of whale blubber," the guard screamed in the fat man's face.

"Please, d-don't shoot me."

The fat man rolled onto his belly and surrendered in front of the restless crowd.

"Ignore it, sir," advised one of the officials as he escorted Dimitri to the podium. "We have a schedule to keep."

Handax kept an eye on the two armed guards by the side entrance to the building. They turned away to look at the commotion at the front of the building. "What's going on over there?"

"Okay, an unexpected gift, guys," Handax whispered to Leif and Moses. "Get ready. Looks like Vasilov is about to do his thing."

The two guards at the side entrance stepped away from their markers, taking a keen interest in the fat man's arrest.

"Denny, can you see what we're seeing?"

"I'm too far away. It looks like a fight has broken out, or something."

"Some fat guy did us a favor," Handax hopped over the cordon and waved Moses and Leif over to the door. "The guards at the animal compound have moved off. I don't know for how long."

"Okay, " Denny said. "I'm ready."

"Good luck, everyone."

A USARIC official stepped up to the podium and moved his face to the microphone. Feedback from the speakers wailed across the grounds, diverting everyone's attention from the fat man. "Citizens. Can I have your attention, please?"

"We want answers," the crowd roared back.

"You'll get them in due course. I would ask everyone here, including our respected journalists, to keep the fuss to a minimum."

Dimitri scanned the blood-hungry mob from behind the safety of his security team. The guards weren't messing around. A contentious moment such as this needed order.

"Dimitri?" The official turned to the elderly man and offered him the podium. "Let's get this over with as quick as possible."

"Oh, I intend to," Dimitri moved through the sea of officials and reached the microphones. The crowds whooped and booed at the sight of him.

He leaned into the microphone. "Good people, please, allow me—"

"U-SUCK-RICK! U-SUCK-RICK!"

A security guard quelled the noise by firing three shots into the air. "Shut the hell up." The crowd fell silent and obedient in an instant.

Dimitri smiled and nodded at the guard. "Thank you."

"No problem."

Dimitri cleared his throat and reached for a sheet of paper from his blazer pocket. "I understand that you are all angry and want answers. I have a prepared statement and I will not be taking any questions."

The angry crowd allowed the man to have his say, poised to scold him at the first opportunity.

"I, Dimitri Vasilov, wish to deny any and all allegations of sabotage. To be clear, USARIC's Infinity Clause, in accordance with the Bering Treaty of 2085, stipulates that no Russian national may join any manned mission to space, or beyond. Despite our reluctance to these terms, the Russian contingent of USARIC had steadfastly agreed to them and continue to do so."

"You're talking *lessense*," a woman yelled from the crowd.

"Please, let me finish," Dimitri continued. "USARIC can confirm that we received communication from Space Opera Beta advising that two Russians had made themselves known amongst the crew. This was shortly before the disappearance of the ship, which also had the winner of the Star Cat Trials, Bisoubisou, amongst its crew members. Despite her Russian nationality it was deemed acceptable that she join the mission on account of her being the most suitable candidate—"

Dimitri's chest opened up in a haze of blood, sending him crashing to the ground.

The crowd screamed bloody murder and dispersed in all directions, pushing into each other.

A violent and desperate dash to escape the shooter - wherever he or she was.

Civilians crushed against and over each other in a dash to get to safety. Men, women, and children. The security guards fired indiscriminately at the crowd, hoping to catch the perpetrator.

The bleeding Dimitri lay on the floor, coughing and spluttering. The bullet had torn through his lungs.

"My God, did you see that?" Dreenagh billowed into her forearm, fending off the stampede rollicking behind her. "Look, look. Dimitri Vasilov has been assassinated."

Her drone buzzed around the podium along with many others in an attempt to get a decent view of the carnage.

BAM!

Two security guards fired at the wasp-like drones. Their bullets hit some of them, punching them out of the air.

"Target eliminated," Denny's voice came through Handax's earpiece over the sound of a car engine firing up followed his instruction. "Over to you, guys."

"Okay, go!"

Handax, Leif, and Moses stormed over to the compound side entrance and pulled their balaclavas over their heads. The door was bolted shut but unguarded.

"Moses, the two guards have moved off. I figure you have about thirty seconds."

"I know, I know," he clamped a rectangular device across the door's bolt. "I only need fifteen."

Handax held his hand gun in both hands and watched the screaming crowd run off. No one spotted Handax and Leif keeping an eye out for security, much less the firearms in their hands.

"Twenty-five seconds, Moses."

"I'm going as fast as I can," Moses lifted the flap of his

device and punched in a three digit code: 4-5-7. "The code is in. Nearly there."

Handax turned to Leif, keeping a tight grip on his gun. "Any sign of security?"

"Not yet, no," Leif watched the ink on her forearm countdown from twenty. She scanned at the corner of the building. "It's only a matter of time before they return. Hurry up, Moses."

"Okay, five seconds till we're in," Moses said, stepping back from the door. "Five… four…"

Leif spotted the security guard walking around the corner of the building with his colleague. "Guys, we got company."

The pair headed straight for them.

"… three…"

"They're coming, they're coming. We gotta get in now before we're seen."

"Two," Moses finished through the earpieces, "One… and, we're in business."

The door didn't unbolt. The tactical device failed and spluttered, slumping against the handle.

"Damn."

"What?" Handax turned to Moses, "What's going on?"

"It didn't work."

"Guys," Leif backed up to the two men, ready to threaten the guards who'd yet to clock them. "We're seconds away from being spotted."

"What do we do?"

"You and your stupid technology," Handax clipped Moses around the back of the head. Fast-thinking, he jumped out from the corner and made his presence known to the approaching guards. "Excuse me."

"What the hell do you think you're doing?" Leif ducked behind the door, unseen by the two guards as they approached her leader with their weapons drawn.

"Hey, you. Citizen. Put the gun down."

Handax pointed his hand gun at them and smiled. Leif

and Moses did the same.

"No, I think *you* put yours down," Handax said.

"We're not messing around," one of the security guards kept his sights focused on Moses and Handax. "This is a private zone. Drop your weapons and remove your masks, or we will shoot you."

Handax kept an eye on the compound door and aimed his gun at the second security guard. "No, I don't think so."

An abrasive stand-off occurred. The five of them pointed their weapons at each other.

"I said lower your weapons, citizen," screamed the first guard.

"Okay, now," Handax blasted the second guard's weapon out of his hand.

The first guard took a shot at Handax's head. Leif barged against guard's elbow, forcing the trajectory of the bullet away.

"Oww."

She jumped onto his back, wrapped her legs around his waist and jammed the barrel of her gun in his temple, "Hey, sweetie. Gonna let us in?"

Moses snatched the shotgun from of the security guard's hands and strapped it over his shoulder. "Be quiet."

Handax kicked the second security guard's gun away, grabbed his collar and lifted him to his feet.

"Wh-what are you d-doing?" the second guard asked in a state of near-paralysis, "Please d-don't kill me."

"We're not the murderers, *murderer*." Handax kicked the guard toward the door. "Now, open the door."

Leif removed the first guard's helmet, revealing a reasonably attractive man underneath it.

"Ooh, you're hot."

"Get off of me. Please."

"Nah, I like it here," she giggled, squeezing his waist from behind with her thighs. "Nice of you to give me a ride."

"Leif," Handax shot her a look of disdain and waved his gun at her. "Stop flirting with the bad guys."

"Aww," she climbed off his back and kept her gun held at his temple, "Maybe after all this is over?"

He squeezed his eyes shut and prayed she wouldn't blow his brains out.

"Get off him. We have work to do," Handax thumped his captor on the back, "Open the door. Now."

"Okay, okay," the guard punched a three digit code on the door where Moses' device had failed. "I'm doing it."

Handax pressed his finger to his ear, pacing around. "Denny, man? Do you read me?"

"Uh, yeah?"

"Where are you?"

"Umm," came his voice, "I'm in the middle of threatening someone right now. Can I call you back?"

A dozen USARIC security cars tore across the airfield after Denny's speeding van. Their sirens wailed and screeched as they gained on him.

"Sure, man," Handax's voice came through the car's speakers. " Just head back to base."

"Very funny," Denny spun the steering wheel to the left, forcing his van to change trajectory. He swiped his forearm, cutting off the call and looked in the rear view mirror. "Come on, cretins. Let's see if you can do one hundred."

The USARIC vehicles grew larger and larger in his wing mirror as he stepped on the gas.

80 mph… 90 mph… "Come on, come on..."

"Driver," a voice through a megaphone on top of an approaching USARIC SUV whirled through the air, "Pull your vehicle over. Now."

"Nu-uh," Denny slammed on the gas with all his might. He rolled down the driver's window and pushed out his hand, flipping his assailants the bird. "Come and get me, scumbags."

Denny's van rocketed across the runway. In the distance, a three-quarter-built cone-shaped spacecraft loomed, facing upright within its scaffolding. On its side in giant, black lettering read *Space Opera Charlie.*

"Huh?" Denny muttered in astonishment, tearing his concentration away from the airstrip. "*Charlie*?"

BLAM-BLAM-BLAM!

Mercenaries in each USARIC SUV opened fired on Denny's van as they zoomed toward the incomplete spacecraft. Dozens of bullets sprayed against the back doors. The left one bust open and flapped back and forth.

105 mph…

Space Opera Charlie got closer and closer as Denny kept his foot on the gas. He pressed his forearm and held his right ear, struggling to keep control of the rickety van. The vehicle wasn't used to these kind of speeds.

"Handax, you read me, man?" Denny yelled. "You read me?"

"Yes, I read you—"

"—Charlie, *man*. Space Opera Charlie. I can see it with right now in the airfield," Denny slammed on the breaks, forcing his rifle to fly off its housing and crash against the windshield. "They're after me. They're going to kill me."

"Denny? Where are you?"

"The airfield. I had no choice, they were on to me the moment the bullet hit Vasilov's left lung."

The van screeched to a halt on the airstrip. Dozens of USARIC vehicles flew past, underestimating Denny's brake application.

A score of handbrake turns sent the speeding SUVs around, kicking dust into the air from under the tires. Some of them tumbled around and upside down.

The remaining SUVs slammed on the brakes, releasing a SWAT-like team of USARIC officials from the back doors. They surrounded Denny's vehicle with their automatic weapons drawn.

"Driver, exit the car," came an furious voice from the megaphone atop the closest car. "We are *not* playing around. Exit the car now, or we *will* open fire—"

"—Okay, okay," Denny screamed and kicked open the driver's door.

"Stay where you are."

Denny closed his eyes and placed his hands on top of his head. This was *it.* This was how it all ended for him, he thought. Mission accomplished and failed in one fell swoop.

A tear rolled down his cheek as he awaited instructions from the one-hundred-strong USARIC army threatening to blow him off the face of the planet.

"Driver, exit your vehicle with your hands behind your head. Place your knees on the ground and hold your arms out. Failure to comply will result in execution."

"Denny?" Handax's voice indicated concern and haste. "What's that noise?"

"I'm sorry, man," Denny cried.

An armed USARIC mercenary pointed his machine gun at the driver's door. "Out."

Denny stepped out of the van with his hands above his head, blubbering like a little girl. "I'm sorry."

"Shut up and get on your goddamn knees," the mercenary kept his gun aimed at Denny as his knees hit the tarmac. He looked at his colleagues and waved them to the van. "Check the vehicle."

"Yes, sir."

Three USARIC mercenaries ran over to the back of the van and tore off the doors.

"You got some balls doing what you did," the mercenary said to Denny. "Why did you do it?"

"D-Do what?" Denny tried to act all innocent.

"Don't act dumb with me, dickhead. You took out Vasilov and tried to escape. Did you really think you'd get away with *that*?"

"I'm sorry."

"And *then* you break into the airfield?" He chuckled with great enthusiasm and nodded up at Space Opera Charlie. "That takes guts. I'm looking forward to yanking them out of your stomach and strangling you with them."

"I said I'm sorry. Please don't kill me—"

"—Oh my God," One of the USARIC trio at the van jumped onto the tarmac and stepped back. "Get back. Get back."

Denny growled and slapped the ink on his left forearm, setting off a series of rapid beeps from the holes in his wrist. "Handax, I'm sorry. It's game over."

"Who are you talking to?" The mercenary grabbed the back of Denny's shirt and hoisted him to his feet. "What's going on—"

"—Get back," screamed the USARIC van inspector, tumbling over his feet. "It's gonna blow—"

KA-BLAAAAM!

The van exploded, vaporizing dozens of nearby USARIC mercenaries - and Denny himself. Dozens of human fireballs catapulted in all directions as the van crashed back to the tarmac-laden airstrip.

Those who didn't get caught up in the explosion opened fire on Denny's barbecuing body. Scores of stray bullets tore into the USARIC official by accident.

The latter's murder was considered a necessary evil.

"Denny? *Denny*?" Handax screamed into his forearm, hearing the real-time death of his friend. A cacophony of fire and bullets rattled into Moses and Leif's earpieces as they held their captives in the compound's corridor.

"Sorry for your loss, man." Moses kept his firearm at the first security guard's head. He could see that murder was on Handax's mind. Quite the irony, considering their mission.

Leif kept her 'hot' security guard at bay with her gun and tried to offer her leader some sympathy. "Handax, man—"

"—Listen to me very carefully," Handax jammed the barrel of his gun into the first security guard's temple. The mist from his breathing plumed out through the fabric of his balaclava, "Do you know who we are?"

"N-No, and we don't need to know," the guard said, aware that his captor was incandescent with rage, "Please, just let us go."

"Get up. Take us to the animal compound."

Moses kept his gun held at the first guard. Leif did the same with the second.

"You'll never get away with this," the second guard said to Leif.

"That's okay,' she flirted back at him, "We don't plan to."

"You're crazy."

"That's right. One of yours just executed one of ours," Handax barked at the pair, "One false move and you get a bullet in the brain. Understood?"

The two guards nodded, convinced they were going to die.

Handax pointed at the far end of the corridor, "Let's go."

Chapter 5

Space Opera Beta

"Let's go," Jaycee's patience ran out. He planted his boot on Tor's lower back and booted him along the corridor.

"Okay, stop hitting me," Tor yelped like a pansy. "I'm *going*."

Tripp and Wool smirked to themselves as they followed behind the pair. The blatant mistreatment of their prisoner felt largely deserved.

The crew entered the control deck.

Jelly snarled at Tor as he reached the communications panel. She hopped onto the swivel chair. The sudden application of her weight made it twirl around a few times.

"Hissss," she dug her infinity claws into the fabric, enacting what she'd like to do with Tor if she ever had time alone with him.

He stared into her bright orange eyes and swallowed hard. Something was very definitely *off* between them.

"What are you looking at?" Jaycee thumped Tor on the shoulder a little harder than necessary. "Get working, you miserable bag of puke."

"Oh," Tor double-took and felt the metal Decapidisc around his neck. He cleared his throat and looked at the comms panel. "Yes. Manuel override set up—"

"*Manuel* override?" Tripp asked in confusion.

"Sorry, I mean *manual* override," Tor felt the rim of the Decapidisc around his neck. "Set up. A-W-A-K-E-4-5-7."

A distinct air of unease fell around the team as the panel booted up. An array of lights sprang to life and flashed. Tor turned to Jaycee and tried for a smile. The comms deck had responded to the command. Progress had been made.

"About damn time," Jaycee said, refusing to share a congratulatory moment with the bad guy. Fighting off the desire to activate the man's Decapidisc proved to be difficult as Tor stared back at him.

"Don't look at me," Jaycee spat. "Get Manuel working."

"He's booting up."

Whump.

Manuel's holographic book appeared few feet away from the deck. The image fizzled and acclimatized to the reboot. Manuel's voice came out as garbled nonsense in an array of pitches and tones.

"G-Good after-m-morrrr-ning,"

"He's back on," Tripp stepped forward and stared at the flipping pages finally shining to life. "At least he's not completely destroyed."

"Manuel?" Tor asked. "Do you read me?"

"Yes. I r-r-r-read y-you."

Tor typed a command on the keyboard at speed. "I'm going to run a diagnostic on you. We need to know you're fully operational."

"Okay."

"Just a couple of easy questions. Please don't take it personally. Are you ready?"

"Yes, I'm ruh… ruh… r-ready.'

Jaycee pointed at Manuel with disdain, "Are you sure Max Headroom, here, is in a fit state to answer questions?"

"Let's find out," Tor hit the return key on the panel and took a step back. "Manuel?"

"Yes, Tor?"

“What does USARIC stand for?"

All eyes turned to Manuel as he drifted over to the control panel. "The United States and Russian Intergalactic Confederation."

"Correct," Tor hit a green button on the control panel. "Second question. What was the primary remit of Space Opera Beta’s mission?"

"Oh, that’s easy," Manuel said. "To visit Enceladus to decipher Saturn Cry."

"Almost," Tripp said. “The journey was to Saturn. We didn’t know about Enceladus until we reached orbit.”

“The answer is good enough for now,” Tor licked his lips and punched in a command on the keyboard. "Last question before flushing to disk."

"Okay."

"Where are we?"

Manuel went silent. His pages rifled together, creating a sound similar to that of a deck of cards being shuffled.

"Manuel?" Tripp grew impatient. His crew members’ lives were at stake. "Where are we?"

The book slammed shut and shifted over to the communications deck, “Right ascension, declination, *position*," Manuel arrived at the most honest answer he could muster.

"Well?"

"I don’t know,” Manuel said. “I’ve retrieved the *geodata* in accordance with the Galactic coordinate system. It makes little sense."

“Much like you, then” Jaycee’s unhelpful retort agitated the others.

“Shut up, Jaycee,’ Tripp said.

Tor shifted Jelly’s chair to one side and set the keyboard onto the panel. “Sorry, pet.”

“Hisss…” Jelly opened her mouth and made sure he could see her sharp fangs.

Somewhat frightened, he turned away from the disgruntled cat and over to Manuel. “Display the coordinates, please."

"I'm not sure how much use they will be. But here they are."

One by one, the numbers beamed into the middle of the deck from Manuel's data page.

00h 00m 00.0000s, −00° 00' 00.0

Tripp's face fell, along with Wool's.

Jaycee couldn't believe the result, either. "Just a bunch of zeros?"

"The format isn't even correct," Manuel said. "Most of the zeros we see shouldn't even be showing. It's scrambled, unintelligible and downright wrong at best."

Jelly took the opportunity to clean her right paw with her tongue.

"*Nowhere*?" Tripp muttered. "No, this can't be right. We have to be somewhere."

An idea jumped into Tor's head as he took in the display. "Manuel, ignore the coordinates for now. We know we went through Enceladus. Do you have *any* idea where we are?"

"I am running a scan, now."

"And the oxygen levels?" Tripp asked. "Botanix took a substantial amount of damage."

"Opera Beta's oxygen supply expires a little under seventy hours from now," Manuel said. "But according to the scan, there is no oxygen present on board. No habitable atmosphere."

"Well that's wrong. We're still here," Tripp took a deep breath and exhaled. "Yup, that's oxygen all right."

Wool grew anxious and began to tremble. "Oh, God. We're dead, aren't we? That's it, there's no rescue."

Tripp took her arms in an attempt to calm her down. "We don't know the full facts, yet. The readings must be wrong."

Her hyperventilation didn't help matters, "Seventy

hours of oxygen? We're going to die, Tripp."

"Calm down. Just breathe."

"That's the whole *problem*, Tripp. I don't want to breathe. We have to conserve—"

"—Well, this is interesting," Manuel interrupted. "I'm not sure how to tell you this."

"What?" Tor asked.

"We are *not* aboard Space Opera Beta."

Everyone looked around the flight deck. They were definitely aboard the spacecraft. Jelly hopped onto the communications deck and walked across the keyboard, swishing her tail. "Meow."

"What do you mean we're not on Beta?" Tripp asked Manuel. "I think you need another reboot, you know."

"Also, something strange is happening to my clock."

"You don't say?" Tripp sighed. "You've got the oxygen report wrong, our location all scrambled - and wrong. Are you trying for the hat trick, now, with us not being on our own spacecraft?"

"Tripp, time is moving very slowly. I am not trying to be humorous. For every hour we have been at these coordinates, Earth has advanced by one calendar month."

"Okay, that's enough. We're switching you off and on again."

"The equation between Earth time and here is an approximation, of course. Not an exact figure."

Tor whispered to Tripp. "I think Manuel is several gigabytes short of a terabyte. He's clearly confused."

"I can assure you I am not confused," Manuel said with a great deal of sincerity. "My calculations are correct. We are *not* on Space Opera Beta. Take a look around. Do you recognize anything you see?"

"Yes! You moron," Tripp screamed with frustration and thumped the control deck "I recognize *everything*. See, I can touch stuff. We're definitely on board Beta—"

"—I think you may be suffering from delusion, Tripp," Manuel interrupted, much to the amazement of the others.

"Might I suggest a couple of hours of rest to fully acclimate yourself to your surroundings—"

"—What are you talking about?"

Tripp turned to Wool for her reaction. To say she was anything other than bamboozled would be a vast understatement.

"He's nuts," she walked over to Jelly and opened her arms. "We're dead. Plain and simple. Jelly, come to mommy."

Jelly jumped into her open arms and nestled herself in the crook of her elbow.

"Meowww-wwwaaar…"

The entire ship rumbled to life just as she made herself comfortable.

Tripp, Tor, and Jaycee looked around and breathed a suspicious sigh of relief. Finally, an atmosphere that suggested progress, and one that was familiar to them.

"Beta. She's back on," Tor looked up and around. "I'm rebooting Manuel. This is a good sign. It looks like we're in business again."

"Tor, please do not reboot me. It is unnecessary. I am one hundred percent operational—"

"—Good call, Tor," Tripp said. "Let's get the controls up and running and find out where we are, at least."

"No, don't do that—"

"—Rest, Manuel." Tor snapped his fingers, shutting off Manuel's holographic representation. "Get some rest."

Jaycee took a few careful steps forward and lifted his K-SPARK toward the door. "Wait. Something's *not* right."

"Not right?"

He looked around the walls and ceiling. The lights flickered. A distant, angelic humming grew louder from behind the door.

"You hear that?"

Jelly snarled, startling the others. She swiped her paw at Wool's face, catching her off guard. Two of her infinity claws tore across the woman's cheek, forcing her to release

Jelly to the ground.

"Oww," Wool yelped, confused by Jelly's lashing out. "Jelly, what are you—"

"—Roowaaaarr!" Jelly hit the ground and tumbled onto her side.

Tripp, Jaycee, and Tor turned to the irritated cat. Her whiskers fizzed with tiny beads of electricity. She sat up right straight on her hind legs and allowed her whiskers to do *whatever they were doing.*

"Muuuuh…"

"What's h-happening to her?" Tor gasped. "What's happening to her face?"

Boom-boom-boom…

Three distinct thuds rattled from behind the door. Jelly ignored it as her whiskers perked up and fizzed. Her face and body vibrated with small, swift shocks.

Wool felt the bloodied scratch on her face and looked at her fingers. Pink liquid trickled between them.

"Jelly?" Tripp muttered in astonishment, "What's happening to you, girl?"

Jelly's metal whiskers lit up and stood on end in a fascinatingly unnatural way. Much like her ears did whenever she heard something she hadn't expected to hear. She lowered her head and stared Tripp in the eyes.

"Meoowww…" she whined - only this time in a slightly lower octave than everyone expected. "Muuuuhhh…"

Boom-boom-boom…

Everyone turned to the door. It shunted open through the ship's intense vibrations.

"What's going on?" Wool cried for her life.

The angelic humming barreled down the walls and into the room, along with a fine pink mist.

"Come to me, sweetie…" A familiar voice accompanied the mist as it pervaded the entire control deck.

Wool's jaw dropped. She lowered her hand, exposing the fresh, bloodied scratch on her cheek. "What's h-happening?"

Jelly howled at the mist hanging around the walls and floor. Her infinity claws spasmed, almost involuntarily. Her whiskers vibrated a storm, creating a spark in her pupils.

"Muh… muh… mwaaah… loo… " Jelly croaked and gave up trying to speak.

"Jelly?" Tripp approached her, only to be met with a fiery resistance. She held up her infinity claws and clenched them tight.

"N-Nnn…" she coughed up a blob of pink phlegm and spat it to the ground. "*No…*"

Tripp could scarcely believe what he was seeing. The same reaction came from Tor, Wool, and Jaycee, who lowered his gun in astonishment.

"Jelly? *No*?"

"She just *spoke*," Jaycee held his shotgun at Jelly as a precaution. He looked around the deck as the pink gas-like substance filled the room from the corridor. "This is weird. I don't like it."

The female voice flooded the room with terrific volume. "Jelly. Come to me, sweetie…"

Jelly turned to the door, jumped to her paws and scurried towards the corridor. She let out a low-pitched growl as she hopped through the opened door.

Jelly Anderson was on a quest. What's more, she seemed to know *exactly* what was going on.

Tripp, Tor, Jaycee, and Wool watched her dart out of the room.

"After her!" Tripp said, chasing after Jelly. "Go, go."

Jelly bounded along the level one walkway. She was headed somewhere unknown. The pink gas wafted out of her path away as the others chased after her.

"Where's she going?" Jaycee stomped along the ground after her.

"How the hell should I know?" Tripp kept up the pace

and turned to Wool as she ran alongside him, pressing her fingertips against the raw scratch mark on her cheek.

Jelly skidded on her paws and bolted around the corner. The chorus-like voice seemed louder, now. Wherever they were headed, they were getting close to the source.

"Jelly, girl," Tripp hollered after her. "Where are you going?"

She ignored them and kept running.

"I think we're going to Medix," Jaycee grabbed Tor's arm, careful not to knock his Decapidisc. "Come on, keep up."

"I am, I am," Tor hoped Jaycee wouldn't knock him out or press the button on his glove.

"Come to me, sweetie," the sleepy, female voice shot past their ears as they ran, "You're such a *good* girl."

"That voice. Is that *Haloo*?" Tripp pointed dead ahead at the opened door to the Medix chamber. "Jelly, what—"

She bounced into the room and disappeared in a cloud of smog.

Whvoom!

"Go, go, go," Tripp said as he reached the Medix facility.

Wool screamed after Tripp. "Are you sure it's safe?"

"No."

Tripp launched himself into the room and into the pink cloud. Wool, Jaycee, and Tor followed him in…

Tripp walked through the pink gas and into Medix proper. Much to his surprise the room was exactly how they'd left it.

Several beds, machines, and the unmistakable bright white walls, ceiling and floor. Nothing untoward as far as the room was concerned.

Jaycee, Tor, and Wool kept a keen eye on Jelly as she nosed around the trolley containing Haloo Ess's covered body.

"Mwaaaar," Jelly snaked around the metal legs, pawing at the casters. "H-Haaa… loooo."

Jaycee scanned his surroundings, ready to blast whatever presented itself to smithereens. "What's going on?"

"I don't know," Tripp nodded at Jelly as she made a fuss over Haloo's bed. "Jelly, what are you doing?"

"Meow."

She seemed calmer, now, backing away from the bed.

The sight of the sheet shuffling around over Haloo's body suggested she wasn't dead.

"My God, stay back," Tripp held out his arms and waved everyone away. "Haloo?"

"What's happening to her?" Wool asked, terrified.

"I don't know—"

Haloo's body sat upright on the bed. The sheet dropped from her chest and landed on her lap. Her eyes were closed, her face still sunken.

Tripp took one step closer to the bed, careful not to antagonize the woman. "Haloo?"

Her eyes opened the moment he called her name. She turned to him with a robotic movement and focused on his face. Her pupils were bright pink.

"Are you okay?" Tripp asked, cautiously.

"Tripp," she whispered.

"Haloo. It's me, Tripp. Are you okay?"

She burst out laughing and held her hand to her mouth. "Oh, I'm sorry, Tripp."

"Huh?"

"I'm feeling *great*," she clocked Tor, Jaycee, and Wool. Aghast, they didn't how to respond to the fact that their colleague was alive.

Tripp pointed out the obvious, "We thought you were dead?"

Jaycee lifted his gun and pointed it at her. "This is insane. She died right in my arms. Don't go near her."

Unmoved by Jaycee's reaction, Haloo turned her

attention to Jelly, who looked up at her from the ground.

"Ohh. I'm not *dead*," she patted her lap, offering Jelly a hug, "Come on, girl. Come and give your auntie Haloo a cuddle."

"Meow."

Jelly hopped onto the chair, and then onto the bed itself. She confidently strode along the surface intending to take up Haloo's offer of a hug.

"Meow."

"Haloo? What are you doing?" Jaycee's trigger finger grew restless. "It's weird."

"Mmm," Haloo scooped the willing Jelly into her arms and planted her lips on her fluffy forehead. "You're such a *good* girl."

Wool blinked a few times, hoping she'd wake up from this bizarre *daymare*. It didn't work - what she saw was *very real indeed.*

"Haloo?" Wool asked, sure that something bad was on its way, "Tell us what's going—"

"—Mmm," Haloo hugged Jelly as tight as possible and smiled at Tripp. Jelly loved every second of it. "She is a good little girl, isn't she?"

"Okay, that's enough." Jaycee aimed his firearm at the sitting corpse. "You don't just wake up from death like this, Haloo. We want answers."

She giggled, enjoying how little the others seemed to understand. Suspense filled the room as a result.

"Oh, Jaycee," Haloo swung her legs over the side of the bed and pressed the soles of her feet on the floor, "Something fantastic is coming."

Chapter 6

USARIC Animal Compound
Sector Z118 - Medix

Handax stormed across the metal veterinary walkway. The fluorescent bulbs emitted a white light that was initially blinding to those who'd never been inside before.

A distinct waft of something very familiar crept under his nostrils - like that of a hospital.

"Right, is this the place?" Handax turned to Moses' guard. "Is it?"

"Yes, this is where they keep them."

"Good," Handax turned to Leif and Moses. "Now, no messing around. Once we're in, we grab what we can. We're looking for the release mechanism."

"Release mechanism?" asked the first guard, who nearly soiled himself. "What are you going—"

"—Shut up," Handax spat in the man's face and removed his balaclava, "You don't say a goddamn word, you hear me?"

"No, don't show me your face."

"Hey," Handax grabbed the first guard's chin and turned his face to his own. "Look at me. Remember my face, USARIC scumbag."

"Okay."

"*We* are going in there and doing what we need to do. Who's in charge at Medix right now?"

"Wool ar-Ban."

"Don't lie to me," Handax slapped the guard's face and tightened the grip no his chin, "ar-Ban is on Beta along with the others. For the last time of asking, who's in charge? Give me a name."

The guard knew he had two options. He could tell his captor the name of Wool's replacement, or head butt a bullet.

"Her name is Katcheena."

"What a stupid name. How many people are in the compound?"

"I dunno, maybe twenty or thirty?"

"That many?" Handax pushed the man against the sliding door, "We need your palm print. Take your glove off."

The guard did as he was told.

"Hanny?" Leif asked. "You want us to keep our guests, here, on display?"

"I want these two cowards front and center. Use them as body shields."

"Oh, no…" the second guard burst into tears, "Please d-don't—"

"—Stop crying," Leif lowered her gun in an attempt to calm the man down, "As long as you do what we say, you'll be fine."

"B-But I d-don't want—"

"—Bluergh, waaah," Handax interrupted in severe mockery mode. "I don't wanna die," he finished and returned to his usual, venomous state. "Try telling that to the poor animals you bastards have locked up in there."

Moses took this opportunity to play the hard man. "Yeah, shut the hell up."

Handax turned to him. "Moses?"

"Yeah?"

"Be quiet."

Handax turned to the first guard and grabbed his bare hand, "We good?"

"Yes."

He grabbed the back of the guard's hand and slammed his palm against the glass plate. The door flew open, inviting them inside the compound. Handax turned to Moses and Leif. "If they run, shoot them. I reckon we have about two minutes. Someone is bound to set off the alarm."

"Let's do it," Moses jammed the barrel of his gun against the first guard's head and walked in with him. Leif did the same with her guard.

Handax pulled his balaclava over his head and thumped the guard on his back. "Let's go."

Handax entered the room and took a look around. A vast laboratory about the size of a football stadium.

Dozens of medicians in white coats busied themselves at their computers to his immediate left. None of them saw him or his colleagues enter the compound.

To the right, a series of metal cages containing dozens of chimpanzees. Many of them hopped around and made a noise. The rest were asleep or covering their ears trying to get comfortable.

Dead ahead of them was the main console. A woman with red-rimmed glasses attended to the control bank. On the far wall behind her stood three doors.

USARIC medicians swarmed the place. It was hard to know where to start.

BLAM!

He fired a shot into the ceiling. It startled everyone in the room. They turned in fright to see a masked Moses and Leif threatening to kill the security guards. "Good people, can I have your attention please?"

The medicians held their breath and threw their arms up in total and utter surrender. The woman with the red-rimmed glasses dropped her clipboard to the ground in shock. “Oh, my word.”

"Now, I know this looks weird," Handax held out his arms and clutched his gun tighter than ever. "I can assure you we are not here to hurt anybody. In order to make sure none of you hit the alarm, I'm gonna need you all to get on the floor. Nice and slowly—"

The cheering and hollering from the caged chimpanzees threatened to overwhelm Handax's statement.

"—Would you shut up, please."

They wouldn't shut up - they were chimps. If anything, the fact that a stranger had made contact with them exacerbated their excitement all the more.

"They're chimpanzees," said the woman with the red-rimmed glasses hit a button on the console. "Leave them alone."

Psssccccchhhhh…

Handax swung his gun at the woman. "What did I just say?"

"It's not an alarm, look," she said, nodding at the chimp cages. A soft, pinkish gas emanated from the seams in the wall. One by one, the more excitable creatures slowed down and fell asleep. "I'm just quietening them down."

"That pink stuff doesn't hurt them, does it?"

"It's absolutely harmless."

"You better not be lying to me," Handax hopped over the bench in front of him and reached the woman. "USARIC's track record in truth-telling department isn't exactly one hundred percent, is it?"

The woman squinted at Handax. "I can assure you, they are perfectly fine." She couldn't see past the balaclava. Inside, she was puzzled. She felt the need to keep an exterior air of confidence for the sake of her team. "Who are you?"

"It doesn't matter who I am," he said, clocking her USARIC name badge. "Consider me a freedom fighter. *Katcheena Brooks*."

She turned her head away, angry at Handax's intrusion on her person.

"Why are you wearing glasses?" He removed them from her face. The wired rims had no lenses in them.

"I like them."

Handax chuckled, "Do you think they make you look intelligent?"

"—Hey," Moses screamed from the door to the compound. He caught a medician reaching for the alarm button under her desk. "You. Get down on the floor or I'll blow your damn head off your shoulders. Do it."

Close to tears, the medician fanned her arms across the floor and sobbed against the tiled floor.

"Moses," Handax called out, feeling a little sorry for her, "Come on, man."

"She was going for the alarm, you know."

"Just keep your gun on the guard."

Moses turned his gun on his captive and thumped him on the arm. "Trying to distract me."

Handax dropped Katcheena's glasses on the floor and nodded over at Moses. "I'll cut straight to the chase, Katcheena. My friend over there is going to absorb USARIC's data. My other friend and I are going to release all the animals."

Katcheena burst out laughing. "Oh, really?"

"Yeah. *Really*," Handax jammed the barrel of his gun into her temple. He found her strange laughter puzzling, "And if you don't do exactly as we say, I'm going to paint a pretty little death smile on your pretty little face."

Katcheena's flippant reaction was met with dumbfounded reaction from her many colleagues.

"I don't think so," she turned to her frightened crew and screamed at the top of her lungs. "Everyone, follow the agreed-upon course of action."

She thumped the red button on the console, setting off the security alarms. The white walls turned blood red from the spinning cascade of the emergency lights.

Handax shot Katcheena in the shin and kicked her against the console, "Stupid woman. Where are the animals?"

Her colleagues tore across the room and made for the opened emergency exits.

Leif and Moses didn't know whether to take potshots at the fleeing USARIC medicians, or train their guns on their captives.

"Handax, what do we do?" Leif called out over the screaming and crying.

"Shut up, I'm thinking."

"Handax? *People Against Animal Cruelty* Handax Skill?" Katcheena went for her bleeding leg, trying to fight off the urge to faint. "Just kill me, you dumb animal-botherer. I'm telling you nothing."

"I mean it," Handax pointed his gun at her chest. "Tell me where they are."

"Never," Katcheena's eyelids closed slowly as she slumped off the console and hit the ground. Handax watched the last of the medicians barrel through the door to freedom.

"Damn it," he screamed over the alarm and waved Moses over to the console. "Do it. Now."

"On it," Moses made a dash for the console and unfastened his shirt sleeve.

"How long to absorb the records?"

"Depends on their interface," Moses lifted the plastic cover from the flat screen on the deck, "Last check, they're storing fifteen terabytes of data so, maybe, two minutes?"

"Get on it," Handax watched Moses press his forearm to the screen.

"Cee-Cee, connect," Moses yelled at his arm as the ink reformed into three lines. "N-Gage. Four, five, seven."

"N-Gage connection complete," advised the calm female console voice, "Commencing data download."

"We're in."

Handax and Moses shared a brief smile. Something resembling victory was forthcoming - as long as they got out in time.

"Hey, babes," Handax shouted at Leif, who kept her gun on the two security guards from behind. "Take care of those two and come help me break these doors down."

"Sure."

BLAM-BLAM!

She shot each guard in the back of their right leg. Both men wailed in pain and dropped to their knees, clutching their wounds.

Moses raised his eyebrows in shock at what she'd done.

"What are you doing?" Handax shouted over the alarm. "I meant tie them up, not shoot them."

"Tie them up with what?" Leif bolted towards him. "I don't have any ties."

Handax grabbed her hand and pulled her across the console. She jumped to her feet and ran with him to the three doors on the far wall.

"That was unnecessary. You didn't have to injure them."

"They're only human. It doesn't matter."

"Guys," Moses hollered after them, effectively chained to the console by his forearm. "The data's downloading. I dunno what you have planned, but whatever it is, make it fast."

Handax turned to the first door and aimed his firearm at the handle. "Stand back!"

KERR-ASH!

The door burst off its hinges, leading into the second compound. A pungent smell of death greeted Handax as Leif followed him into the frosty cryo-chamber.

"Ugh. What's that smell?"

"Smells like rancid butter," Leif stepped forward and accidentally knocked Handax's heel. "Ugh, I think I'm gonna be sick."

The lights fizzed to life and illuminated the contents of the small room. Leif's face fell when she peered from behind her hand. "Oh my God."

Handax took a look around and felt his soul machete through his chest and run away from his body, "I don't believe it."

More cages. But this time, stuffed to the brim with animal carcasses. Most of them had tails and were long dead.

"No, this is a mistake. This can't be right."

One of the in-built storage units caught his attention. He slid the compartment out and stared at the gray feline carcass inside it. One of the lucky ones, by all accounts.

He lifted its hind leg. What was once a Russian Blue was no more. Attached to its foot was a tag with a name written on it.

Bisoubisou Gagarin

"Bisoubisou?" Handax muttered. "But she's—"

"—She's on Opera Beta?" Leif interrupted. "Has been for nearly two years."

"Guys," Moses hollered from the central control unit, "I'm nearly done. Get ready to get the hell out of here."

The illness Leif felt in the pit of her stomach was hard to take. Handax lowered the cat's hind leg as gently as he could to the surface of the cage. "She never went."

"I hate USARIC," Leif freaked out and thumped the cage, inadvertently shuffling the carcasses around, "We were supposed to set them free. How can we set them free when they're all dead?"

"Calm down," Handax took her by the shoulders and tried to shake her back to reality. "Leif, please."

"They're all dead. USARIC killed them all."

"Leif, you're hysterical. Calm down and listen to me."

"Let go of me, I have to rescue the animals." She pushed him back and darted out of the room.

Moses looked over at her running towards the second door. "Leif, what are you doing?"

"I'm going to rescue whatever's behind that second

door," she aimed her gun at the door handle and blasted it with her gun.

BLAM!

Handax chased after her with trepidation, "Leif, don't go in there. You don't know what you'll—"

"—No, Handax. I'm going in."

He closed his eyes and allowed her to carry out her quest.

A series of cages housed more than a hundred cats in the second enclosed compound. They howled at Leif as she entered the room, each of them vying for her attention.

"Oh my God," Leif clapped her hands together in delight. "They're here."

Handax bolted into the room after her and took a look around. "Oh, *wow*."

A torrent of 'meows' flew from the cages, each and every one of them desperate for freedom.

"What are they doing here?" Leif asked. "Why is USARIC keeping them?"

SNARL … SNASH … HISS!

Two of the caged cats displayed their frustration at having been kept holed up in their metal cells.

"I dunno," Handax scoured the room and attempted to count the felines on display, "There must be a switch or something that releases them all. It'd take forever to open them one by one."

"Hey, little guys," she approached the cages and addressed the wailing felines, "It's okay. We're here to set you free."

Leif clamped eyes with a white American bobtail who seemed happy to see her, "Hey, gorgeous. What's your name?"

"Meow."

Handax looked around the room for the release switch. "I can't find anything here. The cages are bolted shut. No individual releases. I'll check with Moses."

"Okay," Leif didn't turn around to see Handax run out of the room. She focused her attention on the fluffy white creature and read the name on the tag attached to her leg.

"Fluffy? Ha. Figures, you sure *are* fluffy."

"Meow."

Fluffy ran the side of her face against the metal bars.

"Why are they keeping you here, Fluffy? What's going on, pet?"

"Meow."

Handax hopped up to the control bank while Moses absorbed the data from the control panel. The inked loading bar on his forearm snailed toward the crook of his elbow. "Careful, man. Don't knock me or you'll sever the connection."

"How's the transfer going?"

"I figure sixty seconds or so. Security are gonna be here any minute, now. We gotta get ready to run."

"We gotta find that release switch," Handax perused the console like a madman, "I'm not leaving those cats in there."

"Cats?"

"Hundreds of them," Handax said. "All caged up."

"Ugh," Katcheena spluttered from the floor, slowly waking up. Her leg bled a storm across the floor, "Ugh."

Both Moses and Handax looked down at her.

"She's seen better days, hasn't she?"

Handax snorted, knowing full well that she was an unfortunate casualty of her employer's war. "We'll get her help when we get what we want. How long, now?"

Moses looked up at the panel and eyed the absorption bar. "Less than a minute. I hope."

"You'll… you'll…" Katcheena tried through her bloodied mouth.

"We'll what?" Handax asked, put-out by her drama.

"You'll never get out alive."

"That's as maybe, but as long as the animals do, we don't care."

By now, everyone had gotten used to the screaming alarms.

Handax crouched down and felt Katcheena's neck, "I reckon you have about two minutes before you bleed out."

Defiant, she spat in his face, "Go to hell."

He duly ignored her instruction and wiped the phlegm from his face. "You can make this right, Katcheena. Tell me where the release switch is."

"Never."

"Suit yourself," Handax rose to his feet and hollered at the second compound door. "Leif, get out of there."

Leif ran out of the room and up to Moses and Handax. "Yeah, what's up?" She spotted the bleeding security guards screaming for their lives by the main door.

"Katcheena, here, won't tell us where the release switch is. It must be here somewhere, judging by the look on her face *lift*."

"How *dare* you," she retaliated and press her fingertips to her cheeks. The oily, plastic skin pushed around her skull, "I have not had a face lift."

"Keep telling yourself that, sweetheart," Moses nodded at a green button on the control deck, "Try that one."

"No, don't press that," Katcheena cried. "It's the fire alarm, you'll soak us all."

Handax looked at her dead in the eyes. "Really?"

"Yes, really," she insisted. "The whole place will flood. If we don't run, we'll drown."

"I guess it'll release the cages if that were to happen, won't it?" Moses kept an eye on his forearm. Hundreds of little black dots formed across his skin. "That would be a mighty shame. For you."

"Ugghh," Katcheena rolled around the floor in pain and clutched at her bullet wound, "Don't press it. Please, don't press it."

Handax and Leif shot each other a knowing glance.

"Leif?"

"Yeah, babe?"

"Hit the green button."

"You got it," she thumped the button and turned to face the second compound.

SCHTANG-SCHTANG-SCHTANG!

The cage doors burst open one by one and released the one-hundred-strong tidal wave of furry felines to the ground. They tumbled, shrieked and scratched their way into the central compound area.

"Run, my darlings," Leif pointed to the main door, "Over there. Run, run, run."

Fluffy, the white American bobtail, led the charge. A huge variety of cats chased after her as they dispersed around the console.

"No, no," Katcheena screamed at the top of her lungs. "What have you done? They're not ready for release—"

"—We're only doing what USARIC claims to be doing,' Handax shouted at her. 'Maintaining their welfare."

"You idiots. You don't know what you've done."

A few cats became fascinated by the workstation's swivel chairs. They spun them around, and dug their claws into the upholstery.

"Gaaah," Ketcheena screamed as the influx of furry little felines descended upon her. "Get away from me."

SCRATCH! GNASH!

Twenty-six cats tore away at Katcheena's work suit and face, tearing her clothes to shreds and much of the skin from her face.

"Meow," one particularly vicious cat who resembled Jelly Anderson clawed at her eyes, hungry for revenge.

"That's one furious pussy, right there," Moses gasped at the attack and turned to his forearm, "Nearly done."

"Good," Handax watched as the majority of the cats storm through the entrance and into the corridor, "They're going."

Leif pointed at the far wall in haste, "The third door?"

"No time for that, now—" Handax caught sight of the door leading to the corridor. Furious gunfire, followed by screeching from some of the felines, rattled along the walls and into the compound. "Oh, *no*."

Just then, twenty-odd cats ran back into the room, trying to hide from danger.

"Someone's coming,' Handax yelled. 'Someone's coming."

Moses kept his forearm held to the plate. "I need more time."

"No, there's no time," Handax grabbed Moses' shoulders, "Security's coming. There's only one way out."

"If we're going to die, I'm taking as many of those bastards with me," Leif lifted her firearm and pointed it at the corridor.

The returning cats fanned out around the room and took refuge behind the chairs and desks.

"Security breach in Sector Z118," a stern-sounding voice thundered down the tunnel, "Shoot to kill."

"Forget that," Handax slid the machine gun Moses had confiscated from the security guard from his shoulder, "Mind if I borrow this?"

"Hold them off till I'm done," Moses reached into his belt for his hand gun with his free, right hand. He aimed it at the door and kept an eye on the absorption process. "Twenty seconds. I'm right here with you."

The sound of charging footsteps grew louder and louder.

Leif hid behind the console and held her gun in both hands. Handax inadvertently stepped on Katcheena's glasses, crunching them against the ground. "Whoops." He slid across the console deck, crouched behind the chair and aimed the machine gun at the door. "Ready, guys?"

"Oh, yeah," Moses held his hand gun at the corridor. "Let's give 'em hell."

"Leif," Handax shouted over the console. "Protect

Moses till he's done transferring."

Leif cocked her weapon and knocked the side of her head against the console, enjoying the adrenaline rush. "You got it, babes."

"Here they come."

A USARIC mercenary ran into the room, ready to open fire with his USARIC-issue machine gun. He took a look around and saw Moses in the middle of the room with his arm pressed to the console plate.

BLAM!

Moses fired a shot at the mercenary. "S'up?" The bullet smoked in the wall a few inches to the right of the man's head. He saw the barrel of Moses' handgun facing him. "The next bullet won't be so kind, my friend."

"Okay, okay," the mercenary unhooked the gun from his shoulder and set it to the floor, "Don't shoot."

"Get on the floor and lie down, face-first."

"Whatever you say."

The mercenary carefully placed his chest on the floor. In doing so, he caught sight of Leif and Handax hiding behind the console. To his left, dozens of scared kitties peered from behind the chairs and desks.

"How many cats got out?" asked the mercenary.

"A few. I don't know," Moses said. "Now it's your turn to answer my question. How many of you scumbags are coming?"

“Dozens. We've been ordered to shoot—”

“—Shut up.”

"They're already here,” the mercenary said.

"What?"

The mercenary pushed himself onto his back and reached into his boot strap. "Advance. One on the console, and two behind the deck."

"Huh?" Moses double-took as everything slowed-down to a crashing halt. "What the—"

The mercenary pulled out a Rez-9 from his boot and

fired at Moses. The charge hit him in the shoulder, breaking the skin and sending a charge down his body.

Handax closed his eyes, hearing a bunch of footsteps enter the room. "Okay, now."

He jumped up from behind the console and fired off a round of bullets at the USARIC militia.

Thraa-a-tat-a-tat!

Seven armed mercenaries returned fire, their random bullets smashing the furniture and walls to pieces.

Leif screamed and launched herself sideways, firing at them. Her bullets caught two USARIC militia in their legs. They dropped their weapons to the ground and screamed blue murder.

"Reloading," Handax unbolted a side magazine from the machine gun's housing and thumped it into the grip.

"Come out, now," screamed a USARIC mercenary as bits of the console pinged and burst apart from the gunfire.

"No. Put down your weapons," Handax screamed as he witnessed Leif try her luck. She launched her behind onto the console and blasted ten successive shots at the five remaining USARIC mercenaries, hitting two of them in the chest. The latter of them swung his arm to the console and pulled the trigger.

BAMM-SCHPLATT!

Leif's forehead opened out like a flower as the bullet careened through her skull, killing her instantly. The back of her head thumped against the console. Her dead eyes stared at Handax as her grip loosened on her firearm.

"Leif, no," he screamed and hulked the machine gun over the console, yanking on the trigger, "Die, you scumbags."

Pow-pow-pow-pow-click-click-click-click.

Blind-firing got him two kills on the spot, leaving two injured USARIC mercs to back away from their fallen colleagues.

Handax threw the empty machine gun aside and

reached for his handgun. He daren't peer up from the console for fear of getting hit in the face by a stray bullet.

He slowed his breathing in a futile attempt to decelerate his heartbeat - the organ in question ready to jump up through his throat and shoot through his mouth.

"Is that all of them?" asked one of the mercenaries.

"I think so. That guy on the console. Headshot on the girl."

"Good. Check the corners and clear the area."

Handax kicked himself against the back of the console and checked his gun. He was so close to hyperventilating and giving himself away.

"What do we do about these damn cats?" a mercenary pointed to the petrified kitties cowering behind the debris.

"They'll be here in ninety seconds. Mark the area as clear, then we execute."

"No, no, no, no—" Handax whispered through the sweat forming on his lips. He turned to his left and saw a congregation of terrified cats look to him for rescue.

Clomp, clomp, clomp…

"Oh, God…" Handax knew it was a matter of seconds before the mercenary found him hiding. He took a final breath and booted the chair next to him away from the console. It provided a distraction as he jumped out from behind the console and unloaded his magazine.

BANG-BANG-BANG!

The approaching mercenary opened fire on the chair without compromise. The bullets tore through it, breaking it into sections across the ground.

Handax spotted his opportunity. He slid over the console and blasted the man in the back, busting his shoulder apart. The mercenary dropped the gun and hit the floor, dead.

"Oh, *God.* Moses," Handax saw Moses' corpse sprawled across the console. By his sneakers, Leif's body had fallen to the ground. Both his friends were dead. "I… I…"

"—Sucks, doesn't it?" came a voice.

"Huh?" Handax double-took and turned to a mercenary chuckling to himself at the entrance. He'd lost his weapon and wasn't quick enough to reach the discarded firearm on the floor.

"Wh-what?"

"Both your friends, there. Dead. And then you go and kill one of mine."

"But, but—"

"—I guess that's your buddy barbecuing out on the airfield, too, right?

Handax didn't know how to respond. He stood still, flummoxed, and lifted his gun at the man's face. He wondered why the mercenary wasn't firing at him.

"You're not going to shoot me," the mercenary said. "Do you know why?"

Handax's nerves got the better of him. He could barely keep the gun up. The anxiety reflected in his voice when he spoke. "No, why?"

"Because there's only one way out for you. And that's in a body bag with your friends. And, of course, all these furry little turds."

"What…" Handax closed his eyes and shook away the sweat. "What is USARIC doing with these cats?"

"I dunno. Who cares," the mercenary kicked himself away from the wall and approached the console. "I don't ask questions. USARIC pays my wage and I get to feed my family. Do you know what they're paying me to do, now?"

"What?" Handax kept his pathetic hold on the man as he got nearer.

"Kill you stone dead," he smiled in the face of execution and nodded at Handax's gun, "You gonna use that on me?"

Handax glanced at the shaking cats and created a compromise, "Will you let me go if I walk out of here?"

"Your two buddies did it. I never saw you. You're wearing a mask. "

Handax thought over the offer for a few seconds. Freedom beckoned.

"Go on, get out of here."

Handax kept his gun aimed at the man and gripped the top of his balaclava with his free hand.

"Hey, no. What are you doing? Don't show me your—"

Off came the balaclava, revealing Handax's tear-strewn face.

The mercenary thumped his fists together in a state of fury, "You imbecile. I've seen you, now."

"Yeah, you know what this means. Don't you?"

The mercenary held up his hands in shock, "You don't have to do this, you know."

"I *have* to do this."

BLAM!

Handax shot the mercenary in the chest, killing him. He blinked a few times and attempted to process what he'd done. "I can't run," he muttered and accepted his fate. He turned to the cats, "But it means *you guys* can. Go on. Get out of here. Quick."

The cats stood looking at him, suspended in disbelief.

"Don't just stand there staring at me, you morons. Run."

Still no response. Any moment now, USARIC would breach the compound and terminate anything turning oxygen into carbon dioxide without question.

Handax did what he had to do. It was for their own good. He ran at them barking like a dog as loud as he could, "Woof, woof!"

The cats shrieked and jumped into the air. Most of them bolted toward the door and down the corridor.

"Go on. Go, go," he shouted after them and waved the few that remained toward the door. He stomped forward, acting the violent beast, "Grrr."

The final few startled kitties chased after their counterparts and vacated the compound, leaving a thoroughly disheveled Handax to take a deep breath.

Leif and Moses were dead.

Handax would join them thirty seconds from now. He stepped up to the console and lifted Moses' left arm. The absorption process was close to completion. The data that had successfully transferred was useless in the body of a dead man.

Handax carefully set his friend's arm to the console and took a seat in the chair. He rolled up his sleeve and swiped the three inked lines across his forearm.

"Individimedia, access. Enable broadcast. Handax T. Skill."

The ink formed a row of dots across his skin. His thumbnail lit up a soft green and pink, throwing a shaft of light at his face.

A screech of tires slamming to a halt barreled from the far end of the corridor. The worry vacated his mind. He looked at his forearm and moved his thumb to allow the light emission to reach his eyes.

"This is Handax Skill from P.A.A.C, People Against Animal Cruelty. I hope someone is watching. We take responsibility for the assassination of Dimitri Vasilov. We breached the animal compound at USARIC's headquarters at Cape Claudius, which is where I am broadcasting from.

"If it moves, shoot it," a voice shouted form within the corridor.

Handax continued his last will and testament into his forearm. "I know someone out there is watching. What USARIC has done is unforgivable. What we found when we breached the compound is even worse…"

The footsteps grew louder and louder, as did the angry shouting of orders to kill everything on sight.

"Remy Gagarin's cat, Bisoubisou, never boarded Opera Beta. We found her body at the compound along with hundreds of others. Those we found alive we set free. USARIC has killed three of my team. Moses, Denny, and Leif. They'll deny it, of course. They'll claim they went missing and have no involvement. In a matter of seconds, I'll be joining them."

"Over there," yelled an umpteenth USARIC mercenary as he entered the room, "Hey, you. Put your arms above your head and drop to your knees."

Handax obliged the official and faced his forearm, still broadcasting, "Can you hear that? Here they are, look."

He tilted his forearm forward, displaying a dozen USARIC mercs looking back at him with their weapons drawn. In that very moment, Handax's broadcast evolved into a live feed for his inevitable execution.

Chrome Valley

Northwest London, United Kingdom

One viewer who saw Handax's Individimedia broadcast was seven-year-old Jamie Anderson, who watched the events play out on a holographic image in his bedroom.

"Handax? Is that *you*?" Jamie muttered in astonishment.

Upside-down footage of the heavily armed USARIC mercenaries greeted the viewer.

"We will not lie down until USARIC reverses its decision to use animals for space exploration," Handax's voice emitted over the broadcast as the image lowered to the ground. He'd dropped to his knees.

The first mercenary hooked his finger around the trigger of his gun, "Hey, *blue hair*. Are you broadcasting?"

"Death to human scum who practice inhumane—"

"—Stop that Individimedia broadcast, right now!" ordered the mercenary.

Handax squeezed his eyes shut and yelled at the top of his lungs. "Death to human scum who practice inhumane treatment of animals—"

BANG-BANG-BANG-THUMP!

Jamie shrieked and held his hands over his mouth as the point-of-view of the live feed crashed to the floor. Not seeing the violence play out on the footage was much worse than seeing it. Handax's arm slapped to the floor, offering viewers a front-row ticket to a first-person death.

Jamie Anderson's mind went into overdrive. He stared at the screen, open-jawed and traumatized. After a moment or two, he turned to his opened bedroom door, "Mom!"

Chapter 7

Botanix

Space Opera Beta - Level Three

"I don't get it. I saw Haloo die *right in front of me*. On the operating table. No pulse, nothing."

Jaycee's suspicion didn't subside as the crew approached Botanix. The door had been shattered - the result of an explosion.

He vented his frustration quietly, and confidently. He kept his grip on Tor's Decapidisc, forcing the man forward, "Ain't that right, Russian?"

"I don't know," Tor said.

"Yeah. You don't know very much, do you?"

"Whatever that pink stuff is, it's done no lasting damage," Tripp whispered back. "You *think* you saw her die. But you're no medician."

Wool glanced at Tripp as they approached the door to Botanix. "Well, I *am* a medician, and something isn't right, here."

Haloo reached the door and ran her palm over Jelly's head. "Look, girl. We're here."

"Meow," Jelly shuffled around in her arms, wanting to get down. Haloo wouldn't release her. Instead, she kissed Jelly on the head and looked into her orange eyes.

"Are you ready, honey?"

"Mwaah," Jelly's saw something in Haloo's face that

terrified her. She squealed and jumped out of her arms, landing paws-first to the floor, "Meow."

She made a bee line for Wool legs and took refuge behind them.

"Hey, girl. What's up?"

Jelly whined and tilted her head up to Wool. The cat's inner-suit had split across her two front arms.

"You've damaged your suit, girl," she crouched to her knees and held Jelly's arm, "How did that happen—?"

"—She's grown, Wool," Haloo smiled, held out her hand and threatened to press the panel on the wall. "She's growing."

"Growing?" Wool collected Jelly in her arms and inspected her suit.

The underside, covering the belly, had torn at the seams. Her two hind legs bulged through the legs of the suit. Even the stitched named tag - *J. Anderson* - hung from the material.

"She's gotten heavier."

"What's going on, Haloo?" Tripp was ready to take out his gun. He saw that Jaycee was already a few steps ahead of him in that respect.

"Oh," Haloo giggled palmed the panel, "It's okay, don't be nervous. Something fantastic is coming."

"Yeah, you keep saying that," Jaycee squeezed the handle on his K-SPARK, "It's not helping."

"Good people of Opera Beta. I have something fantastic to show you."

The door to Botanix slid open.

A thunderous draught flew along the walkway and shot through the door, carrying whatever remained of the pink mist with it.

In the distance a chorus of classical music wailed around. Quite unusual for Botanix. Haloo usually liked it quiet and peaceful in there, being the crew's botanist.

Haloo's hair lifted and rippled across her shoulders as

she embraced the opened door, “Come, see," she said as she drifted into the brilliant white light.

Tor took a deep breath and tilted his head. He was greeted by the metal disc housed around his neck. "You’re not going to follow her, are you?"

"She seems to know what’s going on," Tripp said. "It’s a room full of plants and fresh water—"

"—Correction, Tripp," Jaycee interrupted, taking a step back, defying all reason to enter the chamber. "It *was* a room full of water and plants until that bomb went off. How do we know it’s not contaminated?"

Tripp considered the facts and pulled out his Rez-9. "Good point. You stay here with Tor. Make sure he doesn’t run off. Wool?"

"Yes, Tripp?"

"We’ll go in and see what Haloo’s got to say. We’ll take Jelly with us."

"Okay," Wool double-checked the proposal with Jelly. She did this by smiling at her face, waiting for as positive a reaction as a human could expect from a cat. Jelly licked Wool’s glove, excitedly.

"Okay," Tripp thumped Jaycee on the back, forgetting that his exo-suit was made of much stronger stuff than flesh and bone. "Ah, damn."

"What did you do that for?" Jaycee asked, failing to get the joke.

"Just trying to be friendly.”

"Well don’t," Jaycee snapped. "Just get in and get out."

"We’ll be right back, as they say."

"No, don’t say that," Jaycee huffed. "Don’t say *anything*. Just go in there and get the hell out."

"Yes, good idea."

Jaycee yanked Tor’s Decapidisc around, ensuring it caused the man a healthy amount of discomfort, "If you’re not back in three minutes, I’m coming in there all guns blazing and leaving this headless piece of crap to paint the floor red. Is that acceptable, Captain?"

Tripp stared at the opened door, thinking over his response. "Yes, very good. Wool, let's go."

He waved Wool - and Jelly - along with him. Seconds later, they disappeared into the haze of white light...

***

They expected to see a ruined Botanix. Initially, that's what they saw.

Rows of plants stood before them in various states of charcoaled destruction.

Wool looked to the left. Jelly's sectioned-off area in the corner sat relatively unscathed from bomb's blast.

"Some damage done. Seems we can salvage a lot of it," Wool turned to Tripp and gasped. "Tripp?"

He stared dead-ahead, eyes bulging, unable to speak. She turned her head forward and saw what he was marveling at.

"Oh… my… *God*," she exclaimed. "It's… *beautiful*."

Jelly turned her head. A puzzled expression on her face formed, along with her two humans.

"Good people," Haloo's voice chimed around them, "Welcome to *life*."

The immediate vicinity of Botanix was as it always was. The walls, however, broke apart like a shattered toy fifty feet ahead of them.

The rows of plants subsided, adjacent to the walls.

The second half - the farthest from Tripp, Wool and Jelly - transformed into a magnificent utopia.

A blue sky with white clouds and flying birds. Where the ground sunk, a glorious beach front, complete with crystal white sand ran all the way up to the horizon.

Looking down, they saw the water filtration system pumping its wares into a beautiful lake of sparkling blue water.

Even the air was a pleasure to breathe.

Tripp closed his eyes and took in a lungful. "It's heaven." He exhaled slowly and rubbed his face, ensuring he wasn't stuck in the middle of a particularly comforting dream.

Wool walked forward with Jelly in her hands, wanting to involve herself further. "Did we die? Is this *heaven*?"

"No, this isn't heaven," Tripp whispered in quiet ecstasy. He walked alongside Wool, steadily approaching the end of the burnt plants. The glistening white sand crunched below their boots with every step, "Where are we?"

Haloo moved in front of them with a glorious grin on her face. She held her hand out, introducing the pair to the perfect rendition of life awaiting them.

"Where are we, Haloo?"

"Welcome… to *Pink Symphony*," Haloo moved her hand to the sprawling ocean to their left, "Where everything began. And where everything will end."

Tripp fell to his knees in utter awe. He cupped the lukewarm sand in his hands and let it waterfall through his fingers.

All the blemishes and varicose veins that had formed through years of service in the American Star Fleet fell with it. A thorough and vital rejuvenation.

Jelly was less impressed. Her whiskers buzzed to life, as did her infinity claws. She dug them into the fabric of Wool's inner-suit, "Meow."

"Whoa, Jelly."

The cat landed on the sand, finding it a little too hot for comfort. She bolted toward Haloo in a haze of fury.

"Hey, girl," Haloo kept smiling and opened her arms. "Come to me. I have a gift for you. You like gifts, don't you?"

"Hissss."

Jelly kicked a bunch of sand into the air as she skidded on her claws. She had no intention of going anywhere near the woman.

"Oh," Haloo pulled a dramatic and sad face. "Don't you love me, anymore?"

"Hisss."

Jelly bushed her tail and flapped it around in circles, certain that danger was close by.

Haloo fell to her knees and wept. Quite the theatrical performance, she began muttering to herself as if she was speaking to someone else, "But I tried. Really, I did."

"Maaah," Jelly knuckled down and sat on her hind legs ten feet away from Haloo. She took no pity on the poor woman.

"What's she doing?" Wool turned her attention to a giant tree shooting up a hundred feet or so from the center of the ocean. "And what's that?"

Streaks of pink lightning streaked across the sky as Haloo continued muttering to herself through her sobs. "She's here, now. She's here."

The light breeze turned into a gale. The clouds bleached across the perfect sky like spilled paint hitting a canvas.

"Aww, no," Haloo fell sideways to the sand and lifted her hands to her face. "Please, leave me to die in peace. Haven't I done enough?"

"Haloo?" Tripp stepped forward in an attempt to help her. Jelly scowled at him and forced him to stop. "Jelly?"

The cat heaved and spluttered tearing the rip in her inner-suit apart. "Traaah… Traaah…"

"What's going on, girl?" Wool watched Jelly tumble to her side and claw at her inner-suit. She wanted out of it as quickly as possible.

Haloo screamed through her tears and grabbed her lips in each hand. "Gnaawww."

"Jesus Christ," Tripp held Wool back as the woman lifted her lip over her nose, coughing a plume of pink gas across the sand. "Gwaaar."

"Haloo," Wool squealed, unable to watch.

"Treeh," Jelly tore chunks of her inner-suit away with

her claws in a feisty fit of anger. "Treep… Trep…"

Haloo's shoulders hulked several inches above the ground. Her head and her body below the abdomen hung, suspended, as her inner-suit broke away.

"My G-God," Tripp pushed Wool back. "Get back, get back. We need to get out of here."

Suddenly, a classical tune emitted from the tree in the middle of the ocean, catching their attention.

It billowed at an increasingly high volume - enough to fill the air. Four, simple chords, twice repeated.

Da-da-da-dum. Da… da… da… *dum.*

"What the hell?" Tripp shouted over the gale and the music.

"The tree is singing?" Wool snapped, not knowing which way to turn. "What's going on—"

Jelly squealed and shredded the last section of her suit. She sprang to her feet and exercised her infinity claws, wrenching them in and out.

She launched into the air and took two swipes at Haloo's levitating body as it rose toward the sky. Her titanium claw caught the woman's left ear and tore the skin.

"Waaah," Jelly screamed in a furious rage, unable to jump higher as Haloo's body tilted to a halt twenty feet in the air.

"Oh, Jesus," Tripp quipped. "Let's get back to Beta, *right now.*"

"Jelly," Wool let out an ambitious, final call of hope that Jelly would return with them.

It fell on deaf, furry ears.

Jelly thudded to the floor, pushing grains of sand away from her. She howled at Wool, terrifying her.

"No, no, no," Wool threw Tripp's hand from her forearm. "I'm not leaving her here—"

Jelly roared, negating the desire to be rescued. She'd grown a few inches, more resembling an orange panther than the common, domesticated cat.

Her growl was near adolescent in nature. Even her face had matured.

Jelly Anderson was… *evolving.*

Tripp and Wool's attention was caught by a rumbling, buzzing noise shooting from the violent pinkish purple sky.

Haloo's chest broke apart and emitted a pink beam of light into the heavens. The back of her head hung down, pushing her chest upwards. It was as if her heart and soul tried to escape from her body.

"Take me," she screamed with a disconcertingly calm manner, "Take me home."

The pink beam blasting from her body thickened and ruptured, seeming to imitate the launch of a spacecraft.

Her knees broke, flinging her legs behind her ass. The back of her head recoiled under the small of her back, snapping her body in two and shattering the bones.

Then, the beam carried her body into the sky and crashed to a close into an electric storm of thunder with the clouds.

Jelly shrieked at the light show and ran toward the ocean in a fit of anger.

Tripp and Wool didn't stick around to watch the unnatural event. They bolted across the sand, backtracking across their original footsteps.

The sand turned from hard ground into scattered mud. Rows of blackened plants and tiled walls appeared beside them.

The fluorescent lighting in Botanix crept along the floor.

"The door, quick," Tripp pulled Wool along and darted for the opened door. As they gained on the rectangular structure, Tripp covered her from behind pushed her through the door to Botanix.

"Tripp," Jaycee lifted his shotgun and aimed it at the door, "What the hell's going on out there?"

"It's a long story," Tripp spat as he ran through the plants and thumped his fist against the panel on the wall.

SCHUNT.

The door slid shut, cutting Opera Beta off from whatever that place was beyond the door.

Tripp caught his breath and coughed up a storm. Wool paced around, trying not to emote. She held her chest, hoping her heart wouldn't grow limbs, climb up her throat and jump out of her mouth, "I feel sick."

"What happened out there?" Jaycee stomped his foot to the floor and thumped Tor on the back for some semblance of satisfaction. "Where's Anderson?"

"No time to explain," Tripp turned to the door and hit the glass, making damn sure nothing could get in - or out. He spun around and pushed past Tor. "You."

"Me?" Tor asked.

"Yes, you," he said, pushing Tor forward by the shoulders. "We need to get Manuel back online right now. Let's go. Come on."

"Okay, okay."

Wool chased after Tripp as he stormed off, "Where are we going?"

"The flight deck. It's time for some answers."

Jaycee kicked Tor along the corridor and showed him his glove. He delighted in threatening to activate his Decapidisc, "Speaking of answers, can you tell me what happened out there?"

For the first time in his career, Tripp felt that his crew might not believe his next statement.

"The dumb bomb Baldron threw into Botanix before we passed out?"

"Yeah?"

"It created a hole on the far wall and opened us up into a whole world of trouble."

"What trouble?" Tor tried.

Jaycee hit him on the back of the head. "Hey, idiot, *I'm* asking the questions here, okay? You're the convict who gets to shut up. Do you understand me?"

"Yes, I understand."

"Good," Jaycee spat. "What trouble, Tripp?"

Wool knew her captain wasn't in the mood for explaining as they turned the corner and made their way to the control deck.

"We've landed on another planet. Haloo said it was called Pink Symphony. Then, she, uh, died again."

"Died *again*?"

Tor started to sniff. "I'm s-scared."

"Shut up, Russian scum," Jaycee shouted in his ear, "Say one more word and you're dead."

"I'm sorry."

Jaycee, at the end of his tether, thumped the man on the back of the head to underscore his point. "And stop apologizing."

"I'm sor—"

"—Something strange happened to Jelly," Wool interjected, saving Tor from himself, "She went on the attack. She didn't want to come back with us. It was like she turned bad or something."

"Enough," Tripp entered the control deck. He pointed at Tor and then at the communications panel. "You, over here."

"Come on, sweetheart," Jaycee pushed Tor against the chair in front of the console. "Let's get to work."

Tripp scratched behind his ear and evaluated his orders before speaking them. "Okay, call up Manuel. He said something about us *not* being on Opera Beta. At first I thought he was mad but he might have been onto something."

"How can we trust him?" Tor asked.

An instant pang of irony stretching across Tripp's face, "That's rich coming from you."

"Look," Tor thumped the console in a fit of despair. "I'm just as scared—"

"—Do not speak back to me, okay? I am your

captain—"

"—No," Tor screamed into Tripp's face, determined to have his say. He calmed soon as he realized that his wish was granted, and sat into the chair.

"I'm just as scared as you are. I don't know what's going on. If I stay here, I'm dead. If I go out there - wherever that place is - I'm dead. Run out of oxygen? Yeah, that could happen, or this hulking ignoramus will take my head off. In fact, even *if* we make it back home, I'll be arrested, tried and sentenced to death. I'm a mathematician. I figure the odds of being alive for much longer are about six million to one."

"The odds will be considerably worse if you don't reboot Manuel and get him to function," Tripp slapped Tor across the face and pointed at the console. "Do you understand what I've just said? *Russian*?"

Wool and Jaycee looked at each other for a response. Their captain was about to lose his mind once and for all.

"Yes, I understand."

"Good," Tripp moved his face into Tor's and stared him out. "One false move and it's all over. Do you understand?"

"Yes," Tor blurted, deeply upset. "I understand."

"I wasn't talking to you." Tripp rubbed Tor's hair like a child, and winked at Jaycee. "I was talking to *him*."

Tor and Tripp looked at Jaycee's glove. He teased the button once again, "Just give me the word, Captain. Any excuse to press this button."

Tor cleared his throat and swallowed. He threw his arms forward and hit the live switch on the console. "In my country I am considered a hero. In the vacuum of space I am considered a traitor. A scumbag." He rose from his seat and snapped his fingers. "USARIC communications officer Tor Klyce, reboot autopilot four, five, seven—"

"—that's not even his real name," Jaycee whispered to Wool, trying to lighten the mood. She didn't laugh so much as roll her eyes.

"—Manuel, do you read me?" Tor finished and snapped his fingers.

"Yes, I read you."

WHVOOM.

Manuel's holographic book image sprang to life in the middle of the room. He rifled through his pages and floated over to Tor, "Good whenever-it-is. How are you?"

"I'm well, Manuel."

"No, *I'm* Manuel."

"No, I said *I am well*, not *I'm Manuel*."

"I beg your pardon?" Manuel shuffled back, slamming his front and back covers together, trying to work out the joke. "I'm sorry, I don't understand—"

"—Never mind that," Tripp stepped in and watched the book float around the room. "How are you feeling, Manuel?"

"Full of the joys of a typical Spring day, Tripp. Yourself?"

"Good. He recognizes us, at least."

"Soul count returns a number I was not expecting," Manuel said.

"How many souls aboard Opera Beta?" Tor asked. "We're counting me, Tripp, Wool, and Jaycee. That should make four."

"I am expecting eight. Haloo Ess, Captain Daryl Katz, Miss Anderson and the series two Androgyne unit."

Tripp squinted at Manuel in confusion. "Eight? Do you know what happened to them?"

"I do not. I apologize," Manuel ruffled his pages and emitted four beeps. "I am in full operational order. Quite without anomaly."

"Without anomaly?" Jaycee shook his head and let out a chuckle of utter disdain. "You know stuff-all about what's happened to us."

"Hey, leave him alone," Tor said. "I don't know how much data was flushed to his disk before we went through

Enceladus. I need to run a test on him. Try to pinpoint the exact time he failed to recollect—"

"—I am running a geo-scan on the ship," Manuel said. "But I cannot locate it."

Tripp turned to Tor and patted him on the shoulder. "See what I mean?"

"Wait. Let's run a test. Ask him something, anything, about an event prior to us going through Enceladus."

Tripp went quiet, thinking of a question to ask. He arrived at one. "Manuel?"

"Yes, Tripp?"

"What's my son's name?"

"Your son's name is Ryan Healy."

"And his date of birth?"

"October seventh, twenty-one-eleven."

Tripp shrugged his shoulders. "Perfect answer."

"No, wait, wait," Tor thought aloud. "That's too far in the past. Manuel?"

"Yes, Tor?"

"Data Point, run exposition scan. Open quote, what is Pink Symphony, close quote."

Manuel's holograph fizzled in mid-air as he spun through his pages. Tor turned to the others and smiled.

"He's recalibrating," Tor lowered his voice to a dead whisper, "If he remembers anything about Pure Genius and Jelly's attempt to decode Saturn Cry, then we know he's up-to-date."

The Manuel

Pink Symphony

Pg 616,647

(exposition dump #139/2a)

Cats exist to live a life of comfort and privilege if they are lucky. Should they find a good home, their work extends to that of capturing a mouse. Sometimes, even, defending their territory - if they can be bothered.

Those less fortunate and without a compassionate home are forced to survive. They become territorial, and deadly so.

Nevertheless, one attribute stands true. Cats are stupid. Dumb, ill-mannered creatures to a man, especially in relation to human beings. They have no concept of intelligence and, as discovered in the year 2080, failed to advance in the way humans did given a lifetime of experience.

Humans went on to grasp the concept of fire, for example. A cat doesn't even know what a box of matches is. Ask an adult human with reasonable common sense to watch a boiling pot of water and he will. Ask a cat the same thing, and it will - it'll watch it burn the house down.

The above-mentioned facts are important in understanding the breakthrough that was achieved in the year 2119.

Space Opera Beta launched the previous year. It's mission, to decode a message from what was originally thought to be Saturn. It transpired that it was actually coming from its sixth largest moon, Enceladus.

In conjunction with Opera Beta's on-board computer, Pure Genius, crew member Jelly Anderson managed to crack the code.

Whether or not she was aware of her success is neither here nor there. The fact remains that she cracked it - which is more than can be said for the humans.

A series of numbers presented themselves, which Pure Genius quickly configured to be the standard English alphabet. The translation of twelve numbers returned the phrase Pink Symphony.

Nothing is known of its derivation, origin, or even what it means. Much like humans in space, or cats on Earth, the answer one can reasonably derive that the discovery is as follows: completely and utterly vague, and of no use to man or beast.

***

"Yeah, okay," Tripp suppressed the urge to accost Manuel for his matter-of-fact rudeness. He turned to Jaycee with his thoughts on the matter, "Very snarky. Inelegant to a fault. He evidently remembers what happened before it all started."

"Well, that's a start."

"Very good, Manuel." Tor held out his hand and prompted Manuel, "Now that you're operational, I need you to run a—"

"Tor?" Manuel asked.

"Yes, Manuel?"

"I do not have you listed as an official crew member of Space Opera Beta."

"What do you mean?" Tor shot Tripp and Jaycee a look of extreme consternation. "Explain, please."

"A little over two hours ago, Opera Beta received a communication from Maar Sheck at USARIC, suggesting that you and Baldron Landaker were not who you said you were."

Tor felt around the rim of his Decapidisc. He hoped the revelation wouldn't anger Jaycee. "It's a long story, Manuel."

"Is it true?"

"Yes, it's true."

"For my records, I need to know your real name and rank. I presume you are an employee of USARIC?"

"Yes, I am."

Manuel opened his bookends out. Tor's head shot, along with his assumed name - Tor Klyce - appeared as a sheet of transparent paper in the air.

"May I have your real name, please?"

Tor cleared his throat, hoping the answer he'd give wouldn't anger the others.

"Viktor Rabinovich."

"What?" Tripp walked through the photo form and sized up to Tor. "You're lying. Rabinovich was poisoned and died."

"No, I wasn't. And I didn't."

Jaycee didn't take the news very well. "Okay, that's enough. I'm pressing the button." He placed his finger on his glove, activating the Decapidisc.

A white light beeped on the surface of the disc around Tor's neck, followed by a tinny-sounding voice. "Decapidisc armed. Warning, Decapidisc armed."

"No, no," Tor yelped in fright, stepping away and tried to remove the disc around his neck. "Please, make it stop.

Beep… beep…

The second of the three white lights lit up, filling Tor with a palpable anxiety.

"Jaycee," Wool shouted, "Don't do this."

"I figure you have about fifteen seconds to explain yourself," Tripp grinned with Jaycee. "Or your head comes off."

"No, no, please." Tor fell to his knees and begged Jaycee to deactivate the inevitable.

"Tell us what happened, *Viktor*."

"Okay, okay, I'll tell you," Tor stumbled over the chair. His breathing quickened, the realization that he had better give an accurate account of events within the given time frame - or risk death.

"Dimitri Vasilov. It was all his idea. I was stationed in Moscow, developing the Androgyne series with Baldron. He tracked me down and head-hunted me—"

"—Now *that's* ironic," Jaycee chuckled to himself.

"Shut up, let him speak."

A stream of tears squirted from Tor's eyes as he hurried his explanation. "He gave us new identities and hurried us into the Opera Beta mission."

"What was your primary objective, Tor?" Tripp folded his arms, enjoying the man's torment.

"To get Anderson to decode Saturn Cry and terminate the crew."

The third and final white dot on the Decapidisc appeared. The beeps grew louder and louder…

"Oh, God. Please, no," Tor stood up, frantically clutching at the disc.

"Hey, ass hat," Jaycee said, "How did you think you were gonna get away with killing us all?"

"When Androgyne boarded Alpha we knew you'd follow. It was perfect. I primed her to detonate and take you down with the ship."

The Decapidisc beeped quicker and quicker to a near flat line sound.

"Oh *Jesus*," Tor's sweat fountained down his face. He hoped the next ten seconds weren't going to be his last.

"So you decode the message and save the day? Return home as heroes?"

"I'm sorry! I'm sorry!" Tor gave up on the disc and gripped the arm rests on the console chair. He was close to throwing up.

"Sorry you were caught?" Tripp spat. "Or genuinely sorry?"

"Both."

"It all makes sense, now," Wool said. "If that plan had worked, they would have been heroes."

"A perfect ruse to get USARIC to allow Russians to join future endeavors?" Tripp kicked the chair away from Tor, throwing him to his ass. "Sound about right to you, *Tor*?"

The beeps feathered out into a constant flat line noise.

"Moment of truth, Rabinovich, my friend," Jaycee said.

Tor rolled onto his side, his neck pushed up at an awkward angle against the cylinder jamming against the floor. He closed his eyes, adjusted his breathing and accepted his fate.

"I'm ready."

SWISH-CLUNK!

The Decapidisc unbolted, separating out into a metal '3' shape. The whirring inner blades sluiced together, nicking his skin as it clanged to the floor.

Nanoseconds away from death.

Tor thought he'd been executed. His eyelids opened, scraping away the tears. His Decapidisc danced around his feet.

"Am I d-dead?"

"Sadly, no," Jaycee showed him his glove, "You're not dead. But we got the truth out of you and that's all that matters."

Tor fell to his knees and burst into tears, "I wish you'd killed me."

"So do we. But we're not mercenaries," Tripp offered the man his hand, "Get up."

"I can't stand this any longer," Wool said, "Stop torturing this poor man."

Tor wrapped his arms around Tripp and hugged him as tightly as possibly, "Thank you. Thank you."

"It's okay. We're not the bad guys," Tripp pushed the confused and discombobulated man away from him. "You and that boyfriend of yours have that all sewn up. Next time, though, you won't be so lucky."

"I understand."

"The only reason you're alive is because you know how to operate the communications panel and Manuel. Remember that."

"Pick up the Decapidisc, Viktor," Jaycee said.

The man did as instructed and swiped the metal execution device from the floor.

"Back on your neck."

"No, please. Don't make me wear it again—"

"—I said put it back on," Jaycee screamed in the man's face. "Do it. Now."

With a great deal of reluctance, Tor slid the neck hole under his chin and clamped the disc shut. He looked utterly miserable and deflated with the compliance device around his neck once again.

"Right, that's enough," Tripp said. "Tor, you stay here and run a diagnostic on Manuel. Find out precisely where we are."

Tor kept his head hung. The best he could do was nod his head in acknowledgment of his Captain's order.

"Wool, come with me to N-Vigorate."

"What are we doing?"

Tripp made his way out of the control deck. "We need to wake Bonnie up. We don't know anything about where we are. The air out there could be toxic. It certainly seems to be having a strange effect on cats and dead people, anyway. Jaycee?"

"Yeah."

"Go and wake up Tor's boyfriend in N-Carcerate. Bring him straight back to the control deck and fill him in on what's happened."

"You want me to tell him *everything*?"

"He'll find out sooner or later, so yes. Tell him everything," Tripp opened the door and let Wool through, "Tell him if we need to fight for whatever reason that he's first in the firing line. Like a human shield, kinda thing."

"My pleasure," Jaycee stormed toward the door and threw Tor a look of evil joy. "You better be here when I get back."

"I will," Tor turned to the communication panel and continued his work. "Manuel, run oxygen level diagnostic, please."

Jaycee reached Trip and walked through the door with him. "Oh, and… Jaycee?"

"Yeah?"

"When you wake up Baldron try not to batter him too badly, okay?"

"Who, *me*?" Jaycee snorted and punched his knuckles together, "The thought never entered my mind."

Chapter 8

New Los Angeles, USA
Howe's Medician Facility
Five years ago…

A wave of muffled voices flew around the darkness. The feeling of an expanding coat hanger pushing through her internal organs was getting too much.

"She's losing consciousness," a female voice flew into the air, "Dr. Whitaker? Can you hear me?"

A horizontal sliver of light burst across the darkness, revealing a blurred vision of a delivery nurse. Bonnie opened her eyelids and looked down to find her knees splayed across flooded, spongy floor.

"Welcome back, Dr. Whitaker," the nurse said, holding her up by her left arm. The image of the woman focused into crystal clarity. The bottom half of her body remained blurred through the plastic case attached to her face.

An oxygen mask.

"Level off the gas, please," said another nurse, who kept an eye on a monitor to the left. "No need for the Entonox. She's doing fine on her own."

"Keep pushing, Bonnie," the delivery nurse said, holding her hands out between her legs, "Nearly there."

Bonnie tilted her head to the right. Holding her hand was her husband, Troy, doing his best to keep her calm. "You're doing great, Bonnie."

Bonnie's cries fogged up the oxygen mask. Her

stomach felt like it had been stuffed with a thousand lit fireworks. She bent her knees apart and tried to push said fireworks out from between her legs.

A man's voice echoed around her head as she suffered her birthing pains, "Good people, it is our pleasure to introduce to you the next level in the Androgyne series. The *third* generation."

Nine Years Ago…

The USARIC 2110 summit - attended by all twelve board members and their guests - was the highlight of the company's year.

In his late twenties, the devastatingly handsome Xavier Manning spoke to the audience from the stage. Two twenty year-old women stood either side of him in black underwear.

"The Androgyne Series Three model is an ultra-simple machine. In every way, vastly superior to its previous incarnation. Take a look at both my friends, here. One of them is a genuine human being, born of flesh and blood. The other is not. Can you tell which is which?"

The first woman stepped forward and place her hands on her hip, posing for the audience.

In the front row, Maar Sheck felt along his forearm, pushing the ink around and taking a keen interest in the display.

The second woman stepped forward and turned one-hundred-and-eighty degrees for the crowd of onlookers.

It was impossible to tell the difference between the two women. Xavier found the audience's awe most amusing.

A diagram of what looked like a human body appeared on the screen behind him.

"What a difference advancements in technology makes. No more amnesia, except for where it counts. The Androgyne Series Three comes equipped with a fully customizable remit. You need an engineer to carry out tasks for you? You got it."

Xavier lifted the back of the first model's hair and lifted it up. He opened a plate in the back of her neck and pressed a button. "Sleep, Bonnie."

The woman's head faced down, appearing to be offline. He turned to the second woman and smiled. "So, I guess you figured out which one was the genuine woman, huh?"

The audience giggled. Maar whispered in Dimitri's ear. "This is incrediful."

"I know. We should consider stocking future ventures with them."

"What do you mean?"

"Think of the savings on life insurance, if nothing else. If something happens, the repair bill will be a lot cheaper than the insurance pay-out."

"I see you're thinking what I'm thinking, Dimitri."

The USARIC chiefs turned to the stage to see the second woman turn her back to Xavier. He reached for the back of her head.

"Well, everyone, you chose wrong. Belinda, here, is *also* a Series Three unit."

He lifted her hair and revealed a removable panel. The casing slid across her neck, revealing the circuitry inside. Her scalp slid off into Xavier's hands.

"Fully integrated organs. Lungs, stomach, pancreas, kidneys, and a fully functioning brain. Every single series three unit is, for all intents and purposes, a real life human being. Calibrated with a lifetime's worth of carefully selected memories. In essence, utterly indistinguishable from a genuine human being."

The audience clapped and cheered as Xavier replaced Belinda's scalp and reactivated her.

"Belinda?"

"Yes, Xavier?"

"Tell me about yourself."

"What would you like to know?" She smiled and winked at him, much to the amusement of the audience.

"I don't know. Tell me your age and where you're from."

"Oh, you're *so* forward," she giggled to knowing chuckles from the audience. "I was born in South Texas, but grew up in New York City. I'm twenty-years-old."

"Excellent," Xavier said. "Tell me about your family?"

"My folks live in South Texas. I have two older brothers."

"What do you do for a living?"

"I'm an engineer for the Manning/Synapse company, out of Moscow. It's a pleasure to be here with you, Xavier. You've always been a hero of mine."

The audience muttered to themselves with great curiosity. Standing before them was an android who believed she was real and had no reason to believe otherwise.

"Sleep, Belinda," Xavier said.

She kept her eyes open and powered down, standing still on the spot.

"Obviously, I don't recommend that command when you acquire your own droid," Xavier chuckled. "This is for the purposes of the demonstration. You can customize your shut-down command, too. You, the shareholders and major partners have spoken. We at Manning/Synapse listened. The series three model will forget that they are a droid with every power-down. No more recharging chambers, either. When they sleep, they replenish their internal core and battery, just like us humans do. They wake up fresh, and remember everything - except that they are not human. Just the way it should be. Being alive is depressing enough without that knowledge. Am I right?"

A burst of giddy excitement came from the audience. The diagram on the screen behind him faded out, replaced by the Manning/Synapse company logo.

"We believe the days are gone where technology and humans are distinguishable. Soon, the differentiation between the two will be a thing of the past. A unit that believes it is human. A unit that can reproduce and never die. Imagine the reduction of risk for your company, given the nature of the work you undertake. No more injury or, at least if there is, it's easily fixed. No more death."

Maar and Dimitri looked at each other knowing full well what the other was thinking.

***

Bonnie screamed and thrashed around as she heaved through her oxygen mask. Her knees threatened to buckle.

The woman was in so much pain squatting over the birthing pool, kept in place by her husband and a nurse.

"Okay, Bonnie, keep pushing," the delivery nurse said, "The head is coming through."

"Nggg…" Bonnie lifted her hips and stomped her false leg to the ground in an attempt to fling the volcano of hurt away.

"It's coming… keep breathing. Push, push."

A final flex of the muscles did the trick. She slammed the back of her head against the padding and exhaled through her tears.

The sense of relief was immeasurable, and only nearly as affecting as the cries of a newborn baby that followed seconds later.

Bonnie opened her eyes to find Troy marveling at what lay in the delivery nurse's arms. "Oh… my God. Bonnie, look."

"Congratulations, Dr. Whitaker," the nurse said, holding the detritus-covered baby in her arms. "It's a boy."

Bonnie lifted her arms, unable to quell her happiness. "It's a miracle is what it is."

Troy smiled at her. "Well done, honey. I'm proud of you."

"Can I hold him?"

"Sure," the delivery nurse helped her to her feet.

Her colleague handed her newborn son over, "Here he

is. Ten fingers and ten, tiny toes."

Bonnie took the crying human being in her arms and scanned him up and down. "My little angel."

By all accounts, the her son was perfect. Ten fingers and ten, tiny toes. The comfort of his mother's embrace was enough to stop him crying and relax.

Finally, he opened his eyes. The first thing he ever saw in his life was his mother smiling back at him. The second thing he saw was the gracious smile stretched across his father's face.

"Do you have a name in mind for him, Dr. Whitaker?"

Bonnie kept her eyes trained on the child and giggled, soaking up every atom of his body.

"We were thinking Adam."

"Huh?" The baby stopped kicking around and shot his mother a look of confusion. "Adam?"

"Yes?" Bonnie felt hurt by her son's protestation. Confused, further, by his ability to speak at a mere ninety seconds old, "Why, what's wrong with that?"

"That's a bit of an obvious name, isn't it?" The baby said, barely able to contain his disdain, "The first human being ever created? Bonnie?"

"But, I—"

"Bonnie?" The baby snapped his fingers, "No, it's no good. I don't think she can hear me."

Bonnie screwed her face. A deep-rooted feeling of illness socked her in the gut, "Who are you talking to—"

A shooting pain stormed across the back of her head, followed by a prolonged and intense tingling in her ears.

"Yaarrggh!"

The baby in her arms fizzed in and out. He opened his mouth and spoke once again. "Bonnie, can you hear me?"

"No, no, it's not right—"

"She's speaking," the baby said, nonchalantly, "Bonnie, I know you can hear me. If you can hear me—"

N-Vigorate

Space Opera Beta – Level Three

"—Just nod your head," Tripp finished his sentence. He crouched in front of her as she sat in the electric chair.

Bonnie jolted in the seat and pressed herself back against the headrest in fright, her eyes wide open.

"Oh, God. Oh, God."

Her breathing quickened as she attempted to acclimatize herself to her surroundings.

Tripp looked at Wool for a response. "There we are, we're back online."

"What am I doing in here?" Bonnie spluttered and caught her breath. "Why did you plug me into the electric chair?"

Tripp's face soured. He rose to his feet and stood next to Wool, looking down at her. "Bonnie, we have something to tell you."

"What is it?"

"We know you're confused," Wool said. "But we want you to know the truth."

"Okay, I'm listening."

Tripp folded his arms and cleared his throat. "There's no easy way to say this, Bonnie. So it's probably just better to come right out with it. You're an Androgyne Series Three Unit."

Bonnie stared at Tripp, waiting for the "ha-ha, *got you*" moment that would never come.

Sure enough, even after Tripp's pregnant pause, it never came.

"Bonnie?"

She blinked and scrunched her face. "Are you serious, right now?"

"I'm afraid so."

"What *lessense*. Only Series Three units recharge in N-Vigorate chambers. That's old school," Bonnie stood out from the seat and extended her arms, ironing out the kinks on her muscles. "Anyway, I have a husband and a son. I was born before the first Androgyne series was even invented. Your jokes are starting to wear thin."

"No, Bonnie," Wool said. "We figured it was better to be honest with you. When you time out, or otherwise lose consciousness, you seem to be suffering from amnesia."

"We think your battery was damaged in the fight. You're not operating properly."

"Is that so?" Bonnie lifted her metal leg and placed her foot on the seat. She unraveled her pants leg across her shin and wiggled her metal toes around. "I lost my leg in a vehicle accident, before they abolished flying cars."

"No. You didn't. USARIC programmed you to think you did."

Bonnie didn't believe a word coming from her captain's mouth. "Why would they do that?"

"To keep their options open."

Bonnie held her right hand at the pair, dismissing their stupidity. "Shut up."

Wool walked to the N-Vigorate chamber door. "We don't have much time, Bonnie. We need your help—"

The stripped lights stretching across the ceiling dipped in and out as the walls began to rumble.

Concerned, Wool looked up and around her immediate vicinity, "What's that?"

"Seems Manuel's got the engine working."

Bonnie walked into the middle of the room and scanned the harshly-lit walls. She closed her eyes and inhaled. "Are we still lost?"

"Yes," Tripp said.

The humming from the power behind the walls underscored Bonnie's recollection of events. "The last thing I remember was a pink gas. My eyes went funny. Anderson rescued us," her speaking slowed as she remembered something vital, "Tor. Baldron. They tried to kill us."

Tripp raised his eyebrows, curious that Bonnie had

remembered. "That's right. You remember?"

"Anderson," Bonnie added with maternal instinct, "Where is she?"

Wool wasted no time in hurrying up the expedition. "That's what we want to find out—"

The entire chamber rocked back and forth like a fairground ride. Dust coughed around them from the ceiling. The near-deafening chaos and vibrations never abated.

"Jesus, what was that?" Tripp grabbed Wool in his arms and ran with her to the door, "Quick, with me."

Bonnie twisted around on the spot and watched the far wall crack apart. It shot sifts of white and pink light through the ceramic. "What is *that*?" Quick-thinking, she followed the cracks crawl up the wall and shatter the ceiling, threatening to propel a chunk of it at her face.

Whoosh.

Chunks of debris whizzed past her head. She splayed out her legs and hit the ground. It stabbed down and created a vicious dent in the ground. Just two more inches to the left and Bonnie could have been sold as scrap metal.

"Quick, get out of here," Bonnie stomped her metal foot to the floor and propelled herself into the air, thumping rocks of falling detritus against the far wall.

Wool and Trip ran through the door, but the spectacular light show was too enthralling to run away from. Wool skidded on her heels and tugged at Tripp's arm, forcing him to stop.

"No, wait. We can't leave Bonnie there, we—" she couldn't finish her sentence. The sight beyond the frame of the door was too much to handle.

"Where are you?" Bonnie screamed at the splattered, milky sky that had opened up around her. "You coming for *me*? Come and get me."

"Bonnie," Wool wailed at her as she ran away from the door and into the beautiful sand-drenched horizon, "Bonnie, come back."

"What the hell is going on here?" Tripp muttered as he witnessed the N-Vigorate chamber break away into nothingness. The walls smashed against the sand, kicking a wisp of saturated rock into the air.

"Manuel said we weren't on Opera Beta," Wool clasped Tripp's hand and ran with him along the corridor, "I'm starting to believe him. We gotta find Jaycee, quick."

Tripp barreled along the walkway with her, their footsteps clanging against the metal grills. He held up his left forearm and screamed into his Individimedia ink.

"Tor, this is Tripp. Do you read me?"

The ink on his arm swirled into the shape of a tick and bled out into a black-and-white rendition of Tor's face. "Yes, this is Tor. I read you."

"Tor, listen. Something has happened to N-Vigorate," he said, losing his breath while running, "We're in danger."

"Danger? What danger?"

"That *place* we saw earlier. It's starting to appear everywhere. We think Manuel is right, we're not on Opera Beta—"

The walls of the walkway shunted back and forth, putting a halt to Tripp's comments, and a slight pause in progress. "Oh, wow."

Breathless, Wool slowed down to a jog and tilted her head to the ceiling. "It's happening again."

"Tripp?" Tor's voice shot out from Tripp's arm, "What's going on?"

SCHUNT!

A chasm split along the ceiling, shattering the material like a broken eggshell. "Run!"

Wool and Tripp wasted no time. They bolted along the corridor as the crack opened up above their heads, spilling pipework and sharp bits of ceramic all around them.

"What do I do? Tor asked from Tripp's forearm.

He turned to the ink on his skin and kept running. "Stay where you are. Do not leave the control deck. Lock the door and await further instru—"

KERRAANG!

A lump of metal daggered through the corridor wall. Tripp yanked her forward just in time for it to avoid severing her hip. The resultant tear on her inner-suit was imminently more preferable than losing a vital organ.

"Thanks."

"Don't thank me, just run," Tripp quipped as they picked up the pace, "Don't even think about stopping."

Wool looked over her shoulder as she quickened her pace. A dozen pipes fell across the path, blasting various liquids and gases across the walkway.

"Oh my God, we're—"

The ceiling cracked apart like a budding rose as they turned the corner, on the path to N-Carcerate.

"Tripp, Tripp," Wool pulled him back and pointed at the opened sky, multi-colored sky. A serene sound of ocean waves and cool air rolled around the opening.

Tripp couldn't believe what he was seeing. His ship was breaking apart all around him like a detonated tomb with a grudge.

"Come on. No time to admire the view." He spun around on his feet and stormed toward N-Carcerate with Wool in tow. "Jaycee, open the door."

The N-Carcerate door edged closer and closer as Tripp and Wool clanged along the stern surface of the walkway. He opened out his palm and shoved his arm in front of his face, intending to slap it against the panel.

"Get ready," he screamed, trying to outrun the metaphysical destruction erupting around them.

The door slid open before Tripp had the chance to manually open it. "Whoa."

He pushed Wool into the room, turned on his heels and drew the door shut by its handle.

Seriously out of breath, he placed his hands on his knees and gasped. "Ugh, no more. No more… this… is too much."

"You okay, Tripp?" Jaycee's voice lumbered from the other side of the room.

Tripp closed his eyes and caught his breath. At last, a reassuring voice and some confirmation that Jaycee was perfectly fine. He stood up straight and was about to speak, when he laid eyes on the giant of a man.

His face fell a few light years from his body. "Jaycee?"

"Yes, Captain. Look who woke up."

Tripp blinked over and over again, trying to process what he saw. Wool held her hand over her mouth and gasped as she finally laid eyes on the scene. "Oh, my God."

"Jaycee?" Tripp took a careful step forward, hoping not to attract any undue attention. "Don't… *move.*"

"What are you talking about?" Jaycee knocked Baldron's arm. The Decapidisc sat around his captive's neck, resting heavily across his shoulders.

Of course, this was to be expected. Jaycee was never one to miss an opportunity to instill fear in people - particularly a traitor. Both he and Baldron faced Tripp and Wool. The opposite direction of the cause of concern.

"He's g-going to kill me," Baldron sobbed and rubbed his arms.

Tripp averted his gaze over Jaycee's shoulder, staring at the wall behind him "Not if that… *thing*… kills you first."

"What *thing*?" Jaycee turned around and nearly soiled his exo-suit pants. "Wha—" He elbowed Baldron toward Tripp and slung his K-SPARK gun at the wall. "What in God's name is that *that*—?

A giant ball of pasty-white human flesh with twelve limbs clung to the wall like an absorbent slug. Balled-up like a spider, it retracted its "arms". It measured at least five feet wide and eight feet tall. The sheer enormity of the *thing* was devastating.

The mid-section of the beast heaved in and out, squirming as it slid down the wall. Two of its *limbs* reached the ground and thumped out, trying to orient itself as it crawled to the ground.

"Get back— My God," Jaycee aimed his shotgun at it and teased the trigger. "What's going on here?"

"Up there," Wool whispered, afraid to alarm the creature as it flopped to the ground and squealed. "Look. The crack. It must have got in through there."

She was right - a crack had formed where the ceiling met the wall.

Jaycee focused on the creature and aimed down his sight. "*Damn*, that's one ugly-looking lump of flesh."

"Jaycee, no. Don't shoot it—" Tripp quipped as the multi-limbed sack of flesh extended six of its twelve fleshy tentacle-cum-limbs across the ground. The central tumorous slit opened up and squealed in anger.

"Night-night, sweetheart," Jaycee spat.

BANG-SCHPLATT!

The bullet rocketed through the air and hit the creature. It exploded in all directions. Bits of pink-colored flesh and blood splattered the crew.

"Gaaoooww," Baldron screamed as some of it went in his mouth.

The bullet blasted right through the creature and smashed into the wall, forcing a crack ten feet above them to break apart. Chunks of ceramic crashed around Baldron and Jaycee.

"Get out of here, now!"

"Baldron, let's go," Wool took his hand and made for the door. Tripp thumped Jaycee on the back, ready to accost him, when he caught a glimpse through the crack in the wall.

"Oh… no, no, run. Run, run, run!" Tripp's soul nearly flew out of his mouth, as did Jaycee's.

Several hundred feet in the sandy horizon thousands more of the same creatures scuttled toward the ship.

"This can't be h-happening," Jaycee stammered, unable to move. "Where are we?"

Tripp pushed him toward the door. "I dunno, but we're not sticking around to find out—"

CRAA-ACCK!

N-Carcerate's ceiling shunted apart like a pressurized ribcage, flooding the prison chamber with pink light. The iron bars on each cell punctured away from its housing and crashed to the floor, creating a series of obstacles on the path to the door.

"Tripp," Wool shouted over the commotion, "Come on, we gotta get outta here!"

Tripp jumped over the fallen bar and pulled Jaycee with him. "God, you're heavy."

"It's the exo-suit, man."

"Yeah," Tripp yanked him by his mammoth waist, "And it's not water retention, it's cake retention."

"You calling me fat?" Jaycee took aim at the chasm in the wall. The creatures scurried forward, squealing for revenge.

"No, I'm calling you *dead* if you don't get out of here," Tripp hoisted himself over the debris and jumped toward the door. "Head for the control deck."

"What?" Jaycee pushed through the door and into the walkway. "Why?"

"We need to get Tor before those *things* do." Tripp slid the door shut mere nanoseconds before the first of scores of fleshy creatures slapped against the glass door, splattering its pink saliva up the glass window.

"What's happening to us?" Baldron cried and shook his head. "What kind of perversion is this?"

Jaycee bopped him on the back of the head with the butt of his K-SPARK as they hurried toward the control deck. "Shut up, Russian."

"It is a perversion of science," Baldron sobbed. "Those things—"

"—Yeah, and those *things* are going to have their way with us if we don't figure out what the hell is going on, here," Tripp lifted his forearm and spoke into his skin ink. "Individimedia. Open channel, please."

"You're not giving Rabinovich the heads up, are you?" Jaycee asked.

"Huh?" Baldron shot Tripp a look of despair. How did they know Tor's real identity?

Tripp didn't look at the man. He was more determined to get the crew to the safety of the control deck. "Don't act the numbnuts with us, *numbnuts*. We know who *Tor* is. Speaking of which, Tor, can you read me?"

"I read you, Tripp," came his voice. "What's the situation?"

"We have Baldron and we're making our way to control right now. Something's happening."

"What?"

"A Tango got on the ship. It's okay, we took care of it."

"Took care of what? What Tango?"

"Hey," Tripp screamed into his arm, "Don't quiz me. Just do as I say."

"Sorry."

"We are ETA ninety seconds to the control deck. Is Manuel online and ready to go?"

"He's online," Tor said. "Whether or not he's ready to go is another matter."

"He'd better be, or I'll have Jaycee remove your head. Do you understand what I have just said?"

"Yes."

"Good, now get ready."

"But, can I—"

"—Can you shut up and do as I say? Yes, good idea." Tripp swiped the ink on his arm to his wrist, severing the communication. He quickened his walk to a sprint and moved ahead of Wool, Baldron, and Jaycee. "First N-Vigorate, then the cells. We're not going to have much of a ship left if this continues."

"Tripp?" Jaycee shouted from behind Baldron. "What about those monster things?"

Tripp's temper neared to a close, "How the hell do I know, Jaycee? I know as much as you do."

"Yeah, but they could be anywhere."

"They *are* anywhere. They're outside. They're all over the damn place," Tripp rubbed Wool's shoulder as he faced front and continued walking. "One thing's for sure, at any rate. We *know* we're not in space. This walkway is bound to subside just like every other part of the ship. Keep moving. As long as we're moving we're not sitting ducks."

"What are we going to do when we get to control?" Wool asked. "Do you have a plan?"

"Yeah."

"What is it?"

"Survive."

Wool rolled her eyes. Fortunately, Tripp couldn't see her reaction as he was ahead of her. If he'd have caught her flippant retort it might have proved to be the final straw.

Tripp was as angry as the others were frightened. He was the captain of Space Opera Beta. The human being in him was frightened, too. The captain in him, though, was a whole different person altogether. Nothing stood in his way.

"The plan right now is to survive."

Chapter 9

A trail of tiny paw prints nestled in the fine, white sand. Two on the left, two on the right, a few inches apart.

They belonged to Jelly.

For such a young cat she sure had a lot of energy. She couldn't remember the last time she'd eaten or had a sip of water. She felt a rumbling sensation in her stomach commensurate with a similar occurrence in the pink sky.

Jelly paused, shifted her behind in the sand and tilted her head back. A permanent smile struck across her face as the glint of the nearest white blotch of white - a sort of *cloud* - reflected in her pupil.

A few laps of her tongue across her mouth and she was off to the oceanfront. As she trundled ever nearer to the shore, she stopped occasionally to turn around and see if the Opera Beta was there.

It wasn't.

She might as well have jumped through a portal for all the good her bearings were to her. Usually, she'd be on point in that respect. Geography had always been her strong suit - a sense of belonging and territory.

In the infinite vastness of Pink Symphony she felt naked and alone.

The crystal blue water lapped against the white sand, turning it a strange yellow color as it rolled across, settled down, and clawed thousands of grains of sand with it into the water.

The journey to the ocean took longer than Jelly expected. Storming forwards, exercising every muscle in her body, the faster she sped the slower the ocean arrived.

A perplexing mirage for a cat.

On the way there she passed the odd fish bone. One of them resembled a ribcage with a skull in the shape of a helmet.

A quick sniff around confirmed what she knew all along. Whatever this thing was had well and truly expired.

She felt the pink-colored sky watch her every move. If she moved her left paw the clouds tilted to the left like an angry lava lamp.

The right claw moved forward taking with it the clouds in the sky. They didn't move as they had back on Earth. Calling them clouds were as comparable as possible to what they really were. More like explosions of distant galaxies; silky and smooth, as if someone had poured full fat cream into a sky full of candy floss.

Jelly might well have had second thoughts about moving in any direction. The water, at least, seemed benevolent enough.

Eventually, she reached the shore. A careful probe with her infinity claws resulted in the wet sand tearing apart as expected.

The metal claws fizzed subtly as the waves crashed around her paws. She stepped forward and lowered her face, exploring the liquid with her tongue.

Two successive gulps - and success. A fully lubricated mouth. A wave of relief ran through her entire body. She felt better, energized, and ready for more.

Lap, lap, lap… the refreshing water soaked into her coarse tongue and swirled around her mouth. Above her in the sky, the white ink-like clouds bled out, creating a harmonious voice for the duration of its travel.

Jelly's ears pricked up as she continued to drink the water.

The thought occurred to her that she should get back to the ship and alert her crew of the seemingly plentiful supply of H2O. Said thought evaporated when the oncoming ripples of water grew higher and turned into medium-sized waves.

"Meow," she squealed and hopped back, fearing the wave would entrench her entirely. She loved the water, but the concept of swimming was way beyond her grasp.

In fact, she didn't even know if she could swim.

Stepping back wasn't enough. She had to run around and run across the sand just in time for the end of the wave to envelope her hind legs.

"Meow," she yelped in defiance, determined to return and satisfy her thirst.

As the wave rolled back into the ocean, her eyes followed it back to the tree dead in the middle of the ocean.

It was a tree, yet it wasn't a tree. It merely resembled one.

Jelly knew what a tree was. Fat at the bottom, thinning out in the middle, with hundreds of blossoming branches fanning out from the top. Usually brown, or dark brown, and made of wood and covered in bark. She'd got stuck in many of them during her young life.

She loved to climb the one in Jamie's garden area. Occasionally, in her good old kitty days, she'd need rescuing.

This *tree* wasn't made of wood. If it was then the wood was made of a spongy, black mucous shooting out from the water and blossoming one hundred feet in the air.

Its towering effect antagonized her.

Where there might have been branches were, instead, darkened shafts of coal about twenty feet in length. It was as if an aircraft's wings had melted in intense heat. They curved around the midpoint, arrowing back toward the water.

The stem bulged in and out as if it was breathing. Jelly

saw the bulge shoot up from the root, causing the water to rupture away. It traveled up the stem and dispersed among the twenty or so *branches* and died out toward their ends.

Jelly sat perfectly still and took in the sheer size of the tree. She blinked hard, expecting it to move. Of course, it had no such intention. Being an inanimate object, it didn't care much for the strange being sitting before of it.

Being curious in nature, Jelly wanted to know more. But she'd be damned if she went into the water to quench her thirst for knowledge.

At least the place was quiet, though. The sky acted strangely. The tree added a perversely morbid air to an otherwise wistful utopia. Jelly rolled around in the wet sand and cooled herself down.

"Jelly?"

She jumped to her feet and turned around. A recognizable shape in the shifting sand seat warbled into focus. The contours of a woman named Bonnie steadily approached her.

"Hey, girl," she finished, confidently striding closer, "There you are."

Jelly hopped to her feet and meowed back.

"I know," Bonnie hollered as softly as she could, "It's nice here, isn't it?"

"Meow."

Bonnie let out a hearty laugh and flung her long, brown hair across her left shoulder. "Aww." She squatted to the sand and held her arms forward. "Come on, pet. Come here and give your auntie Bonnie a cuddle."

Jelly found the human's behavior a little strange. Stuck in a strange place and with little-to-no recourse for rescue, Bonnie seemed uniquely at home.

Her demeanor was enough reassurance for Jelly. She hopped along the sand, digging her infinity claws in with each step for good measure, and raced into Bonnie's opened hands.

She arched her back and held Jelly out at arm's length against the sky.

"Hey, sweetie."

"Meow," Jelly licked her lips and flipped her tail around, wondering when the cuddle would commence. She lifted her right leg for balance.

"God, you're such a gorgeous creature," Bonnie said with a deft admiration, her eyes fixated on Jelly's. "Look at you."

Then, the cuddle came. Bonnie's left cheek nestled against Jelly's forehead.

She took a look at the blackened tree to find a waterfall of dark pink liquid gushing from a slit that tore near the top of the stem.

"Oh, look. It's crying pink."

Jelly took a look and immediately grew concerned. She dug her titanium claws into Bonnie's inner-suit sleeve, wanting to be set free.

"Okay, okay," Bonnie huffed. "Jeez, you're cranky—"

The middle of the tree's stem heaved out, as if taking in a lungful of air. A pregnant pause befell Jelly and Bonnie as they waited for it to exhale.

Where would the exhalation come from, anyway? Apart from the slit, there was no sign of a mouth anywhere on it.

The branches slumped down, appearing to weaken as the tree bent back.

"What is that?" Bonnie squinted at the alien object as it gently lilted around.

Then, a deafening blast of sound rippled in every direction from the root of the tree.

Da-da-da-dummm…

"Huh?" she said.

Dah, dah, dah…. *dum.*

Bonnie clamped her hands over her ears and let out a cry of pain. "Agh."

SPLASH!

A wave crashed out across the sand. A large fish

plopped to the shore and shuffled around in pain, trying to breath. Its rounded lips gaped in and out.

"Meow," Jelly kicked up some sand as she entered the prone position. Her tail bushed out, ready to attack.

"Jelly, honey, what—"

"Shhh," Jelly fixated her eyes on the fat, circular fish as it flapped across the sand and gasped for air, "Shhh."

"Sweetie? How are you saying that—"

"Mweh," Jelly coughed up a lump of pink phlegm and spat to the sand. She darted over to the fish intending to tear it to shreds.

"No, Jelly. Don't touch it—"

The fish bounced over the damp sand in an attempt to escape its impending doom. The back end of the blue creature lifted up and shed its skin.

A bony tail shot out and slapped to the ground.

Jelly screeched to a halt, kicking sand into the air with her paws. She didn't like what had happened and would soon be terrified of what happened next, "Muuuh."

The creature whipped its tail in retaliation. The end thwacked against the sand. The impact sent a shock wave through its bone, shattering its blue, oily skin across its body. The fish's mouth stretched back over its face. A row of sharp teeth jutted out from its skull, as the blue skin flaked away.

It had turned into a bizarre armadillo-type creature. Four small limbs, bent at the middle, with claws.

Jelly widened her eyes in terror as the creature turned to her and growled. A swish from the creature's tail made sure Jelly took a few steps back, hoping not to get murdered.

The beast crept forward on its chunky feet and slammed its razor sharp jaws together.

Da-da-da... dum... the tree appeared to sing.

Bonnie found the whole spectacle puzzling but wasn't afraid of the abnormality creeping towards her. She gripped her metal leg and made sure it was armed in case the creature tried its luck.

"What the hell is going on, here?" she turned to Jelly and raised her voice, "Come here, girl."

Jelly didn't hear the command. She froze on the spot, scared that the creature might lunge at her.

The tree heaved and lilted to the left side as if quietly dancing to its own rendition of a classical tune. The mimicry of organs and trumpets came out like a confused amalgam of croaking wood and belches.

Bonnie recognized the attempt, finding the entire scenario eerily reminiscent of Opera Alpha.

"Is that… *Beethoven's Fifth*?" she gasped, piecing the tree's segments of harmonious rumbles together. "It is, it is…" She turned over her shoulder and saw a transparent spacecraft wreckage in the horizon. The ghost of the deserted Space Opera Alpha.

"Huh?"

Jelly, meanwhile, found herself crawling backwards on her hind legs as the recently-evolved beast threw its spindly arms forward.

"Maaw," she kept her fattened tail up and swung it around. A failed attempted to allay the creature's desire for feline blood.

The beast growled at her, forcing the air molecules to ripple together and throw her fur on end.

"Meow," Jelly screamed back and swiped her right claw in retaliation.

So hard was the creature's roar that the reptilian skin on its face broke apart and slapped against the sand. A gray-colored skull broke forward and shrieked, shedding the rest of its skin. Its skeletal structure fizzed and sparked, cracking onto itself.

The spine curved in the middle and sprung stems either side, meeting around its exposed organs.

A liver.

A stomach.

A pancreas.

The ribbed bones crept around its lungs and heart, forming a protective cage around them.

The pinkish under skin blistered in the intense heat from the pink sky. A sun, previously unseen, introduced itself from behind one of several milky clouds.

The tree continued its interpretation of *Beethoven's 5th Symphony* across the air. Croaky and strangely harmonic, given the absence of a coherent orchestra.

Bonnie unhooked her Rez-9 firearm from her belt and pointed it at the creature. She'd seen - and had - enough, "Don't move."

Jelly turned around and meowed at Bonnie. The look in both her eyeballs screamed *don't shoot.*

"Don't look at me in that tone of voice, young madam," Bonnie said. "Look at it. It's in pain. I'm doing it a favor."

Jelly turned back to the creature.

It resembled more an ape than a scaly reptile. The sunburn blackened most of its skin. Tufts of hair had formed on it as it squealed in immense turmoil.

"Meow," Jelly chanced her luck and crawled nearer to the pained monstrosity writhing around in front of her.

"Enough," Bonnie cocked her Rez-9 and loomed over the crying beast. She held the gun to its head and took mercy, "Peace."

BLAM!

She shot the ape creature in the head and jumped back when the unexpected made itself known.

"What the—?

Instead of busting the primate's head apart and disintegrating the rest of its body, it only exacerbated the transformation.

The impact of the bullet sent a bolt of electricity through its body, cracking its shoulders out a few inches. In retaliation, the ape climbed to its feet and stomped its considerably large feet to the ground.

Bonnie kept her gun pointed at the beast. "Wh-what… *are you?*"

The ape slammed its furry chest with both fists and roared, frightening Jelly enough for her to run behind Bonnie's feet for protection.

"Girl, we better get out of here. Let's go."

Bonnie walked backwards across the sand, keeping an eye on the ape-like creature as it screamed for vengeance. Pink tears shot down its face.

"That's one ugly beast," Bonnie turned around and expected to find Opera Beta sitting in the distance.

It wasn't there. The distant apparition of Opera Alpha in the horizon had vanished, too.

"God, I must be seeing things," she stopped in her tracks and looked down to Jelly. "Girl, where's our ship?"

"Muuuh," Jelly lifted her shoulders up and down, indicating that she had no clue.

ROOOOAAARRRR!

The ape's insane exclamation forced Bonnie and Jelly to pay attention to it. They turned around in tandem, expecting to be set-upon and mauled to death.

Instead of attacking, the ape slammed its fists against the sand. A loud grunt followed before it snorted through its widened nostrils.

Huffing around the grains of sand, it laid eyes on Jelly and grunted again. It held out its left paw, wanting Jelly to make contact.

The cat was much too afraid to oblige.

"Jelly, stay right where you are," Bonnie tuned her ears to the tree's attempt to reproduce Beethoven's classic symphony, "And would you *stop* that damn singing."

The tree, relentless in its insistence to continue singing, upped its volume. In turn, its rendition grew more strained and perverse.

The ape appeared not to hear it.

"Meow," Jelly tried in a bid to win favor - or at the very least, *time* - with the hirsute freak standing before them.

"We have nowhere to go," Bonnie faced the sky for some semblance of geography, "If we run, we could end up running forever."

The light from the intense sun blanketed her face. For just a moment, she felt like she was home. Closing her eyes shut and enjoying the warmth meant the world to her, "It's fantastic, isn't it?"

Bonnie opened her eyes and saw the sun had split into three, larger balls of magnificence. To call it *the sun* was a massive anomaly. It wasn't the sun Bonnie had enjoyed on Earth. The ball of fire she saw in the sky enlarged a few millimeters per second.

A deafening thud came from her left. "Oh, my God."

The ape had dropped onto its side, crying and moaning to itself. Much of its hair had shed and entwined amongst the grains of sands.

The grunting turned to sobbing as the ape balled up in the fetal position. As the hair shed away to reveal a pink-white skin - like that of a human being.

"Stay there, girl," Bonnie's curiosity outshone the cat's, which was a first in all the time they'd known each other. Jelly followed behind her careful not to draw attention to herself.

"Hey," Bonnie said at the five-foot lump of skin burying its head against its stomach, "Are you okay?"

The creature moved its arms forward and covered its face. As it groaned and kicked across the dusty ground with its feet, its ape-like voice normalized into that of a human being's.

"Sch… sch… gwup."

The sand sticking to its sweaty skin as it rolled around.

"Whoa," Bonnie held out her hands and tried to calm the thing down. "Hey, can you hear me?"

It removed its perfectly-formed human hands from its face. A scared and shivering man stared back at her - his face covered in pink liquid sprouting from his tear ducts.

A naked, male human being.

"Shaaa…" he gurgled and lifted his hand up, blocking out the light from the three suns. "Shaa—"

"—Here, get up," Bonnie grabbed his hand and hoisted him to his feet. She took the opportunity to thoroughly check him over. Two arms, two legs, ten fingers and toes. Overall, he appeared to be in excellent shape.

Bonnie's eyes clamped on the one appendage that confirmed his masculinity. She looked at his face and tried to keep professional, "You're not going to hurt me, are you?"

"Whu…" he gasped and scratched his beard as he eyed Jelly. "Wah!" He pointed at her, wanting to know what the furry little creature was.

"Oh, her? That's Jelly."

"Juh… juh…" he tried, closing his eyes, angry about his inability to replicate the sounds Bonnie was making. "Jeh…"

"Meow."

"Meee?" The man repeated - utterly clueless - and shook his head in anger. He thumped his stomach with the underside of his fist. "Meee. Oww."

Jelly looked to Bonnie for a reaction. This *new* human being was clearly insane, and probably quite volatile.

Bonnie chuckled to herself and extended her index finger. She placed her fingertip at her chest. "Bonnie."

"Boh… boh…" the man said, fighting of the perturbation of the singing tree. "Boh… knee."

"Yes."

She clapped her hands together and gave the man the thumbs up. She lifted her index finger and pressed it against his chest.

"Ah," he said, "Shaa…"

"Shaa?"

"Shanta—"

A pink tear rolled down his cheek. She flicked her finger over to his top lip and collected the liquid against her knuckle. "Do you know what this is?"

Jelly tore her gaze away from the man and looked at the tree. "Meow!"

WHUMP.

As the song slowed down the cavernous slit at the top of the tree coughed. Jelly squealed and spun her arms and hind legs around in the air in a fit of apoplectic rage.

Bonnie looked at her, deeply concerned. "Jelly!"

The confrontation between the two lasted exactly eight seconds. Then, the tree spat again.

WHUMP.

Jelly flew into a tizzy, thoroughly agitated by the noise. She extended her claws and made straight for the man standing in front of Bonnie.

"Maaaah," she growled, intending to launch herself into the air and claw the man to death.

He grunted and held out his arms for protection.

"Bad pussycat," Bonnie shouted at her as Jelly kicked her hind legs against the sand and jumped into the air, headed for the man's face.

"Meow."

The man's attempt to guard his face worked. Jelly took a swipe with her extended titanium claw and tore the skin on top of his hand. He batted her away, sending her to the floor.

She landed on her infinity claws and scraped a lump of sand away, ready for a second attack. "Meow."

WHUMP... The tree swayed around and coughed out a third and final sound. Jelly instantly relaxed and gave up her desire for blood.

She needed water, and the oceanfront looked suitably thirst-quenching.

"Shaaa—"

"—Meow," Jelly snapped, cutting the man off mid-grunt. The stern look in her eyes suggested she wasn't to be messed with. Her nose twitched over and over again as her whiskers began to vibrate.

The tree's incessant humming of the tune came to a

close.

Then, Jelly's facial fur stood on end, as if having been rubbed by a balloon, "Meoowwuuurrr…."

Bonnie and the man couldn't tear their eyes away. Something *strange* was happening to Jelly.

Her entire body shuddered continuously.

The tree began to subside and crumble apart.

The sky grew overcast with a milk-like substance.

Jelly's whiskers tingled and sparked, lighting up. The intensity throttled her around, the air dragging her by the shoulders towards the shore.

"Jelly," Bonnie ran after her. Ready to take out her Rez-9 and blast whatever was responsible for pulling Jelly to the ocean, she found herself at a loss. Nothing to shoot - no preventable action could be taken.

Powerless, Bonnie watched Jelly lift into the air, thrashing her limbs around and screaming for dear life.

"Oh, *God…*" Bonnie dropped her arms and witnessed the tree break apart and slink into the pink, bloodied ocean.

"Miyeeeww,' Jelly let out a final squeal of terror fifty feet in the air. The invisible force released its grip and tossed her face-first into the water.

She threw her infinity claws in front of her face.

SPLOSH.

Helpless, Bonnie didn't know where to turn. Perhaps the naked man could help?

"Hey, you," she said. "Where are— oh, *no.* Oh no, no, no…"

She couldn't believe what she saw.

His severed head sat atop the sand, wide-eyed. It looked as if someone had buried him up to the neck for fun.

She retrieved her Rez-9 from her belt and held it at the head, "Where's… where's the rest of your body—"

BOP!

An incredible forced slammed Bonnie from behind,

throwing her chest-first to the floor. "Gah!" Her Rez-9 flew out of her hand and slid ten feet across the sand in front of her. "Damn."

She pushed herself onto her elbows, expected to be blinded by the sun, "Help me."

Instead, the shadow of something insidious crept over her face. Whatever it was scuttled in slow-motion toward her.

Bonnie kicked herself back along the sand, trying to understand the predicament she was in. "Jesus Christ, what the *hell* is that?"

It was an outrageous amalgam of flesh and skin, previously of human form. Measuring eight-foot high and around ten-foot wide. Twelve limb-like legs with stumps on each side working in unison to help it forward. A gaping concoction of gums and teeth opened up in the middle and let out a guttural, terrifying roar.

Seconds away from doing whatever it was it did to people like Bonnie, she decided she wasn't sticking around to find out.

"*Jeez...*"

She scrambled onto her front and crawled along the piping hot sandy surface. Her fists slipped with each grasp forward, slowing her escape down to a near halt.

The creature gained on her.

"Come on, come on..." she squinted at her Rez-9 firearm laying five feet away from her, "Gah, gah... *come on.*"

She made the mistake of looking over her shoulder. The beast jabbed the sand with its four front limbs and pulled itself toward her.

"Aggh," she dug her heels into the ground and pushed the top half of her body back a few inches.

SWIPE! SWISH!

One of its limbs tore her inner-suit with its razor sharp talon at the end of its stump.

Six of its back limbs lifted up, ready to strike, leaving

six grounded flesh poles to move forward.

"No, no… *please*."

The beast roared, spraying pink spittle into the air. Some of it hit Bonnie's face as she trailed back by her elbows, "No!"

SWIPE!

Bonnie kicked her titanium foot at the beast in an attempt to fend it off. It had the opposite effect, enraging the beast even more.

Her leg detached from the ball and joint socket in her hip, the dislodged appendage firmly in the beast's razor-sharp claws.

"Nooo," Bonnie flipped onto her front and scrambled for her Rez-9. She grabbed at it but her fingertips couldn't quite get there.

Just three inches separated her from death and freedom. "Please, please…"

WHUMP!

The beast roared once again and stabbed at Bonnie, spearing its front-left limb into the ground.

"Gah! Cute little thing, aren't ya?"

Bonnie scrunched her face and planted the sole of her right boot on the creature's front limb. The beast howled as she kicked herself back.

She rolled onto her side, swiped her Rez-9 in her right hand and swung the barrel at the center of the monstrosity.

"Hey, you," She flicked the latch on the side of the chamber, arming the gun, "Look at me, you disgusting knuckle-headed bag of puke."

All twelve of the creature's limbs tightened up, throwing its body onto its haunches.

"Go to hell," she pulled the trigger and covered her face.

The hole at the end of the barrel focused into the creature's view, followed by a smothering of white light. It's mouth opened up and screamed in her face.

"Shantaaaaaaa—"

KA-SCHPPLLAAATTT!!!

The creature exploded into a zillion, gloopy pieces. It's stuck front limb stood upright like a tent peg as the rest of it splattered across the ground, coating the sand a wet shade of pink and red.

Bonnie held her position - and her breath - wanting confirmation that the thing had been obliterated.

Her detached leg slumped to the middle of the gore-strewn sand a few feet away from her.

She took a deep breath and pressed the back of her head against the sand, thankful she hadn't been killed.

As the harsh, radioactive light from the three suns cooked her face, she realized she didn't have to worry about sunburn. She was an Androgyne unit, after all, despite her memories suggesting the contrary.

Bonnie moved her head to the side. The waves crashed against the shore.

The tree was there a few moments ago but had disappeared during the fight. Its absence brought Bonnie back into action.

Where had Jelly gone?

Chapter 10

Pink Symphony

A thousand bubbles raced up Jelly's arms as she waded through the clear, blue water.

"Blug-blug-blug," came out of her mouth instead of a meow. Her lungs expelled the oxygen into the never-ending depths of the ocean.

Her whiskers lit up a neon yellow and fizzed at the tips. Her infinity claws acted the same way as she forced herself to keep her eyes open.

She'd experienced water before. Outside of actually needing to drink it, she'd fallen into Jamie's paddling pool in the garden area outside his apartment. It was a torturous affair for her.

But this was no paddling pool. It stretched out in all directions. The surface was only a few feet from her head.

She learned to swim right there and then. A movement of both arms seemed to do the trick. She waded as hard as she could, trying to reach the surface.

It was no use.

Time and oxygen were running out. A feeling of suffocation began to pervade her body and mind. The ensuing panic afforded her that vital few seconds she'd need if she was to ever reach the surface.

Bwup, bwup, bwup…

Jelly felt her whiskers direct her away from the surface -

the opposite direction to her she felt she needed to go.

A dolphin echo from way, way down pierced through the water. Before long, a second and third siren beamed through the density of the ocean.

Her claws opened out and sparked again, pointing toward the ocean bed. It was too far down to be seen with her eyes. It was clear to her that her whiskers were pointing her to the ocean bed.

Jelly had no concept of drowning. She knew she needed to breathe, though - that much was clear. How long could she hold on for without any air?

Whump.

A ripple of bubbles spread apart as she swam down to the bed. With no concept of drowning came little concept of how physics worked. She was a cat, after all, trying to figure out everything on her own terms.

The pervading tail-end of the whump noise rumbling through the water crashed against her, firing up her internal engine. She clawed at the bubbles, hoping one of them might release so much-needed respite.

No such luck.

The other bubbles chuckled away, laughing at her, as she tried to kill them. They were too fast.

Whump…

It was easy enough for her to recoil and tumble head-over-tail in the weightlessness of the ocean. A feeling she'd experienced once or twice during zero gravity training. At least she had that going for her.

That second *whump* sound came from *somewhere* below. Jelly pressed her paws to her face and stopped moving. Her tail drifted up between her fanned-out legs as she tried to block out the fury she felt.

"Bleooowwulp," she squealed, expending most of what little oxygen remained in her body.

Then, a dawning realization set in. No more air. That was her last breath floating in a warbled, glinting bubble dead in front of her face.

Her whiskers buzzed to life once again, sending a tingling sensation down her spine.

Jelly barreled over and plummeted toward the sea bed as fast as she could. On the way, she spotted a school of fish swimming around. The same fish that would go on to beach themselves and turn into those creatures.

She wished she could trade places with them.

Biddum-biddum-biddum…

Her heart-rate quickened. The water felt like it was heating up. Nothing to do with her proximity within the water, rather, her rising body temperature and fear that death was looming.

Death was on the cards if a way out didn't present itself soon.

"Blowaarggh," Jelly let out the last gasp of oxygen she had in her lungs. The closer to the ocean bed she swam, the more her whiskers lit up and fizzed.

Her infinity claws pushed push the water away, almost intuitively. She breast-stroked deeper and deeper toward the ocean bed.

A pink hue burst through the water from below like a discarded floodlight. The strips of light bounced around, offering her a challenge.

Swipe right, fail to catch.

Swipe left, bound forward - still no success.

The light couldn't be caught. The closer she swam to the source the more her whiskers seemed to guide her.

Way, way up above, an unintelligible voice shouted something at someone. Then, the sound of a holy thud creaked across the ocean's surface.

A deathly howl followed.

The blackened branches of the tree bulleted through the water, narrowly missing Jelly as she continued to swim…

And swim…

Her whiskers danced a glorious light show as the

source of the pink beams made itself visually available.

A gelatinous blob of pink throbbed near the root of the tree, surrounded by a sliver of gold haze.

"Glub… glub," Jelly's mouth opened out. Her eyes widened at the view of the spectacular foreign entity calling her down.

Consciousness was about to become a thing of the past…

***

"Jelly?"

"Meow."

"I know you're not a dog. But I have this ball if you wanna play with it?"

Jamie sat crossed-legged in the middle of the garden. He held up a shiny pink object about the size of a tennis ball. Jelly sat a few feet away wondering what the dastardly contraption was.

"Wanna chase the ball?"

She purred up a treat and climbed on all fours, ready for Jamie to roll the ball to her.

"Ah, no, no," he giggled. "You gotta go get it. Ready?"

"Meow."

He tossed the ball toward the bushes by the fence - a little too hard. "Oh."

"Meow," Jelly jumped at the bushes and followed the ball through the foliage.

Jamie scrambled to his feet and called after her. He knew the danger of the bushes all too well. The fence was broken. Worse, the busy main road lay right behind it.

"Jelly, come back!" he yelled as he saw her behind disappear behind the bushes.

She trundled through the leaves and broken sticks and eyed the ball as it rolled through the gap in the fence. "Meow." The sticks broke apart as she trundled over them.

The hole in the fence yawned out and invited her through.

The hole was a bit smaller than she'd have liked. Hoisting her considerable frame through tiny opening was painful. The jagged ends raked through her fur and body as she squeezed through.

The pink ball took center stage in the middle of the road. It seemed to plead for rescue amongst the whizzing cars. She hadn't the first clue how to grab the thing when she reached it.

But it didn't matter. It needed rescuing, and that was all that mattered. She bolted across the first lane of traffic believing herself to be invincible.

NEEAAWW!

A car whizzed past her, nearly taking a whisker away from her face.

More cars shot past at ridiculous speeds. Her head twisted right to left, left to right, keeping up with the vehicular jousting match.

"Jelly, don't move," Jamie's face appeared in the hole of the fence. He'd burrowed through the mud and sticks to try and save her.

"Meow," she turned around and spotted her opportunity to move.

Pounce!

She jumped into the middle of the road, narrowly avoiding being hit by a speeding car.

"Jelly," Jamie hollered. "What did I tell you? Stay there."

She sniffed around the ball and kicked her tail up for balance. She decided she couldn't bite it much less carry it in her mouth. She'd seen dogs do it but knew that they were more adept at carrying items.

Bop.

She knocked the ball with her paw. It wobbled and rested back to its original position.

Maybe two paws?

She yelped and batted the ball from opposite ends with

her two paws. It pinged out of her grasp and rolled across the main road.

Without thinking, she darted after it… but hadn't counted on a speeding car rocketing toward her.

She turned to face the gargantuan hunk of metal blare its horn and flood her face with its head lights.

"Meow."

"No," Jamie ran into the path of the car with his arms out, hoping the driver would slam on his brakes in time.

Jelly closed her eyes and held her breath, expecting the worst…

***

Darkness.

Imagine your arms, legs and midriff are suspended in the air. Like you're lying on cloud, without fear of falling either side. No more noise.

Just complete and utter silence.

That's how Jelly felt for a time once the headlights disappeared. She opened her eyes very slowly.

A horizontal slit let a flood of white and pink light into her retinas. It should have hurt but it didn't. Instead, it had a soothing effect.

Her left paw lifted into view, complete with her titanium claws. She exercised them, retracting them in and fanning them back out. A tiny whirring occurred, followed by a streak of blue shocks.

Her right paw waded in front of her face, blockading the view of the length of her body.

An endless gloop of pink stuff cocooned her outstretched body as if being smothered by a warm duvet.

No more suffocating. No more water. No more *anything.*

She tried to flip around to her side but couldn't. Perhaps she was too relaxed? Not as such. She wanted to move around - but simply couldn't.

Her limbs worked, evidently. She wasn't tired - quite the contrary.

She lifted her face to the side and stared at the sticky, pink substance and tried to meow at it.

But she couldn't speak. Her mouth opened, but nothing came out.

A face emerged within the pink, jellied tomb. A nose, then two cheekbones and a pair of eyes. It moved around and stared back at Jelly.

"Ha… Haloo… ?" Jelly mouthed.

A smile stretched across the image of the woman's face and nodded. "Hello, Jelly," it said, softly.

"Mwaaa-ack,' Jelly nearly squeezed out a sound but it was of little use. She pained when she tried to speak and so decided against it.

Another face appeared directly above her. A Japanese woman Jelly had met on Space Opera Alpha. Her name was Zilla Chin-Dunne.

"Zaaah…" Jelly tried and licked her mouth.

Zillah's face nodded and slowly faded away from the sloppy, pink ceiling.

Jelly made the mistake of blinking. Blackness fell for approximately two-fifths of a second and turned back to pink. Another blink. The gelatinous catacomb turned black.

Another blink, and it turned pink once again.

It frightened Jelly to the point where she didn't want to blink ever again.

Before she had time to display her defiance the entire womb-like tomb rotated around her body. The sound of the movement was intense. She wasn't able to block her ears with her paws. Try as she might, she'd just have to put up with the deafening sound.

"Meeeooowwww."

"Jelly," a voice whirled around the increasing spin of the tomb, "Something *fantastic* is coming."

"Mwaaaah," she screamed and clamped her face with

both paws, careful not to take her eye out with her infinity claws.

Lightning bolts struck around the internal walls of the tomb, briefly illuminating it to resemble the inside of a human brain.

Then, Jelly herself began to spin around sideways.

At first it was quick, but as the tomb's rotation sped up so, too, did Jelly's - in the opposite direction.

Spin… spin… spin…

Faster and faster and faster…

A rocketing thunder clap lit up the tomb as it smoothed out into a perfect cylinder, spinning faster than was comprehensible.

Jelly's meowing bleached into a blend of gargles and growls then to nothing as she rotated several hundred times per second.

The thunder bolts intensified as a pang of white light broke out from her face.

Perfect oblong particles broke along her whiskers, streaking out to her nose and cheeks, shifting them away from her head.

Just then, a storm of choral music piped in, smearing into the brilliant white light as Jelly spun around even faster. And faster. Her body blurred, she was spinning so fast.

Her body ballooned due to the inertia until it reached the insides the tomb in all directions. Jelly's zippy revolutions per second were beyond measure.

Spin-spin-spin-spin… Jelly let out a prolonged growl of pain.

The white light exploded into a miasma of heavenly outreach.

Seconds later it swallowed onto itself, leaving absolutely nothing left… *of anything.*

Chapter 11

USARIC Headquarters

Cape Claudius, South Texas, USA

The staff parking lot.

A quartet of USARIC mercenaries decked out in standard-issue armor bundled an elderly man into the back of a limousine.

"Get in, now," the leader of the squad stood next to the door as the man got in.

"Sheck is secure," he said into his black-coated utility sleeve. The USARIC logo adorned the underside of his forearm, along with his first initial and surname - *K. Too.*

He listened intently to the response.

"Kaoz," Marr shifting his behind across the length of the limousine's back seat, "Are we going or what?"

"Team, listen up," Kaoz addressed his three subordinates and pointed at the peninsula in the not-too-distant horizon. "We've had a major security breach at the Animal compound, Sector Z118."

"What happened?" asked one of the mercenaries, ready to spring into action. "What kind of breach?"

"Most escaped. The perps have been dealt with but the subjects in the second bay escaped."

"Escaped?"

"They're headed for the peninsula."

The reflection of the incomplete Space Opera Charlie vessel smeared across Kaoz's visor.

"Set up a task and finish team to bring them back. They're not regular felines."

"They're not?"

"No. Don't ask any questions. Just find them and bring them back. Dead or alive, I don't much care at this point."

"Understood," Kaoz stepped into the limousine and took a seat opposite Maar. He thumped on the driver's compartment, "Let's go."

The driver slammed on the gas and drove toward the gated exit. A kick of dust lifted from the ground and into dusky haze of the setting sun.

Maar almost freaked out inside the car. He couldn't get comfortable, fidgeting around with the belt clip in the padding of the plush seat.

"Don't be anxious," Kaoz flipped his visor over his head and pinched his mouthpiece, "You're perfectly safe now. ETA, ten minutes."

"Good, good," Maar looked over his shoulder and saw the USARIC building vanish into the distance, "Please tell me this damn car is bulletproof?"

"Of course it is."

"I'm sorry. Can we talk business, please?"

Kaoz and Maar turned to a stern-looking man with silver hair sitting opposite them. He pressed his back against the glass compartment between them and the driver.

"Sorry, Crain. What's the update?"

Crain McDormand - USARIC's head of the legal counsel and the chair of the select committee. Not someone you'd want to get on the wrong side of. He had a manner about him that suggested he'd take you down in court for looking at him the wrong way.

Crain opened his palm and pulled out his thumbnail, "About fifteen minutes after Vasilov was executed someone sent an Individimedia broadcast inside USARIC's animal compound."

He set his cuticle down on the champagne unit next to his knee.

"Some guy with blue hair you might recognize."

The thumbnail projected a paused holographic image of Handax Skill in the middle of the limousine.

"I think I'd recognize a cretin with blue hair," Maar kept his head away from the passenger window. He wasn't terribly interested in a stray bullet flying through his cranium. "Who is this guy?"

"His name is Handax Skill," the man explained, "Sort of the leader of PAAC."

"People Against Animal Cruelty?" Kaoz asked and shook his head. "They're always disturbing us."

"They did a great job in the past hour, I'm afraid to say," Crain snapped his fingers and sat back into the chair, "I could fill you in verbally. The broadcast does a better job of explaining just how bad this is than I ever could."

"They kill Dimitri and there's *more* bad news?"

"Just watch."

Maar leaned forward as the recording played. A sound of gunfire and commotion rattled around the walls of the limousine.

Even though Handax was long dead it felt like he was directly addressing everyone in the vehicle. Maar found it doubly worrying. He'd failed to realize that Handax addressed *a lot* more people than just those in the car.

"Bisoubisou never boarded Opera Beta. We found her body at the compound along with hundreds of others. Those we found alive and well, we rescued. USARIC has killed three of my team. Moses, Denny, and Leif—"

"—Oh no, no," Maar gasped and held his mouth in shock, "Did this Individimedia go live?"

"I'm afraid so," Crain frowned.

"What? How many saw it?"

"Tens of thousands, if not more. Keep watching."

"That's okay," Maar tried to calm himself down, "We'll just deny it and claim—"

"—They'll deny it, of course," Handax's recording continued much to Maar's worry, "They'll claim they went missing and have no involvement. In a matter of seconds, I'll be joining them."

"Over there," screamed another voice in the recording. "Hey, you. Put your arms above your head and drop to your knees."

Handax turned away from the broadcast to a cacophony of bullets. The recording paused, offering Crain, Maar, and Kaoz a view of the ground.

"Oh, for heaven's sake," Maar thumped the seat in anger and wiped his sweating brow, "USARIC shot the protesters dead on a live feed?"

Kaoz and Crain didn't know how to respond. They watched their boss try to calm down.

The roads were empty right now. Maar was surrounded by advisers and bodyguards, two of whom were with him in the limousine. Many more were stationed at USARIC's Research & Development Institute twenty miles away to the north.

"I'm…" Maar whimpered, "This was a mistake. A big mistake."

"What was a mistake?" Crain asked with no hint of emotion.

"The Star Cat Project," Maar pointed around the interior of the limousine, "Opera Beta, all this. How long ago was the broadcast?"

"Thirty minutes or so."

"Ugh," Maar hung his head and sniffed, "All hell is going to break loose."

"Maar, if I may say so. I don't think any of this was a mistake. You made decisions in USARIC's best interests. If you had failed to act on Saturn Cry, or Tripp Healy's request to find a suitable subject, we could well have regretted it. In my view you had no choice."

"Try telling that to Dimitri," Maar looked up and stared Crain out with his now-reddened eyes, "He's not even around anymore to argue with you."

"It's *terriful* what happened to him,' Crain tried to sympathize, 'but this was always going to be a contentious issue. It's just very unfortunate—"

"—They shot him in the chest and practically destroyed the animal compound," Maar interjected with a healthy dose of venom, "They've set a dangerous precedent. You know what people are like. When one maniac shoots a place up and becomes a household name they spawn thousands of imitators."

"I'm sure it won't come to that, Maar,"

"Thank God social media is a thing of the past. Everyone would be getting ideas."

Crain tried for a smile of reassurance. "They targeted Vasilov because of his Russian connection. The two aboard Beta who defected and tried to sabotage the mission."

"You're not the one in my shoes, Crain," Maar said. "I want my wife and son relocated to safety."

"It's not necessary—"

"—Have it done right now, Crain," Maar snapped in a fit of rage, "I can't have them in the firing line. Compounds collapse. Important people get shot. Innocent bystanders die."

Crain slipped his thumbnail onto his thumb and shook his head.

"Crain?" Maar threw the man a look of remorse, "Wives and children *burn*, Crain."

Moscow, Russia

Second Sub District of Ramenki

Seven-year-old Remy Gagarin looked up at his mother with an angelic smile. She spat into her palm and wiped a black smudge from his cheek.

Vera Gagarin held her son's face in her hands and made sure he looked the part.

"Mom?"

"Yes, Remy?"

"Why must I speak in English?"

"Because, son, most who watch will not understand Russian."

She palmed his dark, gelled hair over his scalp and smartened him up. She took a step back and eyed him up and down, "There, that is much better."

Remy held out his arms. Dressed in a very attractive suit and tie, he looked approximately a quarter of a million dollars.

It had been nearly two years since Space Opera Beta left on its mission to Saturn.

Remy looked at the marble mantelpiece as he pulled his shirt down. Pictures of him with various celebrities, including Maar Sheck, adorned the wall.

He'd become famous for a time - the handsome boy whose Russian Blue had won the Star Cat Project.

He missed Bisoubisou beyond all measure. His family's new-found riches staved off the regret for large periods of time. The sickening feeling of giving her up for the sake of the good life crept back in. He'd grown up a lot in the past twenty-four months.

Vera didn't much care about Bisoubisou. She and her son rarely spoke of her.

His mother had never been much of a cat lover. Bisoubisou was her son's pet as far as she was concerned - at least, that's what she'd tell herself whenever she experienced the odd pang of regret.

The most fierce regret came in the form of the occasional sadness in her son's eyes. He walked over to the Bisoubisou action figure perched next to the photos. A five-inch rendition of the cat he once had, which resulted in a brief, but Pyrrhic, smile of affection.

Vera's forearm pulsed. She pushed the black ink around into a circle on her skin and looked at her son, "You still miss her, don't you?"

"She is in space helping the American astronauts," Remy was lost in his own naive contrition. He put the figure down on the ledge, "One day she will return."

"Okay, she is ready," Vera pulled an antique chair across the rug and set it beside their expensive couch. "Come, sit next to me."

Remy sat next to his mother on the sofa. She removed her thumbnail and placed it on the Edwardian-style coffee table in front of their knees. "Now, remember. You speak with precision. No filling time with *lessense*."

"Yes, mother."

"You answer the questions she has with as few words as possible and be polite when you do it."

"I will."

"Very good," she snapped her fingers, forcing a projected holographic image of a woman to appear in the middle of the room.

"Ah, I'm here."

A life-size image of Dreenagh Remix pinged to life in the middle of the coffee table. Her shins were out of view as she stood within the coffee table. "Oh, I'm sorry," she looked down and stepped out through the wooden slab.

"That is quite okay."

"Ugh, I hate these live feeds sometimes," Dreenagh chuckled. Her transparent visual representation shimmied up and down like a drunken ghost trying to maintain the strength of its connection from the ether.

"You know, one time, I appeared in my boyfriend's toilet while he was brushing his teeth. So embarrassing."

Dreenagh's affable humor didn't wash very well with the Gagarin family. She shrugged her shoulders, pulled up her left sleeve and pointed at the chair, "Is that for me?"

"Yes," Vera pushed her long ponytail behind her neck and showed Dreenagh right side of her face. "I prefer if you show this side as it is better than my left."

"You're gorgeous. You have *no* bad sides, Vera,"

Dreenagh held out her see-through hand. A tiny drone built itself from the surface of her skin. "How are you, Remy?"

"I am well, Dreenagh. Thank you."

"You excited about the interview?"

"Yes. I think so."

The drone whizzed from Dreenagh's palm and zoomed twenty feet away. She angled her fist to the right, moving the holographic drone above the coffee table. "Okay, ready?"

"We are ready," Vera held her posture steady for the drone.

"*Amaziant*, here we go," Dreenagh turned to the drone. The light beaming from its iris blasted out and highlighted the contours on each of the three bodies.

"Hey, good people," she smiled at the drone and jumped into professional-mode, "Dreenagh Remix here on Individimedia forty-four. As we approach the two-year anniversary of the Star Cat Project and Opera Beta's mission to Saturn, I'm *here*, so to speak, with the Bisoubisou's owners for an exclusive update."

Dreenagh turned to Remy and gave him a media-strewn smile. "Remy Gagarin. You must be very excited?"

"Yes, I am. My cat is going to help people."

Vera placed her hand on his knee. "Yes, we are most proud of Bisoubisou."

"Now, Vera, as Remy's mother, how has the past two years affected you?"

"Oh, we have been most fortunate. We have the satisfaction of knowing our beloved pet is helping USARIC on their vital mission," she beamed and eyeballed the interior of their expensive front room. "As you can see, the money has helped, too."

"So I see," Dreenagh's holographic image sat forward, impressed by the no-expense-spared decor, "I gather the quarter of a million dollar prize money was just the beginning?"

"Indeed, it was very helpful," Vera smiled at Remy, "Since then, Bisoubisou has become a hero and we have become like celebrities."

"I guess the celebrity endorsements contributed to your wealth, too?"

"My mother had a small part in Star Jelly thirty-eight as a scientist."

"Oh, yes," Dreenagh chuckled politely, "The Star Jelly movie franchise. She was very good at acting, wasn't she?"

"Yes," Remy said, "And I appeared in cat food commercials."

"Meow-nom-nom," Dreenagh enacted the famous line from the commercial. "I'm sure people say that to you all the time, right?"

"Not really," Remy said. "We try to stay away from poor people who eat junk food."

"Oh."

Vera rolled her shoulders and held her neck out, attempting to remove her double-chin from the drone's feed. "Yes, it got very much bad after everyone found out where we lived. So we moved here. Remy is now home-schooled."

"A very wise idea."

"Yes."

Dreenagh's mood softened as she looked at her forearm, preparing herself for the next question. "Remy?"

"Yes?"

"Have you been missing Bisoubisou since she's been away?"

Remy stared at his pristine-suited legs and considered the question. "Yes, I do. But she will be home soon."

It was clear that Vera had no knowledge of recent events at Cape Claudius. She wondered why the aura in the interview was so chirpy. If Remy and his mother and known the truth they might not have been so forthcoming with their answers - or even agreed to the interview in the first place.

Chrome Valley

Northwest London, United Kingdom

Jamie sat cross-legged on the floor of the front room watching Dreenagh's Individimedia broadcast. His mother, Emily, sat on the couch keeping one eye on the floor.

Remy and Vera's holographic representations sat in the middle of the front room awaiting Dreenagh's next question.

A toddler crawled across the carpet, trying to grab at Vera's sparkling shoes.

"No, Jolene," Emily ran over to her and scooped her off the floor, "It's not real, don't touch it."

"Ga-ga," she burped and produced a messy grin.

"Mom, please. I'm trying to listen," Jamie lifted his palm in the air and, along with it, the volume of the broadcast.

Emily lifted Jolene into her high chair, "Not too loud, poppet. You'll upset your sister."

"Not as upset as Remy's going to be, look," Jamie pointed at Dreenagh, "She knows they don't know. She's going to tell him."

"Oh, Jesus," Emily lowered her behind to the couch, entranced by the drama that would surely follow, "That woman is a piece of work. Tony, come and see this."

"History in the making, is it?" Tony appeared at the door to the front room with a cup of coffee. He leaned against the frame and shook his head. "They have no idea?"

"No, Dad," Jamie turned to the broadcast with great intensity, "Everyone knows but them."

Dreenagh cleared her throat and dampened her voice. Remy eyes shot back at her, wistfully.

"Remy, what was your reaction to the breaking news a couple of hours ago?"

"What news?" Vera asked. "What are you speaking

about?"

"You don't know, do you?"

"No," Remy said with innocence, "Is something wrong?"

Dreenagh closed her eyes. On the surface she felt terrible. In her heart, she knew she had the exclusive story of a lifetime. She'd be the first to break it. Enough for her to continue with her USARIC-like grab for power and glory.

"Someone broke into USARIC and found Bisoubisou's body."

"What?" Remy snapped. "You liar. Is it a joke?"

"No, Remy. He sent out a message saying that Bisoubisou was dead and still at USARIC."

"This is quite terriful," Vera snapped. "Bisoubisou is at Saturn helping the Americans find out what the message means."

"I'm afraid not," Dreenagh held out her finger and drew a large rectangle in from their face. Handax's face appeared and the broadcast began to play."

Emily turned to Tony, full of emotion. "I can't watch this."

"No, Mom. We *need* to watch it," Jamie pushed himself onto his feet. Now seven-years-old, he'd grown since he'd last seen Jelly. "It's always better to tell the truth," he turned to his stepfather for confirmation, "Isn't it, Dad?"

"I'm not so sure on this occasion, Jamie," Tony fixed his gaze on Remy's beleaguered face. "Sometimes we have to tell lies. Sometimes it's necessary."

"The scumbags never told them," Emily left the room in a flood of tears. "All this time we thought they knew."

"Sweetie," Tony walked after her and tried to talk her down from her upset. "It's not your fault—"

"—Yes, it is. I took USARIC at their word like a complete fool."

Jamie shut out his mother's grief and concentrated on the interview.

Remy burst into tears and fell into his Vera's arms. She was equally as shocked at the news. His mother's holographic representation pushed through Jolene's face. She, too, began to cry at the visual of Remy doing the same thing.

"Jolene, stop it," Jamie pointed at Dreenagh, "I'm trying to watch."

Vera hugged her grief-ridden son and screamed at Dreenagh. "My God. Is this some kind of sick joke?"

"No, Vera. I'm afraid not."

"It is a lie," she unhanded Remy and stood up from the couch, "You media, you are all the same. Nothing but sensation and lies."

"Well, I'm sorry but—"

"—Get out of my house, you scheming cow."

Dreenagh's transparent image stood up and held out her hands. "I'm not *in* your house, technically."

"That's not what I meant and you know it," she barked back and pointed at Remy sobbing against a cushion, "You invade my home. You come here, spreading lies with actors with stupid colored hair."

"I can assure you I am not lying, Vera. Look," Dreenagh displayed her forearm. The ink swirled around to form a number: 1.4M.

"See that?" Dreenagh asked.

"Yes?"

"That's how many viewers across the world are watching right now. Don't you think just *one* of them might have something to say if they knew it to be false?"

The woman had a point. Remy was way, way ahead of his mother in the grieving process. Granted, that was down to adolescent naivety on his part but, nevertheless, an accurate and fair distance ahead of his mother's reasoning.

"Bisoubisou died right there at the Star Cat Trial finals, Vera," Dreenagh said as she watched the dizzied Russian woman slump to the couch. "I'm sorry, but it's the truth."

"They killed her," Remy hyperventilated through his sobs, "They killed my cat—"

"—Vera, you think the assassination of Viktor Rabinovich and the subsequent expulsion of twenty-three Russian diplomats was a coincidence?" Dreenagh tried to bring the woman to her senses. "Do you see how this ties together?

Vera stared at the floor in bewilderment. "How could I have been so blind?"

"You may hate me, Vera, and that's fine. But I'm a journalist," Dreenagh smiled at her drone and gave it a sly wink, "My job is to report the truth. You saw it here first, viewers."

Jamie couldn't decide which of the three images were more compelling.

Remy, with the look of fear and devastation on his face.

Vera came around to the idea that her life and career was over.

Dreenagh Remix suppressed her desire for fame and fortune at the expense of tearing a family apart with the truth.

It was at this moment that Jamie Anderson realized two things:

1: The world didn't work the way he thought it did. The same could be said for the universe at large but there was no time to expatiate on it. The world suddenly showed its playing cards as the ruthless, vindictive and painful place it had always been. The same place his mother and, until a few years ago, his biological father had tried to shield from his innocent eyes.

2: Bisoubisou's death and subsequent absence was known to him and his mother. Jelly went in her place after accidentally murdering her. Actually, *murder*, he thought, was a complete misnomer. She was merely defending herself and fought for honor. At the time Jelly was signed up, he and his mother signed a contract non-disclosure agreement. Judging by the Gagarin family interview, it seemed they had avoided a major hassle. Jamie and his mother received the prize money. When he turned eighteen he'd be in receipt of the bulk of it.

A thought occurred to him as he sat in the carpet.

If everyone now knew that Bisoubisou didn't join Opera Beta, then *which cat did*?

He assumed that anyone wanting answers - which was *everyone* and their grandmother - would come knocking at the Anderson household looking for answers.

One such feisty journalist named Dreenagh Remix could be the first of them.

"Mom, Mom," Jamie climbed to his feet and ran out of the front room. He used the sound of his mother's sobbing as route to find where she was. "*Mom.*"

Tony stepped into Jamie's path, preventing him from reaching the bedroom. "Hey, son. She's a bit upset. Give her a few minutes, okay?"

"No, Tony. This is really—"

"—Don't call me Tony. I'm your father."

"You're not my *real* dad," he barged past and nearly made the door, only to be caught by the back of the shirt. Tony crouched down and glanced at his vindictive little stepchild in the eyes.

"What did you just say?"

"I'm sorry, I—"

"—I'd appreciate it if you referred to me as *Dad*," Tony finished, noticing Jamie was desperate to get to his mother. "What's wrong?"

Jamie raised his eyebrows with great sincerity. "If everyone knows Remy's cat didn't go to Saturn they might think Jelly went, instead. Everyone still thinks she's the runner-up"

The boy had a hell of a point. The knock-on consequences of this revelation smacked Tony in the face. "You're right."

He stood up straight and made for the bedroom with

Jamie's hand in his. "Come on, son, let's go tell her."

Emily's incessant sobbing flew out of the bedroom and showed no sign of halting.

Tony peered around the door, not wanting to disturb her moment of sadness. "Emily?"

Jamie looked up at him with an cherubic smile. His stepfather couldn't help but feel a shudder roll down his spine. Moments ago he viewed Jamie as just an average little boy. Now, with the astonishing connection he'd made, the little boy seemed more mature.

Certainly wiser…

USARIC Research & Development Institute

Port D'Souza

(Ten miles northeast of Corpus Claudius)

USARIC's R&D institute, much like its headquarters at Cape Claudius, was so big it had its own zip code. Maar had become the major shareholder of the company now that Dimitri Vasilov was no longer breathing.

The research and development institute housed hangers designed to test thruster and engine capabilities. Much of Manning/Synapse's beta testing of the Androgyne series with the American Star Fleet had taken place at this location.

This evening, it also served as a discreet embassy to protect the one man who'd yet to be assassinated - Maar Sheck.

He stepped out of the tubular elevator cage and into a vast scientific laboratory.

Like the animal compound at USARIC HQ this clandestine set-up was as sinister, if not more so. Though he rarely frequented the science division (the nerds and tech-heads had that all covered) he always marveled at the technology on display.

No such luxuries could be afforded now, though, as Kaoz marched him and Crain along the observatory gangway several feet above the work parapet.

"How long do I have to stay down here?" Maar walked past a colossal slab of ceramic being polished by six men wearing breathing apparatus.

"As long as it takes, Maar," Kaoz said. "News has just broken of what's happened, so you'll be down here for at least another couple of months."

"*Couple of months*?"

"At least."

"Ugh, this is a nightmare."

"Unless you want to go up for air and risk getting your head blown off, then yes."

"God damn it," Maar pointed at the dead of a wall at the end of the gangway. A dim red bulb rotated just above it. "Are they here?"

"Yes."

Maar continued down the metal strip and waved them on. "Good, I want a full report on the subject capture, please. They better have good news for me."

The wall split in two as the men approached toward it. Kaoz lifted his mouthpiece in front of his lips and hit a button on his wrist. "Oxade, this is Kaoz. Come in."

The sound of an attack vehicle roared through his earpiece. "This is Oxade, over."

The clandestine bunker lit up as the three men entered. Maar placed his hands on his hips, "So, this is home, is it?" he asked himself as he looked around the featureless room.

"For the moment, yes," Crain said. "You're safe here."

"Do my family know?"

"Oh. Good Lord, no. They can't know your whereabouts."

Kaoz hit a button on the wall, forcing the doors to shut behind him. "Maar wants a sit-rep on the subject capture."

The moon was full tonight.

A female Siamese sniffed around a patch of fresh grass and mud in a desperate hunt for food. The dried flakes of dust began to rumble back and forth like a marbles on a vibrating trampoline.

Her ears pricked up, alert, "Meow."

The mud cracked apart as the sound of a furious engine blanketed her from behind.

She hopped around and attempted to find the source of the noise. Two giant headlamps blinded her as she howled for her life.

P'TATCH! SWISH-SWIPE!

A brown grid enlarged in front of her eyes. Her feet shot into the air. The tomb of rope tangled in her claws as she somersaulted and landed in the back of a jeep.

"Maaooowww," she squealed through her soft but venomous prison.

"Got her," Oxade yelled at the driver from the passenger side of the 4x4. He thumped the USARIC logo on the outside of the door. The Siamese squealed in terror as it clamped eyes on a dozen captured cats in the back. The roped cats slammed into each other as the vehicle sped along the ground.

"Sorry, Kaoz. You were saying?"

He clutched the window-mounted machine gun and flicked the attached flashlight to life. The ground illuminated as they sped up, searching for more of the escapees.

"Maar wants to know how many you've caught."

"Uh, hang on," Oxade turned to the back of the 4x4 and performed a hasty head count, "Around twenty or so. We have other units out looking for them. You know what herding cats is like."

"Okay, I'll tell him," Kaoz said before cutting the connection dead.

Two American bobtails - one orange, one white - hid behind a tree, exhausted from their escape from the compound. Not the fastest of felines, they'd become separated from the others who'd stormed ahead.

The 4x4's headlamps began as dots in the distance but expanded the closer they got to them.

"Meow," the orange bobtail nudged the white's behind, running toward the Port D'Souza peninsula on the Gulf of Mexico - a glorious stretch of water lit up by the full moon.

Orange bobtail found the strength to continue toward the section of land that encroached the water, leaving the fatigued white cat behind.

VROOM, VROOM!

"I think I can see another one," Oxade said to the driver, "Quick, to the left. Look, there. You can see its stupid cat's eyes."

"Meow," the white bobtail exclaimed and ran away from the vehicle's path.

Oxade took both handles of the gun as the driver floored the gas, frightening the life out of the cat. It jumped into the air and hissed, bushing up its tail.

He opened fire on the cat.

THRAAAA-TA-TAT-A-TAT!

"Here, kitty-kitty-kitty…" he shouted as the bullets chewed up the grass as it hopped around like a cowboy having its feet fired at it by a drunken ne'er-do-well.

"Rowwaaarrr," she screamed, tumbling around the exploding patches of mud.

"We got a live one," Oxade yelled at the driver, "I think this one's for the net. Back up."

The vehicle screeched to a halt, flinging mud out in front of its bumper.

The hellish red reverse lights sprang on, flooding the white bobtail's scared face. She turned around and ran off in the opposite direction.

VROOOOM!

The vehicle spun its wheels and darted backwards at full speed. Oxade swung the machine gun toward the trunk of the SUV and aimed it at the cat as the vehicle backed towards her.

"Faster, man. C'mon!"

"I'm trying," the driver shouted into the rear view mirror. He carefully avoided veering off the already-beaten track.

"Closer… *closer*… come on to daddy, you dumb critter," Oxade whispered, aiming the sight down on the cat's behind. "Now!"

He yanked back on both triggers.

P'TATCH!

A net blasted out from the barrel and javelined over her as she ran.

"Got her!"

SWISH-SWIPE! The net swished across the mud, wrapped itself around the white Bobtail's hind legs and swung into the air like a fierce fairground ride.

"Meeooooowwwwaaaaahhhh!"

She slammed to the opened deck in the back of the vehicles with dozens of fellow captives. The black Siamese clawed and chewed at the rope, trying to burst free. She looked up at the nasty man sitting atop the roof.

"Attention, please, my furry friends," Oxade squatted and clapped his hands together, "Now, all of you have been *very* naughty, haven't you? And you know what happens to bad pussycats, don't you?"

"Hey, Oxade," yelled the driver as he stepped on the gas, "Stop flirting with them. They've had enough."

Oxade hissed at the petrified cats, scaring them half to death, "Ha-ha!"

He thumped his foot on the roof and shouted over his shoulder. "We must have at least thirty of them, now."

"Where are the rest?"

"I don't know, but we'll get them," Oxade took a final look at the feline captives, "Won't we, my little pedigree chums?"

The 4x4 sped off past the trees and into the horizon. The noise from the engine dissipated only to be replaced by crickets.

Ten seconds later, a wet nose appeared from one of the trees. All clear.

Then another nose moved out from another tree…

… and another…

… until twenty or so female felines of different breeds, sizes and colors emerged, knowing they were safe - for now.

The leader of the pack, a gorgeous panther-esque Egyptian Mau with silver eyes, howled at the others and caught their attention.

Scores of tiny spiders crept across the ground, snaking in and out of their paws.

The cats clawed back at them, stomping, and squishing a few of the spindly creatures as they scuttled away.

Mau snarled at the surviving spiders. She roared at the ground, scaring them off.

The cats instinctively formed a crescent around her and sat on their haunches. They were ready for answers.

Mau shifted around, lifted her tail and showed them all her behind. Everyone knew who was in charge, now.

"Meow," the cats replied in unison.

Mau wandered toward the water knowing the others were following her. She averted her attention to the bright moon and stopped at the shoreline.

The cats sat upright behind her.

Mau licked her mouth and shook the fatigue from her head. The light from the moon streaked across her pupils.

"Meow."

The other cats followed suit. "Meow."

A wondrous sight to behold if anyone had seen it. Thirty or so escapees looking at the stars in the night sky. Thankful for the chance for freedom.

The call-outs to the moon occurred again, and again… until the chorus of meows from each cat blended into one prolonged and eerie howl at the moon…

Chapter 12

The Control Deck

Space Opera Beta

Tor held the analog keyboard in his hands, restricted in movement by the wires connecting to the deck. Manuel's holographic book hung in the air as they conversed.

"Manuel, what is your primary function?"

"To serve the crew of Space Opera Beta and to act as autopilot."

"Good," Tor punched the results onto the keys and turned to the transparent screen in front of the deck. He felt the rim of his Decapidisc, lamenting the day ever he fell on the wrong side of his crew. "Confirm coordinates of Opera Beta, please."

Manuel folded his spine and conked out for a couple of seconds.

"Manuel?"

"Yes, Tor?"

"Confirm Opera Beta coordinates, please. Command prompt. One, zero, six, forward slash, one, zero."

The numbers appeared in as a green digital readout over the front of the book.

"The coordinates are precisely the same as before. That is to say, zero, zero, zero, zero—"

"—Okay, stop. I get the picture."

Tor shook his head and typed a prompt on the keyboard, "Commencing scan, please standby."

Tripp and Wool ran into the deck ahead of Jaycee escorting Baldron through the door, "Tor, are we up and running?"

"Yes, we—" he turned around and saw Tripp clutching his Rez-9. It made him nervous, "What's going on? Why the gun?"

"Didn't you hear what I told you?" Tripp scanned the walls and ceiling ready to blast whatever might pop out from the walls, "The whole place is breaking up."

"Breaking up?"

"It's sick, comrade," Baldron spat and caught Tor's attention, "There's these *things* breaking into the ship, Viktor. We're not in space anymore, comrade."

Tor eyed Baldron's Decapidisc. It seemed to him that whoever was wearing one was considered to be the bad guy.

"Comrade," Baldron stepped over to Tor and opened his arms for a hug. The pair found they couldn't hug on account of the metal discs around their necks..

"Hey," Jaycee threatened the pair with his K-SPARK shotgun. "Less of that stupidity. Get a room."

"We *had* a room," Tor chewed down the urge to scream, "We were perfectly safe in N-Carcerate till you forced us out."

Baldron closed his eyes and tugged at his Decapidisc, "No, no, that's where the things got in."

"Will someone please tell me what he's talking about?" Tor asked. "What things?"

Tripp checked signs of damage on the control deck, "They're big and ugly, and vicious. Whatever they are."

Baldron eyed Jaycee, only to receive a knowing wink from him.

"You don't say."

"How's Manuel? We need to get the thrusters up and running and get the hell out of here."

Tor placed the keyboard on the control deck and hit the return key, "Functional, but still confused. I found something, though."

Wool kept her right hand near her belt's hand gun holster. "What did you find?

"A video message. Sent just before we went dark."

"Oh."

Tripp knew the content of the message. He had hoped to keep the details to himself, "The one from USARIC?"

Tor couldn't bear to look at his captain. "Yeah. Look." He hit a key. The holovideo to projected into the middle of the control deck.

Maar Sheck, CEO of USARIC, read from a prepared holographic statement at a podium.

"Following the death of Viktor Rabinovich, Deputy Dimitri Vasilov and the news of Russian infiltration on Space Opera Beta, USARIC will cease operation with immediate effect."

Baldron took a few steps around the holovideo and glanced at Tor, "So, they know?"

"Seems so," Tor nodded as the video played out.

Maar continued, "All diplomatic relations have been suspended with immediate effect. It is with regret that all Russian operatives are to be ejected from American soil, and vice versa."

Jaycee didn't take the revelation very well at all. He stomped over to the keyboard and hit the pause button. "You mean to tell me that Russia and North America are now at war?"

Tripp shook his head, "Not quite *war*. More a divorce, if you like."

"It wasn't our fault," Tor complained. "It was the brainchild of Dimitri Vasilov. We were only following orders."

"Much like my button on my glove, here," Jaycee held up his wrist and teased the button on his glove with his finger.

"Stop doing that," Baldron and Tor screamed in unison.

"Jaycee, stop," Wool tried to placate the angry mercenary as he pushed Baldron against the control deck.

"Hey, imbecile."

"Please don't kill me," Baldron felt along the rim of the deck and pulled himself away from Jaycee. "I swear, it wasn't—"

"—*Earth* is about to start a second cold war because of *you*. I have family back home."

Tripp tried to placate the angry giant's temper, "Jaycee, all of us have family back home."

"You shut up," He pointed at Tripp and screamed at him for the first time - close to two years' worth of pent-up frustration against his colleague.

Tripp lowered his gun, stunned beyond comprehension, "*Okaaay*?"

Jaycee socked Baldron in the face. The side of his body hit the deck, accidentally hitting the play button on the keyboard.

"Oww."

"You're gonna get us all killed,' Jaycee spat and blenched his fist.

Maar's hologram continued speaking, "We send our thoughts and prayers to the souls aboard Opera Beta and wish them all the best on their survival in the vicinity of Enceladus. Beta, may God be with you."

Jaycee ran his gloves through his hair and let out a pained exclamation, "Someone shut that imbecile off!"

"Yes," Tor scrambled to the keyboard and hit the pause button. "I'm sorry."

Tripp held out his arms and walked through the paused image of Maar Sheck. He offered a makeshift peace treaty. "Listen to me very carefully."

The visual cracked apart and vanished into thin air. The entire team turned to Tripp to hear him out.

"Events on Earth can't be changed. What's done is done. I can only run with the facts."

"No," Jaycee said. "We can kill these two right now and

protect ourselves."

Tor and Baldron hung their heads in shame. Jaycee wasn't exactly exercising his subtlety at this point.

"Stop and think for a second, will you? Just *think*. We can't kill them—"

"—you heard the message, Tripp," Jaycee said. "USARIC is no more. We're at war with these commie scum suckers—"

"—I know that. But the fact still stands. We need them and they need us. I don't care about what's going on back home. I just care that we *get* back home."

"This is utter lessense."

Tripp turned to the two men at the control deck, "You said Manuel was up and running?"

"Yes," Tor picked up the keyboard, eager to satisfy his superior.

"I want a trace on Anderson and Dr Whitaker. I want an update on the engine and the thrusters and what we need to do to get back get home."

Tor typed away on the keys with enthusiasm. Jaycee's desire to murder him and his colleague had been overridden by the captain. "I'm way ahead of you—"

BZZZZ-OWWW.

The communications and flight panel shunted around. The lights snapped off and filled the deck with darkness. The generator's hum slowed to a standstill. Even the floor's emergency strip lighting failed to light up.

"Jesus, what was that?" Wool's voice came from the darkness.

"Oh, God," Baldron's trembling vocal chords barreled around the room, "Is this it? Are we dead?"

"Stay absolutely still, everyone." Tripp advised. "Don't move a muscle."

"I can't see anything," Jaycee pressed his foot forward.

"I said don't move. Wool, is that you?"

"Yes, yes, I think so," she said, trying her level best to keep calm, "I can feel your hand."

"Don't move."

The walls and ground vibrated and shifted around. Despite the darkness, most in the room tried to keep their balance by holding onto something solid.

"What's going on?"

"We've lost power," Tripp barked. "Grab hold of something. Anything rooted to the ground or the wall."

The shifting intensified and refused to let up.

Wool grabbed hold of the flight deck. Jaycee pressed his back against the wall. The sound of two metal Decapidiscs clanging together suggested Tor and Baldron hugged each other.

"Christ, we're going to die," Baldron bawled. "This is how it ends."

"Shut up and hold tight," Tripp shouted over the noise and turned to the flight deck's acrylic frontage, "We're not going to— Oh… *my God.* What is *that*?"

Stars formed across the black canvas of space. Lighting up one by one, they added glare and cast a dim light into the control deck.

Everyone staggered around in an attempt to remain upright.

Pink dust crept across the stars and fanned out in all directions. Seconds later, a giant circle appeared to the right of the shield, filling itself with a bizarre amalgam of black and orange clouds.

Six silver whiskers streaked out underneath the circle as it formed into a strangely familiar eye.

The vibrations of the ship conformed to a piece of classical music.

"Is that… *Jelly*?" Wool screamed over the commotion.

It was. Her enlarged eyeball peered against the transparent plastic, reflecting Saturn and its spinning rings. Violent-looking and beyond reproach, her face remained steady - and determined. Fire erupted in her thirty-foot eyeball.

"Jelly!"

Cracks tore down the sides of the control deck. A burst of pink light blasted the darkness away.

"My God," Baldron looked at the eyeball in utter astonishment. He couldn't move out of sheer reverence. "She's…"

WHUMP.

Baldron and Tor blacked out. Their bodies hit the deck. Jaycee covered his face with his arm, blocking out the magnificent light from his eyes. It wasn't long before he passed out and hit the deck.

Tripp and Wool kept their gaze fixed on Jelly's face as the volume of the orchestra loudened.

"She's… she's…" Wool gasped and gripped Tripp's arm. "She's…"

WHUMP.

Overwhelmed, Tripp and Wool's eyelids snapped shut. They collapsed to the ground together.

The cracks in the ship sealed up immediately, plunging the control deck into darkness once again.

Then, Jelly's face vanished in a puff of dust - taking the stars in the sky with it.

A bizarre phenomenon that proved beyond comprehension…

Botanix

The damage from the dumb bomb explosion could still be felt. The walls had been shattered to a point, leading into the sprawling and infinite Pink Symphony landscape.

Sitting with her back to the wall, Bonnie remained unconscious. The back of her hand lay against the ground with her Rez-9 in her palm.

The water tank suffered damage. Broken into three sections, it gushed the contents across the floor and soaked her inner-suit pants and boots. Her removable leg had come free during the fight with the creature. It was missing.

A pink tear collected in her right eye as she breathed. More and more watery effluence added to the build-up, forcing its collected weight over the eyelid and down her cheek.

It plummeted toward the ground and splashed against her good leg, soaking into the fabric.

It was enough to make her open her eyes and inspect the strange sensation.

"Ugh, what happened?" she lubricated the inside of her mouth with her tongue, "Good lord, what—"

She squeezed the gun and brushed her inner-suit down. Splatter from the creature she'd executed outside had soaked into it. Her focus shifted from her stomach to the stump on her right leg.

Fear set in.

Her titanium leg was nowhere to be seen. She leaned over and grabbed at the metal grille, hoisting herself forward. "My leg, my leg…"

She dragged the lower half of her body by her hands along the row of plants, trying her utmost to peek between them. Still no sign of her missing limb.

Instead, she saw a small, furry creature laying on its side. It's stomach and sides pushed in and out. An indication that it was at least alive.

"God damn it, not another one," she gripped her Rez-9 and aimed the sight at the beast, "Hey, you."

Its furry ears twitched at the sound of her voice, but didn't move from the fetal position.

"You want some more, you freak?"

She squeezed the trigger, blasting a warning shot across its body.

A tuft of fur flew into the air having been grazed by the edge of the projectile. The creature lifted its tail and whipped it back to the ground.

"Huh?" Bonnie watched in amazement as the creature rolled over onto its back and held up its paws. Its eyes opened, forcing it to yawn and reveal its front teeth.

"Anderson?"

Its ears pricked up at the call of her name. A slurp of the tongue, and the little thing was back in business. Of course it was Jelly.

"Meeooo..." she squealed at the top of her croaking voice, struggling to get the sound out. She meowed again. This time in much lower pitch.

"Where... where did you go?"

"Boh... Boh..." Jelly rolled onto her back and clawed at her tail. "Boh... knee..."

"You just said my name!"

Bonnie flipped around and dug her shoulders into the ground. Enthralled by what she'd witnessed, she lifted her forearm in front of her face. Her thumb scraped the three links of black ink across her synthetic skin, "Individimedia, access. Dr. Bonnie Whitaker, broadcast enable."

The ink formed three individual dots. They flashed on and off, indicating a successful connection, "This is Bonnie. I repeat, this is Bonnie Whitaker. Does anyone read me?"

She kept her eyes on Jelly, who clawed at her own tail in the throes of turmoil.

"Bonnie?" Tripp's tinny voice flew out of the pinpricks in her wrist, "We read you. Where are you?"

"Botanix. Anderson's with me. Come, quickly."

"Is she? What's she doing?"

"Behaving strangely. Something happened to us, to her. Where are you?"

"We're in control right now. Something happened here, too. We lost power, briefly, but we're back on."

"I'm scared, Tripp," Bonnie looked around at the shattered walls. Behind her stood the door to Botanix. Directly opposite, the infinite landscape of Pink Symphony. "That pink beach thing is still here. I was attacked. I've lost my leg—"

"—Okay, okay, calm down. Just stay there. I'll be right over with Wool."

"Please be quick," Bonnie lowered her arm and relaxed her shoulders.

"Make sure Anderson doesn't run off out there—"

"—But, I can't move."

Tripp waved Wool over to the door of the control deck, "We're on our way. Do you have your firearm on you?"

Bonnie's voice came through Tripp's forearm, "Just my Rez."

An ethical quandary appeared in his mind as he reached the door, "Listen, Bonnie."

"What is it?"

"If you have to..." Tripp ducked his head and thought very carefully about his instruction.

"If I have to *what*?"

"Damn it."

Wool knew what was going on, "Oh, Tripp. No. Don't you *dare*."

"We have no choice," Tripp lifted his arm to mouth, "Use the gun on Anderson if she doesn't comply."

"What?" Bonnie screamed back.

Jaycee, Baldron and Tor threw their captain a befuddled look. "What?"

"I'm not playing around, here," Tripp finished. "If she tries to run off, shoot her."

"Tripp, you can't do that—" Wool tried.

"—I don't trust her, not after what happened a few minutes ago. Come on, we have to get to Botanix."

The duo walked through the door, leaving Jaycee, and his two Russian captives alone in the control deck.

Tor turned to Jaycee for a reaction.

"What are you looking at?" he bopped the man on the back of the head, "Get busy, numbskull. We know where everyone is. We need to know the state of Opera Beta."

"Right, right," Tor snapped his fingers and prayed Manuel would appear, "Manuel?"

The holographic book appeared in front of them, spinning its covers around, eager to assist, "Greetings, good people."

"I want a full report on the ship's system."

"Certainly."

Tor followed Manuel across the room. The book inspected the flight deck.

"Also, run coordinates on our current location."

"As I have relayed *twice*, now, the coordinates are irrelevant. Please excuse me while I run a scan on Beta's functionality."

The holographic book beeped over and over again.

Baldron dared not look Jaycee in the eye. He kept his focus on his boots hoping he wouldn't get thumped.

"Hey, you. Landaker."

Baldron tensed his shoulders and flinched, "Don't hit me."

"I'm not gonna hit you," Jaycee sniggered. "Just wanted to know how you were feeling right now?"

"I'm scared."

"You have *no* idea how happy I am to hear that."

Jaycee intimidated him by slammed the K-SPARK barrel in his open palm. Baldron jumped in his shoes, the weight of his Decapidisc reminding him of his situation. "*Jeez*. I think I'm going to have a coronary."

"We can only hope,' Jaycee grinned. "Hey, can I tell you a secret?"

"Wh-what?"

"I'm scared too, you know," Jaycee whispered in his ear, "I know I don't look it, but I am. Do you know what happens when I get scared?"

"N-No, what?" Baldron bit his lip as his oppressor got a little *too* close for comfort.

"I get fidgety, you know. Dunno what to do with myself. I start hitting things. Me and my temper."

"Oh, G-God," Baldron whimpered and scrunched his face. "Please d-don't—"

"—you ever seen what a K-SPARK shell does to the human body?"

"N-No."

"Total and utter evisceration."

Biddip-beep. Manuel snapped out of his scan. "Aha. Report complete."

Baldron breathed a sigh of relief as Jaycee turned to the holographic book, "Is he on?"

"Seems to be," Tor said. "Manuel?"

"Yes, Tor?"

"Report, please?"

"Certainly."

Manuel darted over to the middle of the room and bent its pages out wide. A vector image of Space Opera Beta projected from its spine and into the middle of the deck.

"Thruster damage in Engine and Payload, Level Ten. Two of twenty modules at more than seventy-five percent damage."

Tor walked around the map of Beta and placed his fingertip on the thruster area at the fat end of the ship, "Ports Y118, and Z409?"

"Indeed."

"Perfect, that's precisely what I wanted you to say," Tor looked at Baldron. "That's one for you, my friend."

"Wanted him to say?" Jaycee asked, quizzically.

Tor held out his hand and corrected himself at speed, "I mean, it's what I was expecting. Two ports down. In other words, Manuel is spot on."

"What's the damage, Manuel?" Baldron felt entitled to join in with the analysis - and away from Jaycee for a moment or two.

The twenty cylinders enlarged into view and spun around slowly, outlining the affected area.

"The affected cylinders disengaged, either during the explosion or the trip through Enceladus. I don't know which, but both need re-connecting."

"Understood," Baldron turned to Tor, who winked at

him in secrecy.

"Is that something you can fix?" Jaycee asked. "I hope so, otherwise you're of no use to man nor beast."

Baldron didn't know where to look, "Yes, yes. I can fix it, provided—"

"—With an emphasis on the word *beast*," Jaycee joked.

"Provided the location is unaffected by whatever that stuff is out there, it's a two-man job with Tor guiding us."

"How long will it take, chump?"

"Thirty minutes, maybe less."

"Okay, *amaziant*," Jaycee booted Baldron in the back. He stumbled forward and crashing against the control deck.

"Jaycee? Seriously?" Tor took pity on his friend, "That was uncalled for."

"No, it wasn't," Jaycee applauded Baldron as he struggled to his feet in serious anguish, "Look at you, withstanding all this pain."

"Stop hitting me."

"No."

"Hey, less of it," Tor held the warring men apart, "Jaycee, please. The last thing you need is an injured man carrying a nuclear device. We're trying to work on getting back home. Baldron is our engineer and he's no use to us if he can't do his job."

Jaycee grabbed Tor's wrist and threw his arm away, "Don't talk to me like you're one of the good guys, you egotistical little turd. Don't come on like you're a hero in all this."

Tor puffed his chest out, ready to take the inevitable beating his next sentence would initiate. "Oh yeah?"

"Yeah."

"We're doing precisely what you're telling us to do. Baldron and I aren't heroes, but we're working with you, aren't we?"

"Only because my captain insists on it."

"Okay, fine," Tor screamed in Jaycee's face, "Kick and

punch us both to death, then. Let's see how far you get."

Jaycee's patience was about to end. He lifted his glove and threatened to active their Decapidiscs.

"Jesus, you and your big mouth, Viktor," Baldron backed away in an attempt to disassociate himself with his comrade. He pointed his finger at Jaycee, "*He's* in control, not us. Don't give him any more excuses to hit that damn button."

"Well said, Landaker,' Jaycee grinned. "I've been instructed to remove both your heads if either of you so much as *fart* in a clear air zone."

Tor backed down. He couldn't argue with *that* statement.

"So, here's what we're gonna do. Tor, you're gonna stay here and complete Manuel's scan, or whatever the hell he does. Baldron, you and I are gonna go to the engine and fix whatever it is needs fixing so we can get the hell out of this pink paradise."

Tor snorted and fought to keep his dignity intact. He didn't acknowledge Jaycee's instruction.

"Do you understand what I've just said, *comrade*?"

"*Yes*," Tor spat, deeply unhappy and full of sarcasm, "I read you loud and clear."

"Good."

Chapter 13

Botanix
Space Opera Beta - Level Three

Bonnie pulled her body across the desecrated row of plants. Inch by inch, she got closer to Jelly, who lay on her side cleaning herself with her tongue.

She coughed and spluttered occasionally, spitting out tufts of fur to the ground. Every time she looked over at Bonnie from between the charcoaled vegetation she froze solid and kept her eyes on her.

"Meow," Jelly licked her titanium infinity claws with her tongue. She'd gotten used to the zinc-like taste over time.

"Hey, girl," Bonnie removed her Rez-9 from her mouth and set it to the ground, "Stay where you are. Help is coming."

Jelly didn't seem the slightest bit concerned. She flicked her ears and shot Bonnie in a vicious look, "Maaoow."

"Stay there, I'm coming for you."

Jelly began to whelp as if overcome by illness. Her throat constricted due to her coughs and splutters.

"Are you feeling okay—"

"Meaooowww," came the creepy response. A deadened, throaty howl of turmoil. Jelly fell back and rolled around, croaking up a storm.

"Jeez, what's wrong with you?"

Jelly hopped onto all fours and shook her entire body. Strands of fur flicked out in all directions. She pushed her right hind leg back, intending to move away into the glorious pink-hued beach front.

"No, no, don't—" Bonnie thumped the grip of her Rez-9 to the ground and took aim at the cat, "Don't go, Anderson."

Jelly took another step back, this time with her left hind leg. Now was the time to test her synthetic human.

"Meow," Jelly spat out a rope of pink drool.

"I mean it, sweetie," Bonnie flicked the safety catch down with her thumb, arming her Rez-9. She blinked hard. A drop of pink liquid fell from her right eye, "Don't move."

Jelly tested the standoff once again, seconds away from an attempt to run off into Pink Symphony.

"What's happened to you, girl?" Bonnie whispered and tightened her grip on the gun, "Tell me what's going on."

Jelly relaxed on the spot and tilted her head.

Swish!

The door to Botanix slid open behind Bonnie's heel. Startled, Jelly launched into the air and flipped around, headed for Pink Symphony.

"Anderson," Tripp screamed after her as she bolted across the metal grille and onto the sand leading to nowhere.

Wool darted after her with her arms outstretched, "Jelly, come back."

Jelly bolted through the opening in the wall.

BOMP!

Her nose and forehead scrunched together, the result of a vicious impact against a transparent barrier preventing her from escape. "Miaow."

Wool's feet splashed through stream of fresh water and ground to a halt. Aghast, she witnessed her feline friend tumbled over in pain.

"Jelly, stop," Wool reached the cat and scooped her up in her arms, "Hey, sweetie. What's wrong?"

Jelly blinked a few times and swiped the air with her claws in a fit of rage, "Miaow!"

"Hey, calm down," Wool lifted her up under her arms and looked into her eyes, "Something's wrong with you, girl," Wool turned to Tripp, "I need to get her to Medix."

"Okay, is she all right?"

"I don't know," Wool ran across the puddle and turned to Bonnie, "What did you do to her?"

"*Me*? I didn't do anything to her."

"Her heart is racing, look," Wool rocked Jelly in her arms in an attempt to calm her down, "Something's hassling her."

"*She*'s feeling hassled?" Bonnie grabbed Tripp's hand and stood on her one, good leg, "Aw, poor thing. She's all hassled, is she?"

"Yes, she is," Wool walked off with Jelly in her arms, "Come on, girl. Let's get you checked out."

"That cat is nothing but a liability," Bonnie screamed after Wool as she exited the area.

Tripp stared at Pink Symphony. Tiny silhouetted figures crept over the sandy dune's horizon and scuttled toward the ship's opening.

"Look, look," he tugged at Bonnie's arm, "Look at them."

"I know. I met one when I was out there."

"Really?" Tripp gasped, "What happened?"

"Came to a pretty messy end, to be honest," Bonnie slung her arm over Tripp's shoulder and nodded at the door, "Seen the state of my suit? It sucks."

"It went down that easy?"

"Right in the middle of its nasty face," Bonnie raised the stump on her right leg. "Take me to the fit room. If I need to fight those things, you need me upright, don't you?"

"No Fit Room for you, Bonnie. We're going to N-

Vigorate to get you re-limbed first."

Hundreds of fleshy, twelve-limbed creatures reached the invisible barrier between the broken section of Botanix's back wall and Pink Symphony.

BAM. THUD-BANG-THUD.

The creatures squealed and slammed their thick talons against the barrier, wanting to get in and murder anything breathing.

"What do you know about these things?" Bonnie asked as she hopped to the door using Tripp for balance.

"Not as much as you."

"Huh?"

"Well, you've disposed of one of them already. I haven't. And I'd rather not if I don't have to."

"Nothing from Manuel?" Bonnie asked.

"No, he's busy trying to get us out of here."

They reached the door and took a final look at what might happen to them if they weren't able to escape. Death by at least one hundred fleshy spider *things*.

"SCREEEEEE!"

The largest of the creatures wailed from its knuckled mid-section. Its front four talons daggered at the see-through barrier.

"I dunno what those things are," Tripp muttered as he helped Bonnie through the door, "But someone had better give us some answers pretty damn fast."

Medix

Jelly struggled for freedom as Wool released her onto her bed. She fought back with an intensity previously unseen by Wool. The claws came out. Swipes were thrown.

"For heaven's sake, Jelly," Wool felt her heart sink as she pinned her forearms against Jelly's. At least she couldn't hit back. "Calm down. You'll work yourself into a frenzy."

"Shaaaantaaa..."

"Shanta? What *are* you saying? You're delirious—"

Jelly screeched up at the ceiling and threw her hind legs forward. One of her infinity claws pierced through Wool's inner-suit by her abdomen, tearing the skin.

Wool pressed her elbow on Jelly's upturned stomach and reached for a syringe on the medician's bedside unit. She pushed the radio out of the way and avoided looking at the picture of Jamie Anderson on the wall next to the window.

She lifted the device in her fingers and caught a glimpse of the horizon stretching over Pink Symphony. "Wow." A large planet hung in the whitened sky. Its three rings moved, slowly, in all directions, like a fairground ride.

Jelly attempted to wriggle free from Wool's pin down.

"Stop it, Jelly. You want the syringe, do you?"

Jelly calmed down the moment her eyes clapped on the needle. Her legs kicked against Wool's thighs. She dropped the syringe and fanned her palm on the crazy cat's head.

"Mwaaah," Jelly sunk her fangs in the webbing between Wool's fingers. Under any other circumstances her actions might have been considered playful. Wool quickly dismissed that notion as she looked into Jelly's eyes.

Both were blood-red with orange clouds formed around each pupil.

"Jesus, what's happened to you?"

"ROOWAARR," Jelly shrieked at the top of her lungs.

Wool pushed herself away in fright and looked down at the tear in her inner-suit. He elbow caught the power cable attached to the radio, knocking the device to the floor.

A glob of blood peeled through Wool's inner-suit. She slid the side of her index finger under the cut and lifted it to her face for inspection.

"Oh, you made me bleed—"

BWUCK!

Jelly spat out a pink fur ball. She rolled onto her front and settled into the prone position, poised to attack. Her tail slapped left and right as she sized up her new opponent.

"Jelly, what are y-you d-doing—"

BWUCK-BWUCK-BWUCK!

Jelly's chest distended, violently. She dug her infinity claws into the foam mattress, puncturing its surface.

"Waaaaaaah!" Jelly's behind lifted into the air like a possessed demon - the start of an event Wool wouldn't forget in a hurry.

"Oh, God…"

Jelly's titanium infinity claws sprung out from her paws. Each digital pad blew open, squeezing out a pink substance across her shedding fur.

"Grrraaaooowww," Jelly's broken screeches bounced off the walls and slammed into Wool's ears.

WHUMP.

Her stomach distended and blew outward, coughing lumps of fur to the bed.

"J-Jelly?" Wool took a step forward, careful not to get too near what was surely some sort of infectious disease.

The cat whined and shook her head, trying to make the pain subside. The more she fought, the worse it became.

Her skin on her arms turned a yellowy white and forced the flesh underneath to blow across to her body.

The stench was overwhelming.

Wool knew she should have sedated Jelly when she had the chance. There was no going back, now.

Jelly's behind ballooned out, pushing most of her fur away. The bone in her hind legs cracked forward, causing her a considerable amount of pain. A sickening sound of contorting flesh breaking into new positions thundered within her limbs. Jelly's intense squeals warbled the acrylic windows back and forth.

"Holy Mary, mother of God," Wool crossed her body with her index finger as she watched Jelly convulse and change before her eyes. "God have mercy."

Jelly's spine arched onto itself, exposing her shoulder

bone through the skin. Strands of fur pushed away from her body.

A final wail of death thundered through the room as her entire body shuddered like a furious cocktail mixer. Her mouth opened out and forward. Jelly's skull pulled back and up, forcing the back of her head to raise thee inches.

The zygomatic bone above her top row of teeth crunched into an oblong and out under her nose. Her teeth fell out one by one. A new set of ivories pushed through her gums, including a pair of sharp incisors.

"Shaaaa," Jelly snorted, fixed to the bed by her infinity claws. Her chin broke away under her bottom row of teeth. A new skeletal structure pushed through in its place.

Her whiskers fizzed away like a perverse light show.

Jelly's entire body thundered on the spot. Her abdomen shunted whatever was left of her former self across the bed in gory segments. Bones transformed and cracked out into new formations.

Fine, dark hair - much like her whiskers - sprouted from the top of her head and fell down her back.

Wool covered her eyes and turned away. Close to a nervous breakdown, she knew what was coming next. Having seen the twelve-legged creatures at a distance - coupled with what she knew of the battle in Pink Symphony - the next stage would prove to be a body apocalypse.

Wool fanned her fingers out over one eye, catching only the briefest glimpses of the horror.

A fur-less cat, dying and effectively melting in a demonic puddle of its own effluence.

"I'm s-so sorry, Jelly," Wool burst out crying and made for the door, "Let's finish this."

"Mwaaoorgh," Jelly blasted her turmoil around the room from the splattered bed.

Wool pulled the door shut and dropped to her knees in

a state of helpless delirium.

"No, please, God. No," she spluttered in floods of tears, "Please."

She knocked the back of her head against the wall in an attempt to block out Jelly's deathly howls from within Medix. Something had to be done.

Her hand slipped around her belt and gripped her Rez-9. A mercy killing was necessary - the second time, now, she'd be attempting to put Jelly out of her misery. Images of having placed a cyanide capsule in Jelly's mouth slammed into her brain.

Wool rolled up the sleeve on her left forearm. She thumbed the ink out into three dots. "This is… Wool," she tried to clear the upset from her voice, "Tripp, are you there?"

No response.

"Tripp, please," Wool sniffed and tilted the side of her gun to ensure it was loaded. The strip light indicated a full magazine. "Tripp?"

"Yes, Wool. I read you."

"She's sick, Tripp. Really sick…"

"Where are you?"

"Outside Medix," Wool blurted and wiped the tears from her eyes. "It's over for her. I need you to come here."

"Dying?"

Wool couldn't help herself. She cried into her forearm like a madwoman. "She's all over the p-place, Tripp. I…"

"—Wool, stay right where you are. Don't do anything."

"She's in s-so much pain, I need to—"

"Wool. No!" Tripp's voice blared through the tiny pin pricks in her wrist, "For God's sake, don't do anything. Stay where you are."

Wool picked herself up from the floor and took a deep breath. She gripped her gun and deliberated the consequences of the action she was about to take.

It was now or never.

N-Vigorate

Three minutes earlier…

The opened utility door revealed a variety of synthetic limbs. One of them had been selected by Bonnie. Much like the others, a titanium-based extensions was the order of the day.

Only, this one was equipped for war as well as balance.

"The Cortex K-12," Tripp attached the magnetic thigh plate to Bonnie's stump, "Interesting choice."

"It really belongs in Weapons and Armory," Bonnie looked down at Tripp and noticed something behind his ear. It resembled a black squiggle. Despite her enhanced vision she elected to look away and braced herself for the forthcoming jolt of pain.

The magnet on her stump sucked the silver plate on the false limb into place with a heavy 'schwump' sound.

"There, you're all set."

Bonnie looked down in time for Tripp to smile at her from between her legs, "Thanks."

"No problem."

"While you're down there?" Bonnie chuckled at her own joke.

"Very funny," Tripp pushed himself upright and held out his palm, "Test it out?"

She grabbed his hand in hers, standing to her feet. She looked down her midriff and swiveled her new right knee left and right, ensuring the device worked. "Feels great."

Tripp smiled obliquely. Something was bothering him.

"What's up?"

"I'm sorry, Bonnie."

"What for?"

"Just, you know. The whole Androgyne *thing*. USARIC has a lot to answer for."

"Oh, that?" Bonnie hopped back to the chair and rammed the calf on the armrest. She arched her back down and grabbed her knees, squinting at her new toe. "I've decided I don't care anymore."

The end of her boot unraveled to the tune of mechanical switches. A barrel formed at the end.

"You don't?"

"Why should I?" Bonnie whacked the side of her hand on a lever on the side of her leg, arming the device. "I'm as human as you or anyone else when you think about it. One thing I don't understand, though?"

"What's that?"

"If I'm a Series Three unit, why do I need the N-Vigorate chamber? Can't I recharge during power down?"

Tripp walked over to the door and pulled out a blast sheet from the hinge, "Your battery took some damage, Bonnie. Once we're up and running we'll need to take a look inside and see if we can fix it."

Bonnie nodded at the sheet, "Can you set up the target?"

"Sure."

Tripp clamped the free end to the wall. The image resembled the common dart board, complete with a bullseye. The USARIC logo stood proudly across the top.

"This okay for you?"

"That's great, step away," Bonnie pressed her elbow to the adjacent arm rest and took hold of her thigh, "I may be synthetic. But my organs are real. My brain is real. I remember everything I need to."

"That's very true," Tripp was relieved that Bonnie had become accustomed to her existence. "You're more human than human, in some respects."

The bullseye focused into view at the end of her brand new limb, "You know it."

Tripp offered her some sympathy, "Sometimes I wish every time I went to sleep I could forget."

Bonnie held out her tongue, taking careful aim at the bullseye on the sheet.

"Be careful what you wish for, Healy."

Bonnie fired off a blast at the sheet. Tripp jumped back

as the bullet burst against the bulletproof sheet and vaporized into a thousand pieces.

"Direct hit," Bonnie smiled and stomped her new foot to the ground.

"Wow. That new leg of yours really kicks ass," Tripp slowed his breathing and approached the sheet, "Umm…"

"What?"

A bullet hole spat out smoke right in the middle of the USARIC logo - her intended target.

"Angry much?"

"As I said. *Direct hit.*"

Tripp's forearm buzzed. The three tattooed lines swirled around to form a name: "Wool ar-Ban."

"Who is it?" Bonnie asked.

"It's Wool. Must be an update on Jelly," he ran his fingers across the ink on his forearm, "Wool?

"Tripp, please?" Wool's strained cries shot out of his wrist.

"Yes, Wool. I read you."

"She's sick, Tripp. Really sick…"

"Where are you?" Tripp's waved Bonnie over toward him.

"Outside Medix," Wool's voice croaked over the transmission, "It's over for her. I need you come here."

"What do you mean she's sick?" Tripp shot Bonnie a look of urgency, "She's crying," he mouthed.

Bonnie raised her eyebrows with suspicion, "Crying?"

"She's all over the p-place, Tripp. I…"

"—Wool, stay right where you are. Don't do anything."

"She's in s-so much pain, I need to—"

"Wool. No. For God's sake, don't do anything hasty. Stay where you are."

Tripp brushed the palm of his hand across his forearm, cutting off the call. "We need to get to Medix. Right now."

"Is she okay?"

"You heard everything I did."

Tripp pulled the door open and stormed into the

walkway with Bonnie.

It was only a two minute walk across the level three gantry from N-Vigorate to Medix. In this very moment, it felt at least three times longer than usual.

Despite the earlier otherworldly happenings, the ship was once again intact. It was as if the cracks and damage had never occurred. A long, distant virus-fueled nightmare.

No creaking, no weird sounds. Everything seemed just fine. The ship's engine was alive - the vibrations that rocked the Opera Beta's interiors provided a welcome and familiar comfort.

That was all Tripp and Bonnie were able to enjoy as they hightailed it across the metal grills on the ground. Plumes of steam shot out around their boots as they snaked around the corner. They prepared themselves for whatever was happening to Wool.

Bonnie eyed around the pipes on the walls, remembering what she'd heard about the ship falling apart. "I don't get it, Tripp."

"What don't you get?"

"Botanix leads out into that weird, pink place. The one with the creature things. Why is everything back to normal?"

"I don't know, Bonnie."

"For our assumed captain you sure don't know very much."

Tripp couldn't take Bonnie's inadvertent rudeness any longer and stopped on the spot, "Bonnie."

Tripp ran his knuckle across his freshly-formed five o'clock shadow. His finger inadvertently brushed against his earlobe - just in time for Bonnie to catch the black text behind it, tucked out-of-sight above his jawline.

A familiar company by the name of *Manning/Synapse.*

"Tripp?" she smiled at him.

"Don't play the dummy android with me, Bonnie. You made be more advanced than the rest of us—"

"—*Au contraire*," she said with side order of snark.

"What's that meant to mean?"

"Nothing."

"No, seriously. What did you mean by that?"

"Drop it, Healy," she nodded up at the far end of the walkway, "Enough pillow talk. Let's get to Wool before she does something stupid."

Chapter 14

Engine & Payload

Space Opera Beta - Level Ten

In any ordinary situation Baldron would have to use the primary airlock to exit the spacecraft. Harnessing the weightlessness of space, he'd use the outer-suit thrusters to "fly" along the exterior of the ship to the fat end to attend to the ship's engine. But this was no ordinary situation. Being grounded on Pink Symphony proved to be a much quicker prospect for fixing them.

Engine & Payload, much like the other chambers on the ship, could be reached by using Opera Beta's lone elevator. Room enough for ten passengers.

The metal cage whizzed down the circular tube.

Jaycee and Baldron each carried a large nuclear canister in their arms. Being close to seven feet in height and built like a tornado fused with a bull, Jaycee barely registered the weight of his nuke.

Baldron, on the other hand, felt the need to place the end of his canister to the floor and rest the tip against the wall of the elevator.

"How many times have you done this before?" Jaycee asked, turning his head away from the whizzing of the panel lights sprawling up and down across his helmet's visor.

"At least a dozen. Delicacy is key, here."

"Like dropping the end on the ground like a big fairy, you mean?" Jaycee chuckled through his internal radio microphone.

"It's heavy. We're not all built like brick houses like you."

"True enough," Jaycee grinned, enamored by the fact that Baldron's Decapidisc fit perfectly under the rim of his helmet, "Still. Nothing to lose your head over, eh?"

Baldron knocked the edge of the disc with his gloved hand, "This is really going to get in my way while I try to work."

"I'm sure you'll live. Probably."

The friendly female announcement whirled around the elevator, "Level Ten. Engine and Payload. Have a nice day,"

The doors slid apart, revealing the enormity of Engine & Payload. Zero gravity set in immediately, lifting the pair's feet from the ground.

"Zero G?" Jaycee asked.

"Yeah. Gravity doesn't help much when you're dealing with ballistics or nuclear paraphernalia," Baldron swung his arms around his canister. He planted the sole of his boot on the elevator wall and propelled himself forward, "Follow me."

Jaycee's boots levitated away from the floor. He enacted the same movement as Baldron and pushed himself into the chamber.

A dimly-lit arena resembling the inside of a set of vocal chords.

Thick, twenty-foot high columns provided an obstacle to the port panel on the far wall. Conversely, it helped the two men kick themselves toward their destination a lot quicker.

"Ugh," Baldron said into his radio mic, "I hate the absence of gravity. It makes my stomach queasy."

"I'm sorry to hear that," Jaycee spat, indicating that he'd run out of rat's asses to give, "Hey, here's an idea."

"What?"

"Why don't you shut the hell up and do your job?"

Baldron pressed his boots against a column and pushed himself toward a gargantuan wall of lit-up rectangles. Thousands of them shone against both men's visors on their approach.

"See those white columns over there?" Baldron pointed to the right of the wall.

"Yeah?"

"The hyper-thrusters," Baldron continued. "Each one of them with enough nuclear energy to wipe out Florida."

"Much like climate change then?"

"Yeah, you could say that. You Americans use nukes to get ahead in the second space race. It's no wonder your country is eroding around the edges."

"Hey, Russkie," Jaycee kicked forward from another column and reached Baldron, "Shall we see if your organs can survive a nuclear blast?"

"What?"

"Keep that xenophobic talk up and I'll shove your head in this canister."

"We're here. Kick down to section *Zee*. We're looking for port loader number four, zero, niner."

The numbers on each of the rectangles ran into the thousands. Jaycee used the locking bolt on a loader to push himself down and read out the numbers on each one.

"Four fifty-two… four twenty-eight…" Jaycee found the one they were looking for, "Here, it's here. Four, zero, niner."

"Good. I'm coming down," Baldron hugged his nuke as he waded down past the loaders, "I gotta say, these things are much easier to carry in here."

"Yeah, I can see that," Jaycee looked up. The butt of Baldron's canister enveloped his visor quicker than anticipated.

"Hey. Be careful," Jaycee kicked back in defiance, "You nearly hit my visor."

"Sorry."

Baldron reached the lock on the panel and balanced the canister upright in the palm of his left hand, "Tor, this is Baldron. Do you read me?"

"Yes, Baldron. I read you,' Tor's static-laden voice bled into Baldron's helmet, "Confirm Port Zee. Four, zero, niner."

"Port Zee. Four, zero, niner. Confirmed."

"Understood, standby."

Jaycee scowled at Baldron and showed him his glove.

Tor spoke before the torment could continue, "On my command you will make contact with the lock. A countdown of three. Do you understand?"

"I understand."

"Reconciling nuclear engagement. Establish contact, please."

The bolt on the lock shunted out, offering itself to Baldron. He grasped it in his hand and cleared his throat. "Contact established."

"From three," Tor's advised. "Three, two, one… and engage."

SHUNT-SWISH.

Baldron's hand turned with the bolt, sliding the port door down.

Jaycee tilted his head to the side and took a look at the interior, "Ugh. That canister thing has seen better days, hasn't it?"

"Yup," Baldron grabbed the port edges and pulled himself inside. "Oh, damn. Can you grab my canister, please?"

Jaycee looked at the cylinder revolving gently in mid-air, "Idiot."

"Sorry, it slipped," Baldron stomped his feet to the ground within the port. Its canister had subsided in its housing. The blackened underside indicated something had gone wrong, "Okay, this is pretty straight forward."

"Baldron," Tor's voice came through the mic, "Sit-rep on Zee four, zero, niner, please?"

"Defective canister. Manuel was right, this one is down. I will confirm on Yankee one, one, eight next."

"Yeah, *Yankee* is about right," Tor chuckled. "Speaking of which, how's our ugly turd holding up?"

Jaycee threw Baldron a look of evil.

"Uh, he can hear you, Tor."

"Damn," Tor's voice fizzled away into silence for a moment. "Uh, Jaycee?"

"Yes, Tor?"

"Sorry about that."

"Don't worry. I'm going to kill you the moment we get back. Nothing serious."

"Yes," Tor tried to make amends, "Joking aside, it might help if—"

"—Oh, I'm *not* joking," Jaycee said, looking at the Yankee section of the loader ports. "I *am* going to kill you."

"Jaycee, please. Listen to me."

"I'm listening."

Jaycee watched Baldron hold the pinkie on his glove to the defective canister housing. The end whizzed around as he inserted it into the first of two bolts at the side of the damaged canister.

"What do you want?"

"We can expedite this event if you start on Yankee one, one, eight. The little finger on your glove will unscrew the housing. You simply remove the dud and clamp the fresh canister into place. Bring the used one back with you for recycle—"

"—You want me to do Baldron's job for him?"

"Actually, *yes*. It would be helpful. Seeing as we're low on oxygen."

"Ugh, fine."

Baldron peered out from the his loader port and held

up his thumb, "Thanks, man."

"It's not a favor, you cretin. I'm doing it to save time."

"Suits me," Baldron winked back at Jaycee as he pushed off toward the Yankee section on the hunt for port 118.

Baldron felt much happier now that his captor had gone away *and* helped him with the task at hand. He clamped the fresh canister into place and screwed it into the brackets.

"Baldron?" Tor's voice came through the mic, "Do you read me?"

"Yes, I read you," he said, screwing the new canister shut with his pinkie.

"Jaycee, do you read me?" Tor asked.

No response.

"I repeat, Jaycee. Do you read me?"

Baldron gripped the edge of the loader and watched Jaycee arrive at port Yankee 118, whistling to himself, "I don't think he hears us."

"Good, I changed the frequency. It's just you and me, now," Tor explained. "He's going start talking at me. He'll want the lock opened."

"Yes, I expect so," Baldron hushed into his helmet mic, "What's this got to do with me?"

"Are you looking at him?"

"Yes, he's nearly at the loader."

"For heaven's sake, get back in, stupid. You don't want him looking at you."

"Okay, okay," Baldron slipped his head into the port and turned to the canister, "What's going on?"

"Now is our chance, comrade."

"What?"

"Manuel was right about the ports needing mended," Tor explained. "But only about why-oh-oh-eight. Zee four zero niner, your loader, is perfectly operational. Never needed attention."

"But, it's been hit by subsidence. The bottom has been hit by—"

"—They're all like that. Standard wear and tear, they're designed to last for decades, if not centuries. You're an *engineer*, remember? You should know that."

"You and I both know that's *lessense*."

Jaycee announced his arrival to his port with a vicious thump on its hatch. The sound echoed through the chamber, "Tor, this is Jaycee. Ready at Yankee-one-one-eight."

"Damn, he's there," Tor lightened his tone and addressed Jaycee, leaving his comrade wondering what was going on, "Understood, Jaycee. One moment, please."

"Hurry up."

"Baldron?" Tor asked.

"Yes?"

"No time to explain. Get the hell out of there, now. And make sure Jaycee doesn't see you."

"What?"

"No questions! Head to the lift and get back to the control deck. Now," Tor changed his tone when addressing Jaycee, "Okay. You heard my instructions to Baldron a few minutes ago, right?"

"Yeah, I get the idea," Jaycee grabbed the bolt on the loader port, "Ready to rock and roll."

Baldron didn't know which way to look, or what to do. "Comrade? What are—"

"—Jaycee, please confirm Port Zee, four, zero, niner." Tor said, no longer available for a clandestine chat with his Russian conspirator.

"Port zed, four, zero, niner. Confirmed."

"Understood, standby," Tor's voice sped up and flooded Baldron's headset, "Get out of there, good buddy."

"Why?"

"Trust me, there is *literally* no time to explain. We're wasting time talking about not talking about it. Go, go—"

"—Okay, I'm *going*."

"Make sure that useless pile of mechanical puke doesn't see you."

"I'll do my best."

"You'll have to do a lot better than *your best*, my friend," Tor switched comms to Jaycee, "Okay, Jaycee. On my command you will make contact with the lock. On a countdown of three. Do you understand?"

"I understand."

Baldron pushed himself out of the port and into the payload chamber. He grabbed the used canister and released it in the air a few inches from the door.

Tor continued with his instruction, "Reconciling nuclear engagement. Make contact please."

Baldron carefully planted the sole of both boots on the adjacent panel and pushed himself into the distance.

Jaycee looked up at Baldron's port but failed to see him move away. As far as he could see, the door was open and Baldron was still inside. His canister revolved around in the air just by the door.

"Idiot."

"Sorry, repeat? Jaycee?"

"I wasn't talking to you," he turned back to the bolt mechanism on the port, "Let's get on with this. Open the damn *thing*, will you?"

"Suits me. Contact established?"

The bolt on the lock shunted out, offering itself to Baldron. He grasped it in his hand and cleared his throat, "Contact established."

Streaks of sweat smeared up the inside of Baldron's visor as he kicked himself away from the next column. The elevator doors loomed fifty feet in the distance. A minute or two from escape.

Jaycee rolled his shoulders and prepared to open his port loader.

"From three," Tor advised. "Three, two, one… and

engage."

SHUNT-SWISH.

The port door slid down into the groove. Jaycee released the bolt and placed the good canister on inside it. "I'm in."

"Good. Just holler if you need me."

"I doubt I'll be doing that," Jaycee huffed and pressed his feet to the ground. He held his right glove to his face and inspected the little finger on his glove. The ends slid apart and released a screw tip, "Here we go."

He moved his glove away from his face and eyeballed the thoroughly worn canister, "Right. Let's get you fixed."

A giant fleshy limb with a razor sharp talon shot out from behind it and swiped at Jaycee.

"Jeeeeeesus *Christ*," he yelped and grabbed the good canister by his knees.

A second, third and fourth limb hugged around the canister, angry at having been disturbed.

The vicious beast snapped the spent canister in two. A blast of gas slammed against Jaycee, pushing him out of the port loader.

The good canister tumbled around at speed over his shoulder and clanged against a column. Jaycee unhooked his Rez-9 and aimed it at the creature, "Tor!"

The creature jammed forward along the port tight walls. It wanted Jaycee's blood.

"Tor, do you read me?"

"Yes, good buddy. I read you. How are you getting on down there?"

"You son of a bi—" Jaycee drew his weapon.

"—What's wrong?"

SNARL-SNASH! The creature's six limbs rapid-gripped the edges of the port, one by one, and prepared to launch forward.

"You know damn well what's wrong—"

"—No need for cursing, that's just rude," Tor fake-chuckled over the comms, "Now, at this point you've probably got your gun aiming right at *it*, don't you?"

"You're Goddamn right I do."

"Yeah, just one thing."

"What?" Jaycee trained his gun at the knuckle-headed midsection of the beast. It opened its mouth-like cave and screeched up a storm.

"Bullets and zero gravity, my friend? You may as well just take a bath and drop a toaster in with you—"

"—You're a dead man, I swear," Jaycee released his finger from the trigger. He threw the gun at the screaming beast's mouth. It caught it with deft expertize and munched away on it, breaking it in two. "You better pray it kills me."

"I've already done that. Send my regards to Daryl and Haloo when you get to Hell," Tor smirked and cut the call.

Baldron reached the elevator doors. He slammed the panel in a desperate bid to open them, "C'mon, c'mon."

"Landaker," Jaycee's voice hurtled toward him as he frantically jabbed at the button on the wall.

"Come on, please. *Please*."

"You and your soviet boyfriend are dead men," Jaycee kicked himself away from one of the many columns, headed straight for the door.

"Close, damn it. *Close*," Baldron rapid-hit the button, praying for a swift escape.

Jaycee flew through the air and threw his hands forward. Baldron's throat needed removing.

The creature, however, was hot on Jaycee's tail, too.

"Baldron, don't close that door," Jaycee shouted as he kicked himself forward, "Keep it open."

"Comrade," Tor's voice came through, "Close the door."

"I am, I am," Baldron hit the panel over and over again, "It won't close."

"Stupid American-made crap," Tor failed to realize his voice came through Jaycee's helmet, "Much like that big hunk of whale blubber."

"What did you call me?" Jaycee screamed.

"Oh, you can hear me?"

"Yeah, I can hear you," Jaycee quipped, angrily, as he zipped towards Baldron in the elevator cage fifty-odd feet away, "Hey, dead man."

"Who, me?" Baldron and Tor asked in unison.

"*Both* of you."

The creature gained on Jaycee. It had learned to propel itself watching the man's actions. Worse still, it had six times as many limbs as its prey to do it with.

Baldron elbowed the button on the elevator panel. The doors slid together very, very slowly, "It's closing," He clapped eyes on the creature in the distance and backed up against the elevator's back wall, "Oh, *shiiii—*"

"—It's trying to kill me,' Jaycee threw his hands forward and opened his fingers in an attempt to grab the doors before they sliced shut, "Stay right where you are, you—"

Too late - the doors were half a second away from slamming shut.

Baldron's face disappeared behind the closing doors.

"I'm gonna tear the skull out of your head," Jaycee clenched his right hand made for Baldron's throat.

"I'm s-sorry, Jaycee—"

SCHLAA-AAM!

The elevator doors clamped shut on Jaycee's wrist, "Gaahh," The severed appendage clanged against the wall and crashed knuckles-first to the ground.

Baldron tumbled to his knees as the cage hurtled up through the elevator tube. Jaycee's grunts and screams dissipated behind the outer door as he fought with the creature.

"Hey, man. You there?" Tor asked.

"Yes, I'm here," Baldron slumped to his behind on the floor and breathed a sigh of relief, "And Jaycee... *isn't*."

"Good job, comrade."

"We're so dead if that thing doesn't finish him off—"

The severed hand's fingers and thumb fanned out and clench into a fist, punching itself to its fingertips. It crawled toward Baldron like a mad, mechanical spider with an opposable thumb.

Thoroughly intimidated, Baldron kicked himself back against the far wall, "His hand. It's his damn *hand*, man!"

"What hand?" Tor asked. "What's going on—"

"—The elevator doors, they… they… *cut it off*. Oh, G-God, it's trying to kill me—"

The hand crept forward, threatening Baldron. sparks of electricity blasted along its trail of wires and metal dragging behind the destroyed wrist.

"Please, no!"

The hand quickly ran out of juice - containing just enough energy left to hold its middle finger up at Baldron as a parting salute.

"Huh?"

It splayed its fingers out and punched the floor with its palm, giving up the ghost. The white button on the wrist flap flashed, begging to be pressed.

"Baldron? Give me a sit-rep, please."

"It's okay. I think it's dead," Baldron quickly arrived at an epiphany, "Wait, wait."

"What?"

"It's… *not real*," he grabbing the discarded appendage by the fingers and looked at the trailing wires and connectors.

"Not real?"

"No."

Baldron slipped the glove from the synthetic hand, "Well, not human. Titanium. Special connectors, with heat-proof underpinnings."

"Classic Manning/Synapse hardware, right?"

"Right," Baldron brushed the tip of his thumb across the synthetic skin on Jaycee's hand, "What do I do with it?"

"What do you do with what?"

Baldron pressed his shoulders against the elevator wall as it rocketed toward level one, "The hand, Tor. What do I do with Jaycee's hand?"

"What? The hand? Who gives a rat's ass? Just leave it there. It's the *glove* we want. For God's sake, do *not* press any buttons on it."

The Decapidisc slunk around Baldron's shoulders, enabling a terrifying prospect, "Oh, God…. Oh, God."

"What is it, now?" Tor asked, near ready to explode.

"The button's flashing on the glove. The disc is gonna take my head off—"

"—It's okay, it's just in advisory mode,' Tor mocked his friend for fun, "I need you to bring that ghastly, five-fingered contraption back to control right now. The elevator is making its way to Level One. Control Deck."

Baldron tossed the hand at the wall and held the glove to his chest, "Are you sure we're okay?"

"As long as you keep away from that activation button, yes," Tor said. "Now, calm yourself down and meet me at control. We'll take care of the others."

"Okay."

"And that stupid cat, as well."

The elevator bolted skyward in a haze of spinning bulbs and lights.

Medix

Wool sat against the exterior Medix wall. She'd resigned herself to the only course of action available.

Jelly's muffled howls of pain muffled from within the room.

"They're not coming," Wool lifted her Rez-9 firearm in her right hand and looked at the safety catch. She pressed it down with her thumb, arming the weapon. Finally, she closed her eyes and took a deep breath.

"Forgive me for what I'm about to do," she pushed her

heels into the ground and slid her back up the wall.

"Wool," Tripp's voice rumbled across the walkway, flying into her ears. She jumped in fright and opened her eyes, instinctively aiming her gun at the emptiness dead ahead of her.

"Tripp?" Wool hollered, prepared to fire, "Is that you?"

"Yes, it's me and Bonnie."

Tripp crept around the corner with terrific trepidation, "Are you okay?"

"No. I'm not okay," Wool thumped the door to Medix. The rectangular slab slid away from its casters.

"Why have you got your firearm out?" Bonnie joined Tripp and readied herself to beat the hell out of whatever had upset her colleague, "What's going on?"

Wool peered through the transparent door's window. An effort that proved to be futile; the surface had fogged up a storm, leaving only a blurry contour of slowing down on the bed.

"She's in there."

Tripp made for the door, "Right, let's rescue her—"

"—No, no. I, uh…" Wool stood in his path and clutched at her Rez-9, "Something's happening to her. Whatever that pink stuff is… it's doing to her what it did to Haloo."

Bonnie frowned and quickly grew angry with their predicament, "For God's sake," she socked the wall with her fist and held her breath.

"It's over, Tripp," Wool sniffed. "She's quarantined in there. Riding it out."

An intense, guttural howl crashed from the other side of the door. Tripp looked down, barely able to soak in Wool's distress. He reached into his belt and grabbed his Rez-9.

"You want me to do it?"

It was the least he could offer to do given the circumstances. Wool and Jelly had formed a bond that was better left on the happiest note available.

"No, no," she wiped a pink tear from her eye, "Let me do it. *Please*."

Bonnie tried to offer some sympathy. "Wool, look. It's the best thing—"

"—What the hell do you know about feelings, Bonnie? You're just a lump of pretty metal, made by men *for* men."

"How dare you," Bonnie protested. Her absence of mind neglected the fact that her follow-on statement would correct the *wrong* half of Wool's accusation, "I am *not* made of metal,"

"Whatever. It doesn't matter anymore," Wool turned to the door, ready to execute the monstrosity in the throes of its last breaths, "We're *all* somebody's bitch at the end of the day, aren't we?"

A wave of sobs crept through the crack in the door as Wool pushed it open, "Wait here. It'll only take a second."

Tripp and Bonnie lowered their heads and nodded.

Wool allowed the door to slide shut behind her. She aimed her Rez-9 at the source of the whimpering with her eyes closed. The sniveling and gasps of anguish were impossible to withstand. All she had to do was pull the trigger, hope to hit a vital organ, and leave without seeing what she'd done. A blissfully ignorant act of mercy, to be sure, but a necessary one if Wool was retain any semblance of mental well-being post-execution.

"I'm sorry, pet."

"Wuh…" groaned a voice more human than she'd expected, "Wuuh…"

In a rare moment of assurance, Wool lifted her eyelids slightly, keeping her gun facing the bed.

"Huh?"

"Wuh-wuh… Wooo… Luhh…"

Wool squeezed her eyes shut for two seconds and then opened them again. She froze on the spot as if having seen God in the flesh.

"Wool," came the voice once again, but lower in pitch.

The surface of Wool's eyeball reflected an orange-white *thing*. It kicked its legs forward.

Blink, blink.

Wool's eyelids wiped the detritus from the surface of her eyeballs. This time, the fleshy, fish-eyed image reflecting back rolled over to its side and stopped crying.

"Wool," the image said, "It… is… *you*."

The gun slipped form Wool's frozen hand and bounced against the white floor tiles beside her left boot.

"I'm… c-cold…" the thing said in a reassuring, young voice, "P-Please?"

Wool finally managed to close her jaw. The reality of the event burrowed through her mind. She wasn't sleeping and certainly not dreaming.

"J-Jelly… you… I…" Wool stammered, "M-My *God*…"

Out in the walkway, Tripp experienced restlessness on a scale he'd seldom encountered. He'd expected to hear a gunshot by now. The desire to run in and assist his colleague was proving hard to shake off.

Impatient, Bonnie paced around and clutched her belt, "What's taking so long in there?"

"I don't know. I really don't like it."

"Maybe a few seconds alone with her?" Bonnie flicked her head up towards the ceiling and licked her lips. "Can't say I blame her."

"*Seconds*? She's been in there five minutes, at least. I'll give her thirty more seconds," Tripp held his forearm in front of his chest. He drew a pattern on the skin with his thumb tip. *00:30*. The numbers counted down the moment his pressed his fingertip against it. "More than enough time."

He needn't have bothered setting the timer. The door slid open and presented a thoroughly relieved - and awe-struck - Wool.

"Done?" Tripp asked.

"Guys," Wool took a deep breath, near ready to cry with excitement, "Come in. Something… something—"

"—*Fantastic?*" Bonnie chimed in with a healthy amount of flippancy.

"Yes, yes," Wool beamed with teary delight and clapped her hands together, "My God, something fantastic *has* happened."

Chapter 15

Level One
Space Opera Beta

The elevator doors slid open. Baldron clutched Jaycee's glove in his right hand, careful not to hit the white button. He stepped into the fluorescent-lit corridor and made for the Control Deck.

"Tor, come in," he tried to unfasten his helmet, "Ugh, this bloody thing."

"Yeah, good buddy. I read you. Are you on your way?"

"Yeah, about sixty seconds ETA."

"Good, I'm working on Manuel, now. You still got that fat idiot's glove?"

"Yeah, left his hand in the elevator," Baldron flipped the visor screen up and took a deep breath as he jogged along the corridor.

"Whatever you do, don't hit that button. It's primed to go."

"I don't intend to." Baldron slipped off his helmet and tossed it against the wall. He thumped the flat, cold surface on his Decapidisc, "I just want this damn thing off my neck."

"You and me both. Just get here, now."

***

"Come get me," Jaycee waved his sparking, wrecked wrist at the creature. His legs levitated above his waist as he tried to wrench the outer elevator tube doors apart.

The monstrosity screeched up a storm and swiped its two front limbs at him.

"Nggg… *c'mon*," Jaycee failed to separate the doors. He pressed the fingers on his good hand through the slit but had no opposing force to wrench it apart, "God damn it."

THRA-AA-APP-PP!

Six of the creature's elongated limbs wrapped around the column. It prepared to bolt like a jellyfish toward the elevator door and attack Jaycee.

"C'mon, c'mon, budge. You stubborn slab of junk," Jaycee turned his body and thumped his boots against the door.

The creature launched forward and squealed as it darted through the air. Jaycee looked over his shoulder and pressed his knees to his chest.

"Come on!"

The creature fanned out all twelve limbs and opened its midsection, like some perverse spider-cobra-flower.

Jaycee's eyes widened. The blasted thing was at least ten feet wide in diameter and about to smother him. "Wow."

SCREEEECH!

The talons at the end of each limb flicked out. The creature spun around and retracted all twelve of its limbs, creating a bizarrely beautiful spectacle.

Not beautiful enough to hang around for, though. Jaycee had to take decisive action to survive.

He kicked himself toward the creature - the two flew through the air towards each other just outside the elevator door. In a few seconds they'd collide and slam the hell out of each other.

Jaycee reached into his belt and took out his secondary Rez-9 firearm. He aimed it at the creature's knuckled center and waited for the perfect moment to take his shot, "Monster go bye-bye."

"Screeeeee," the creature flung its talons forward.

Jaycee ducked as the talon sliced the back of his helmet. "Gaah," He jammed the Rez-9 into the creature's screaming throat and squeezed the trigger.

KA-SCHPLAA-AATT!

Six of the creature's limbs splattered out from his body, vomiting ropes of pink slime in all directions.

Jaycee whipped his hand out from the creature's mouth as its jaws clamped shut. The Rez-9 bounced off its incisors and into the depths of the chamber.

"Screeeee," It wailed against the elevator tube's outer doors. Four of its remaining limbs pushed the door off its railings, forcing the creature's body into the empty travel tube.

Jaycee kicked himself away from the column. He barrel-rolled for the battered door like a twisting dart of metal.

"Let's finish this, ass-face."

The creature slammed three limbs on both sides of its body against the elevator tube. The result looked like a twenty-foot, limb-like cobweb - ready to catch and murder its prey.

Jaycee shot through the broken door and clenched his right fist, "Come get some."

FLICK-SWISH-SCHTANG!

The talons on each of the six limbs fanned out in readiness for its assailant's arrival.

Jaycee's knuckles connected with the beast's screaming slit. Its razor teeth bent down its throat causing it to choke and splutter. It retaliated by swiping its limbs at Jaycee. Each attempt narrowly avoided his body. He was too close and the limbs couldn't tuck in enough to do any significant damage.

A thundering sound of something *very* heavy shot down the tube as Jaycee punched the beast once again.

The sound of heaviness grew ever louder. The tube shuddered more and more…

A shadow stretched across Jaycee's face. Something

rocketed towards him and the beast - the elevator.

"Oh, shii—"

He took one, final look at the beast. The creature roared in Jaycee's face with such force that a hairline crack tore across his visor.

He tightened his grip on the creature's midsection and yelled back over the growing thunder of the whizzing elevator, "Die. You ugly, pink bastard."

Jaycee booted the creature and somersaulted out of the tunnel, banging his arm on the broken door.

The force of the launch sent the creature back against the curved tube.

It looked up as its body blanketed into darkness from the shadow created by the approaching elevator.

"Screeeee—"

SCHAA-PLATTT!

The elevator pulverized the creature against the ground. It exploded in a haze of pink gore and shattered bone.

Jaycee's boots hit the ground, affording him a few seconds of respite.

Streaks of pink blood the size of a rolled-up duvet jettisoned in all directions from underneath the elevator and splattered across the floor.

"Level ten. Engine and Payload. Have a nice day," the female voice announced with a chirpy vigor. The elevator doors opened and released Jaycee's severed, gloveless hand.

He grabbed it in his good hand and pulled himself into the elevator.

The flat surface panel lit up, requesting a level selection. He didn't press any of the buttons. Instead, he looked at the complicated fusion of wires and metal rods jutting out from the wrist of his severed hand.

Tucked inside the trapezium of the hand was a small imprint of *something*.

Jaycee squinted at it at the text and moved it closer to his face. Then, a damning blow crept across his brain as he processed the information.

The logo of a company named of *Manning/Synapse* nestled inside the wrist.

Jaycee blinked three times in succession. The text was still there in black and white - in more ways than one.

He let out an apocalyptic cry of anger and threw his useless hand against the ground, "Bastards."

He kicked the elevator wall with his giant metal boot. He wanted blood, but had to expel the revelation from his mind.

"No, no, no…"

The elevator wall didn't budge. He could have kicked it all day long without so much as causing a chink in the material.

He stomped his boot to the floor and tried to calm himself down, "An Androgyne? I can't—"

THWACK!

He thumped the panel on the wall and shattered the screen. He'd taken himself by surprise with his own violent reaction.

Level Four lit up on the selection panel.

"Thank you," the reassuring voice said, "Lever Four. Weapons and Armory. Please remain standing."

The cage doors closed on a furious Jaycee Nayall.

The elevator shot up the delivery pipe, sending the ultimate - if imperfect and incomplete - execution machine to the top of the ship.

***

Wool, Tripp, and Bonnie entered Medix with a considerable amount of caution. The latter two members of Opera Beta were unsure of what they were about to see and braced themselves.

Wool walked over to Jelly's bed. She encouraging her colleague's eye line to the wondrous event that had taken place on Jelly's bed.

"It's okay, you can come forward," Wool grabbed a blanket from an adjacent gurney and turned to Jelly, "Look at you. You're cold."

Tripp and Bonnie could hardly believe what they saw, "Jelly?" they said together.

"Oh, wow," a joyous grin crept across Bonnie's face, "It's amaziant."

"But, but—" Tripp shook his head and flew into cynical mode, "It can't be?"

"I believe you," Bonnie sat at the edge of the bed and pressed her fingertips against the mattress. "Are you okay?"

"It can be, and it is," Wool pulled out the soft sheet and lowered it onto the back of an orange-white neck and shoulders, "She's fine and healthy. Aren't you, honey?"

A six-year-old girl-cat sat on the bed, shivering, with her arms around her bent knees. Several wires attached to her chest and abdomen sprawled over her arms, attached to a heart rate monitor.

This was no ordinary girl, though.

"Is that better, honey?" Wool smiled and placed the blanket over Jelly's knees, warming her up and securing her modesty.

The girl ran the side of her face against Wool's sleeve.

"Aww. You like that, don't you?"

Jelly had evolved. How much so? It was too early to tell.

Her whiskers had shrunk but still vibrated with life. She retained her slightly elongated infinity claws. Very fine orange hair adorned her legs, arms, and face.

She looked more human than feline, not accounting for the whiskers. By all accounts, an astounding vision of beauty.

Tripp took a step forward and couldn't help but stare, "In all my life, I... I don't know what to *say*."

"Then don't say anything," Wool whispered. "She's had a rough day. I think she'll need some rest."

"Wool?" Jelly coughed inside her throat and ran her coarse tongue across her lips.

"Yes, honey?"

"Water."

Her voice conformed to that of a typical six-year-old's - relatively high in tone but with a discreet cat-like twist.

"She talks, too?" Bonnie's eyes lit up with love in an instant. She pressed her finger to her chest and over-gesticulated her opening statement, "Me... Bonnie."

Jelly ducked her head with embarrassment, "I know… *you.*"

"Wow," Bonnie gasped.

Jelly's cat-like ears slapped back and forth as she lowered the side of her face to her own forearm and purred.

Tripp made for the door in haste, "I'm sorry, I need a few minutes. I'll be right back."

Wool passed by him with a cup of water, "Everything okay?"

"Yes," he huffed, very unsure of himself, "No. I don't know. Just give me…"

He didn't finish his sentence as he walked through the door. Wool shrugged her shoulders and approached Jelly's bed, "Here you are, honey. Some fresh water."

"Mommy," Jelly opened out her half-human hand, fanning her titanium claws out, "Claws. Sharp. Ouch."

Wool giggled. "I'll tell you what I'll do. I'll set it down on the side desk, here. You can pick it up yourself."

"Water," Jelly added.

Tripp wandered aimlessly around the corridor with his eyes shut. He muttered to himself at a rapid pace. Praying was beyond him. Most of the events he'd experienced since leaving for Saturn ran through his mind.

Discovering Alpha.

The escape from Alpha.

The loss of his best friend and captain, Daryl Katz.

The strange happenings with Haloo Ess.

News of what was happening on Earth.

The discovery of Pink Symphony - whatever it was.

He tried to make sense of it all. The answer felt so tantalizingly close yet nowhere near solvable. A frustrating experience aided little with what had happened to Jelly.

"Please, tell me this is all a dream," Tripp crouched to his knees and ran his hands through his hair, "I want to wake up… I feel so alone…"

Jelly wiggled her nose at her own reflection in the glass of water.

Wool and Bonnie watched her sniff around the rim of the glass. A bit too close. Her head jolted back from the corresponding reflection of her nose in the glass.

"You've seen humans drink from a glass, haven't you?" Wool giggled with affection.

"Yes," she opened out her brand new human fingers and blew across her fur. Her metacarpal pad remained in the center of her palm.

She closed her fingers around it. The sharp underside of each infinity claw clinked across the glass as she tightened her grip.

"That's it, honey," Wool beamed and winked at Bonnie, "You're doing *so* well."

The bottom of the glass lifted away from the desk and over her lap. Jelly sniffed around the rim, ensuring its freshness.

"Now, put up to your mouth," Bonnie pursed her lips and mimed knocking back a shot of liquid from a pretend glass, "You'll have to make your mouth move. Like this."

Jelly enacted what she saw. Her lips were new - she'd have fun with them for the next few hours until the novelty wore off.

The rim of the glass pressed against her bottom lip. She replicated Bonnie's actions a little *too* literally. The water fountained down her sheet, going everywhere *except* her mouth.

"Oh no," Wool moved forward and caught the glass from Jelly's hand, "Here, let me take that—"

Jelly burst out crying as the water soaked through the sheet.

"Hey, hey, it's okay," Bonnie took the sheet away and folded it in her arms, "We'll get you another—"

"—Right, I want answers," Tripp stormed through the door and made for Jelly, who instantly cowered behind her arms in fright.

"Miew."

"Jelly, look at me."

"Tripp, what are you doing?" Wool barked at him as he loomed over the frightened young girl. The heart monitor beeped rapidly.

"Be quiet, Wool. That's an order," he turned to Jelly and paused for a second as he looked into her eyes, "Look at me."

"I… I *look*."

"This is quite ridiculous. You expect me to believe—"

"—Tripp, please," Bonnie tried.

"Bonnie, you're outta line. Stand down," he returned to Jelly and demanded answers, "I know you understand me. I'm not playing around, anymore. Tell me what happened to you."

Jelly stopped purring and hugged her knees against her chest, "Big… water."

"Big water? You mean outside there in that pink place?"

She nodded and hoped Tripp was satisfied enough to leave her alone. Very ambitious, given his less than sedentary mood.

"What happened when you went in the water?"

"S-Swim," she stammered, her whiskers vibrating subtly, "Down."

"Why did you do that?"

"Hairs made me," she pointed at her whiskers, "Go to

get gift."

"*Gift?*" Tripp exclaimed and threw his hands into the air, "What gift? What's the gift?"

"Pink Symphony."

"This is useless," Tripp couldn't look at her any longer. He faced the opposite wall in an attempt to calm his nerves.

"Not liking. Angry," Jelly swung her legs over the edge of the bed in defiance, "Not liking *you*."

He punched his fists together with frustration, "Tell her to stop speaking. She's a cat for Christ's sake. Cats don't speak."

Wool wasn't happy with his behavior. She walked around the bed and held her hands out at Jelly, "Tripp, can you try to exercise a bit of decorum, here? Please?"

Bonnie didn't have anything to say.

"Here, honey," Wool held her hands under Jelly's opened arms, "You want to try and walk? Like we do?"

Exasperated, Tripp turned around, baffled with the girls' refusal to question what had happened.

"She's a *cat*. Look at her."

"Tripp," Bonnie shouted at him with disdain and pointed at the little girl, "Look, we know it's ridiculous, but look at her. She's real, she's there, and she's frightened. It's happened, okay? *This* is what we have, now. Do you understand?"

He screwed his face and looked at the floor.

"Hey, Healy," Bonnie jumped to her feet and clapped her hands together, launching into a sarcastic tirade. "Yoo-hoo. Pink Symphony-to-Healy. Can you read me?"

"Yes, I hear you."

"What did you think we'd find when we left USARIC, huh?" Bonnie's heart needed to release way more than just a rhetorical cliché of a question.

"I don't know—"

"—You think we'd all sail up to Saturn and find aliens with two mouths? We use all the weapons and start a big, galactic fight with space ships and guns? Pfft, typical *male*, aren't you?"

"No."

Bonnie licked her mouth and pretend-spat at the floor, "Ugh, you've made my mouth go all dry, now, having to shout at you like that," she thumped her chest in a pantomime fashion, "Me, Bonnie. *You*, captain," she pointed to Wool as she hugged Jelly. "Her? Jelly Anderson. *Star Cat*. Remember that?"

"Yes," Tripp apologized. "I remember."

"This was *your* idea, you know."

"I know."

"Don't *I know* me and act all repentant now that you're being told off by an android. You're feeling lonely? Tough. Hard times out in the big bad universe? Big deal, go N-Gage your wife and kid and cry about it. Start as you mean to go on, Healy. You asked USARIC to help you find the perfect candidate to join us. Now that you've have it you're acting like a puss— no, actually, you're acting like a *bitch*. Kind of ironic, isn't it?"

She stormed over to the bed and scooped Jelly into her arms. She purred up a treat and rubbed the side of her face against Bonnie's shoulder. Wool teared up and moved her face away from view.

Jelly stretched her arms out at the picture of Jamie on the wall, "Want Jamie."

"I know, sweetie. We all have people we miss."

"Miew," Jelly whimpered with a smile on her face. She threw her arms around Bonnie's neck and hugged her, purring up a treat, "Bonnie."

Tripp took in the unusual sight. He knew deep down inside that he'd acted hastily. It was the last thing anyone on Opera Beta needed right now.

"I'm sorry."

"You bet your sweet ass you're sorry," Bonnie ran her knuckle under Jelly's chin and threw Tripp a look of contrition, "Now apologize to Jelly."

"Uh, sorry. Jelly."

"Pathetic. Say it like you mean it."

Bonnie lowered Jelly to the ground. Tripp's eyes followed her down. Her bare paw-like feet hit the tiled ground. Then, a fluffy tail lowered above it.

Jelly waded around on the spot, keeping a firm grip on Bonnie's hand.

Tripp squatted in front of her and held out his hand, "I'm sorry, Jelly. Friends?"

She eyed his fingers and considered his offer.

"No."

"Oh."

For the first time in his entire life Tripp's attempt at reconciliation had failed him. His charm may have worked wonders with others. But with Jelly? Not so much.

"Tripp, we have work to do," Wool said. "I need to make sure she's mobile. I want to run a PET scan on her before I let her leave Medix. Just to be on the safe side."

"A *pet* scan?" Tripp smiled.

"Yes. Problem?"

"No, no. Just appreciating the irony, that's all." He stood up and swallowed the rejection. He caught Jelly peering from behind Bonnie's waist, hoping he'd just go away.

"Miew.'

"Okay, okay. I'm going," he acknowledged his personal rejection, "I'll go and find out what's happening on the flight deck, shall I?"

"Yes, I think that would be best," Bonnie ran her fingers through Jelly's new head of hair.

Tripp exited Medix with as much affability and dignity as his current situation allowed. Which wasn't very much, sadly.

As soon as the door shut, Wool and Bonnie breathed a sigh of relief.

"He's such a butt hole, sometimes," Wool turned to Jelly and smiled, "Do you know what a butt hole is?"

Jelly nodded.

"Yes, of course you do. You've spent enough time cleaning yours."

"No decorum, huh?" Bonnie giggled.

Jelly stared at Bonnie's hand and released her grip, slowly.

"What are you doing, honey?" Wool grew apprehensive about Jelly's desire for independence, "No, no. You're not ready for that, yet."

"Let her try?" Bonnie kept her focus on Jelly's hand in hers, "Go on, sweetie. Try and stand on your own."

Jelly pursed her lips and teased her claws away from Bonnie's palm.

Her arm moved to the side of her waist. There she was, standing upright on her own feet, covered in a damp, white blanket. She resembled a statuesque angel in her own way.

Wool held her mouth in amazement. "Unbelievable."

Bonnie lifted her false leg and planted her right boot a few inches in front of her left, "Like that, Jelly. Like we do."

"Like you… *do*," Jelly repeated.

"Yes. Try it."

Jelly moved her right foot forward and planted the sole of her foot on the ground. She held out her arms for balance and stepped forward.

Then, she remembered she had her tail. She swished it around and evened her body weight out, relaxing into position.

"Now, the other leg," Bonnie demonstrated by lifting her left boot next to her right.

Jelly let out cat-like whimper as she shifted her weight forward. Her right foot rocked sideways as she struggle to balance.

It needed to be done. Wool and Bonnie watched with great intensity.

"Miew," she quipped with fear.

"Try, honey."

Her mouth quivered as she moved her right leg forward. She lost her balance quite out of the blue and fell paws-first to the ground. The bed rocked back and forth on its casters.

Jelly started sobbing on the floor.

Wool raced over to pick Jelly up under her arms, "Okay, that's more than enough fun for today, I think."

"Oh dear," Bonnie sighed. "Looks like we're gonna have to practice this a bit more, huh?

Wool laid Jelly out on the bed and fluffed the pillow, "Bonnie, I need to perform an enhanced MRI. Can you give us about half an hour? "

"Sure," Bonnie made for the door and blew Jelly a kiss, "Good luck."

Chapter 16

USARIC - Weapons & Armory
Space Opera Beta - Level Four

"Level Four," the elevator called out as the cage stopped at the outer doors, "Weapons and Armory. Have a nice day."

"Open the damn doors," Jaycee clutched his severed left hand in his right and yelled at the ceiling. He kicked the cage in a fit of fury.

His boot connected with the Perspex panel, effectively scaring the doors open.

Jaycee stormed onto the sprawling metal gantry that led to Weapons & Armory. A ruthless determination to rectify what had happened swept through his body.

The clanging from his stomping boots echoed across the ground as he spoke into his radio mic.

"Tripp, this is Jaycee. Broadcasting on a secure frequency. Do you read me?"

A burst of static came through his ear piece. The device belonged to his helmet which he'd long since discarded.

"Tripp, do you read—"

"—Jaycee?" Tripp's voice crept into his ear, "Yes, this is Tripp. I read you."

"Tripp?"

"Yes, go ahead. Are you done with Engine and

Payload, yet? I guess you must be if we're able to communi—"

"—Tripp, listen," Jaycee jogged along the gantry at speed, "We need to find Baldron and Tor right now. Have you seen them?"

"No, I've just got out of Medix. Why, what's the issue? Where are you?"

"Heading for Weapons and Armory."

"What?" his voice indicated confusion, "Why?"

"I'm gonna tool up and kill them both."

"What did they do?"

Jaycee arrived at the door and slammed the palm of his severed hand against the open panel. The door slid open and allowed him in.

"Jaycee? Talk to me?"

"Yeah, I hear you."

"What happened?"

"They tried to kill me."

"But you have the compliance device. Weren't they afraid you'd use it?"

"It's a trap, man. They brought me down to E&P so one of those creature things could attack me. Baldron ran off with my glove. He's got the Decapidisc detonator."

Jaycee arrived at the first weapons bay and kicked the door open in a furious rage.

"Tor's on the control deck," Tripp said. "Baldron must be headed there right now."

Jaycee lifted a fresh K-SPARK shotgun from the holster on the wall and strapped it around his shoulders, "I'm tooling up, now, Tripp. Are you *carrying*?

"I've got my standard issue on me."

"It might not be enough," Jaycee grabbed two Rez-9s from the wall and slotted a fresh magazine into each one with extreme deftness, "Don't go there without me. You're outnumbered two-to-one."

"Jaycee, listen. I can't let them loose on the deck. God knows what they'll get up to with all the core commands and Manuel at their disposal.

"Do *not* go into control alone," Jaycee grunted into his mouth piece as he pulled open the second bay, "They probably think I'm dead. If so, who do you think is next on their hit list?"

An array of grenades and assorted explosive weapons and attachments glinted in the bay's strip lights.

"How long are you going to be?" Tripp asked.

Jaycee swiped a handful of dumb bombs and planted his boot on the lip of the shelf, "Dunno, maybe a couple minutes."

"Jaycee, listen. Something else has happened. Something bizarre. To do with Anderson."

The side section of Jaycee's thigh sprung open, providing a compartment to store four red dumb bombs and four black smart bombs.

"Anderson? What about her?"

He dropped the grenades inside and thumped the compartment shut with the side of his fist.

"I'll tell you when we meet. You're not going to believe me. Can you get to control in ninety seconds?" Tripp asked through the static.

"Sure thing," Jaycee reached into the bay and unfastened a yellow claymore from its housing. "Stay out of sight."

"Will do."

Jaycee lifted the claymore up in front of his face and pulled it apart like an accordion. Three additional claymores hung together across a wire, "Make sure it's just you. No one else."

"Sure, just you and me."

"At the corner by the door," Satisfied, Jaycee collapsed the claymores together and clipped them to his belt. He looked at the first weapons bay and saw a second K-SPARK shining back at him.

He had an idea.

"I'm bringing another shotgun with me, this one's floor

mountable. Doubles up as a turret. Go to the deck, I'm on my way."

Jaycee wrenched the heavy artillery unit from the bay in his right hand.

"See you in ninety," Tripp said.

Jaycee gripped the barrel and cocked it in his strong, right hand, "Stay safe till I get there."

The Control Deck

Space Opera Beta – Level One

Baldron stood at the flight deck, staring idly at the controls. He'd placed Jaycee's glove next to the yellow thruster lever. He looked at the view of Pink Symphony through the windscreen and felt the lip of his Decapidisc. His fate, until now, had been in the hands of someone who despised him; someone who could have taken his life at the push of a button - one which Baldron was now in control of.

He took a deep breath and closed his eyes, "One down, three to go."

"Three?" Tor looked over from the communications panel, "Oh, right. Yeah. Including that stupid cat."

Manuel hung still six feet in the air. His pages paused and flickering in mid-flip.

"How's Manuel?"

Tor followed a small white line creeping across Manuel's paused page, "Flushing to disk. Thirty more seconds and we're in business."

Baldron turned to the glorious, opulent pink sky looming beyond the shield. The three suns closed together, the harshness of their beams subdued by a series of pallid, milky clouds.

"A century and a half ago we put the first dog in space. I still don't know why we bothered."

Tor ran his fingers along the surface of his Decapidisc, "Because we could, comrade."

"I just hope Dimitri is okay. Those idiot Yanks have a habit of executing first and asking questions later. They have a history of it."

Baldron turned around and looked at Manuel's holograph. It shimmied around and attempted to speak.

"Remember, Viktor. We may be the bad guys in the eyes of those on Earth. But we had no choice. The others died and we survived. We cracked the code," Baldron pointed at the window, "Now, we have the answer."

"We do. Now we just need to figure out what it means."

Manuel vanished and reappeared in the blink of an eye. The book powered up and spread its ends out like a bird. Healthy and energetic.

"Ah, I'm online," Manuel beamed and tilted the top of his pages at Tor, "Good whenever-it-is, Tor. How are you?"

"I'm okay, Manuel."

Manuel slipped a few meters to Tor's right and nosed in around his neck, "Why are you wearing a compliance unit?"

"It's a mistake, Manuel. Jaycee Nayall attached them to me and Baldron Landaker in error."

"We believe Jaycee has short-circuited," Baldron added as he approached Tor and Manuel, "We are unhappy that a Series Three Androgyne getting with insubordination like this."

"I agree."

Tor raised his eyebrows with surprise, "You do?"

"Absolutely," Manuel flipped to page 453, 770. "See, here? Infinity Clause seven, para one. *No Androgyne unit may act against its humans*. He is in direct contravention of this clause."

"Good," Tor breathed a sigh of relief along with Baldron, "Can you remove my Decapidisc please?"

"Certainly. Give me a moment," Manuel froze solid in the air.

Baldron and Tor smiled and high-fived each other.

***

Tripp peered round the corner wall and stared at the control deck door. He held his Rez-9 in flat in his palm, clocking the white indicator on the side - a full magazine.

"Please, God. Let us survive this one."

He squeezed the grip in his right hand, keeping the gun pointed at the ground.

A series of heavy footsteps clomped away behind his shoulders. He knew who they belonged to.

"You ready, man?"

Time seemed to grind into slow motion as Tripp laid eyes on Jaycee.

The man bounded forward with great purpose. Armed with two, heavy K-SPARKS, claymores and an exo-suit that could probably withstand an atomic blast.

"Jaycee."

"Catch," He tossed one of the K-SPARKs over to Tripp, who caught it in both hands and slipped the harness over his shoulder.

"Got it."

Jaycee flipped his visor down, ready for war, "Let's give 'em hell."

Tripp held him back, "Jaycee, listen. Don't kill them. At worst, a little light maiming. We need them."

"But we can't trust those scumbags."

"I know, but we need them."

"*Need them*? Need them to kill us the second our backs are turned?"

"What happened down at Engine and Payload?"

Jaycee held up his ruined wrist. A bent metal carpal extension protruded through the broken wires and connectors.

"What the—"

"Does this answer your question?"

"Yes."

"—They need killing. So, let's do it," Jaycee put a foot forward, only to be held back by Tripp.

"Jaycee?"

"Yeah."

"You're an Androgyne?"

Jaycee spun his head to the right, no longer able to face reality. "I… I… just…"

"I had no idea."

Jaycee sniffed and held his elbow to his face, "I know you didn't. How could you? Bonnie didn't even know when she found out."

Tripp allowed Jaycee a few seconds to himself.

"If it's any consolation, you're as good as human to me. You know that, right?"

A pink tear trickled down Jaycee's cheek, "I never thought it could happen to me, man."

"Why anyone, buddy?

"My entire life has been a lie," Jaycee wept quietly, "My wife must know. My kids—"

"—Jaycee, I know it's hard to take, but—"

"—Every single time I go to sleep, I forget. I wake up the next day thinking I'm normal," Jaycee's lips quivered. "I remember everything. Everything, except for the fact I'm not normal."

Tripp didn't have the words nor the credentials to try and talk his friend down from his mire, "Hey."

"Yeah," Jaycee wiped the liquid from his face and half-laughed in pain, "Genuine tears, look. They've even got the salt levels right."

"I'm not going to try and tell you everything is okay. I can't imagine what you're going through."

"You have no idea what I'm going through. I just want to die. I never want to feel like this again."

"You're a man, aren't you?"

"Yeah," Jaycee sniffed.

"You have memories? A loving family, right?"

"Yes. I do."

"Then as far as everyone's concerned, you're a human being. What's the difference?" Tripp placed his finger under the barrel of Jaycee's gun and lifted up to the control deck door, "All that anger deep in your gut? Put it to good use. Focus it at those bastards in *there*."

Jaycee sniggered through his tears. The feeling of heartache and self-pity manifested itself into a whirlwind of pure rage.

Tripp could see the realization take place in Jaycee's eyes, "That's right, man. You fire up and take it out on the bad guys."

"I will."

Tripp gave him a harsh but friendly thump on the shoulder, "That's the spirit."

"Thanks, man."

"Oww," Tripp waved his hand in pain, quietly, "Damn, your suit is vicious."

"Yeah, don't hit me again," Jaycee cleared his throat and acted manly once again, "Don't tell anyone I cried, okay?"

"Of course not."

"Because if you do I'll remove your skull, sand it down and give it to your wife as a souvenir cereal bowl."

"That won't work. She hates cereal."

Tripp and Jaycee shared a moment. Certain death was on the horizon. Both men knew it, and elected to laugh right in its face.

"Okay, listen carefully. We're not going in all guns blazing."

"No?"

"Nope," Tripp shook his head and scanned the door to the control deck, "I'm going in first…"

***

"Override compliance unit," Manuel's voice came out

of Tor's mouth, "Decapidisc. Unit Two."

The lights on the disc shut off one by one. Tor stood mannequin-still as Manuel controlled his body.

"Oh, this *is* curious. This is what it feels like to be human?" Tor felt the neck hole unbolt. Both halves of the disc swung out, resembling a huge *three* shape hanging from the back of his neck.

A sharp, purple light bolted out from Tor's eyes, puking Manuel's holographic book image into the air.

"Done. Whoa, what a rush," Manuel fluttered around in an attempt to acclimatize himself to his surroundings.

Tor's blinked back to life and shook the dizziness away, "Wow. Is it over?"

"Yes," Manuel shifted around in the air, applauding the experience with two of his pages.

"Thank, God," He caught the disabled Decapidisc in his hands and placed it on the communications panel, "Thanks, Manuel."

"You're welcome. Thank you for letting me inside you, Viktor."

"What?"

"Your name. Viktor Rabinovich. I took the liberty to run a backup on your entire life in case you ever developed Alzheimer's."

"I didn't give you permission to do that," Tor fumed. "Erase it. Right now, please."

"I'm sorry, I didn't mean to—"

"—Dah, dah, I don't wanna hear it. Erase all that data you *stole* from my head, please. At once."

"Certainly," Manuel paused for nanosecond. "Erase complete."

"Thank *you*. You're out of your mind."

"I know, Tor. I was *in* yours."

"That's not what I meant—*forget it.*"

Baldron got thoroughly fed up with the friendly exchange. He pointed at the button on Jaycee's glove and then to his own Decapidisc, "Hey, what about me? Get inside me and take this thing off."

Tor waved his hand across his face. An eight-foot holographic vector image of Opera Beta pinged to life in the middle of the room.

"Manuel?"

"Yes, Viktor?

"Stop calling me that. Call me Tor."

"Certainly, *Tor.*"

"What's the situation with Pure Genius?"

"The supercomputer is fully operational, now. Everything is well."

"Good," Tor ignored Baldron and pointed to the vector image, "Sit-rep report on all souls aboard Opera Beta, please. Engage coordinates, and show them in purple."

"Certainly."

"Comrade, please," Baldron pleaded, "Have Manuel remove this thing from my neck."

"Look, *comrade.* We need to know where the others are, and I want to make sure Jaycee is dead—"

The door to the control deck slid open. Tor and Baldron averted their attention to the man entering the room.

A stern-looking Tripp Healy, complete with K-SPARK heavy artillery, "Hey, guys."

"Hello, Tripp," Tor clutched at his neck and stood in front of the opened Decapidisc nestled on the comms panel.

"Did you get those nuke thrusters replaced okay?"

"Yes, we did. Everything is… *well.*"

"You're starting to sound just like him."

"Who?"

"Manuel," Tripp smiled and nodded at the vector image of Opera Beta, "What are you doing with that, Tor?"

"Oh, I—" he stumbled over his need to lie, "I was just working out if Pure Genius is up and running."

Tripp clocked Baldron's nerves getting the better of him. He threw Tor a look of suspicion but kept his manner friendly and professional, "I see you managed to get your Decapidisc off?"

"It was hurting my neck," Tor held his breath and watched Tripp walk towards the flight deck. A swift change of conversation was required. "Um, where have you been?"

"Where have I been?" Tripp gripped the back of the flight chair and chuckled with faux confusion, "I'm sorry, I didn't know I had to report my whereabouts to you at all times."

Tor and Baldron just *knew* something was wrong. Tripp knew it, too, and decided to have fun with them. He clocked Jaycee's glove in the corner of his eye but made out he hadn't noticed.

"Where's the big man? Was he helpful?"

Baldron gulped hard, trying not to sweat. His pores had other ideas, though.

"Y-Yes," he stammered and almost croaked, "H-He was—"

"—Why are you sweating, Landaker?" Tripp asked.

"This is unusual," Manuel butted in, "I'm detecting a lot more souls than anticipated."

Tor ignored Manuel and focused his attention on pleasing Tripp, "I'm not. It's just hot in here—"

Manuel activated himself and shifted around the room, "Tor, the sit-rep is available. But I'm afraid to report there are many more—"

"—Not now, Manuel—"

"—Sit-rep? *Souls*?" Tripp stepped toward the vector image, away from the flight deck, "What sit-rep?"

Tor held out his hands in defiance. "Manuel, no—"

"—Ah, hello, Tripp. Tor asked me for everyone's coordinates within Opera Beta. Here they are."

Tor closed his eyes as three purple dots blotted out inside Medix. Three in the control deck, and one in the corridor just outside.

"Those are just the crew, however."

Baldron scrunched his face in confusion at the last pulsating purple icon. Someone was just outside the door. He shot Tor a look and then made for the glove on the flight panel.

Tripp didn't see Baldron snatching the glove - he had his back to him.

"Why do you want to know where everyone is?" Tripp lifted his K-SPARK and slipped his finger around the trigger.

Dozens of purple blobs appeared around the ship's vector.

Manuel flew around the room trying to catch everyone's attention, "I seriously advise you act on this information, good people." A giant blob appeared at the front of the ship's vector image.

"B-Because…" Tor struggled.

Tripp opened his mouth and shouted at the door. "Jaycee, now!"

"What?" Tor didn't know where to turn. He backed up and gripped the edges of the deck, "Quick, the glove."

"I got it, I got it," Baldron wiggled his fingers into the glove.

Jaycee stomped into the room and pointed his gun at Baldron, "Hey, *you*."

"No, d-don't shoot!"

SCHPLATTT!

Everyone turned to the source of the noise. A giant creature slapped itself to exterior of the flight deck windshield.

"Jaaaaysus," Tor gasped at the underbelly of the thirty-foot tall creature thumping the transparent plastic.

"Gah," Baldron looked up at the hundreds of sharp teeth scratching at him from up above. The magnificent beast was darker in color than the other, smaller ones they'd seen, "We're in hell!"

"Shut up," Jaycee aimed down his sight and stomped his foot to the ground, "Hey! You idiot, over here."

Baldron turned around in an utter daze, "Huh?"

The creature shunted the windshield, squealing an ungodly roar at the humans on the other side.

"I want my damn glove back," Jaycee's K-SPARK beamed to life, seconds away from firing a bullet, "Throw it to me."

Baldron squeezed it in his hand, "No."

"I said give me the damn glove."

"No."

CRAAA-AAA-ACK… Scores of hairline cracks blasted across the windshield. It wouldn't hold off the beast much longer.

"Hell's teeth!" Tripp backed up and waved everyone to the door, "Everyone, get out of here."

Manuel flew through the vector image and emitted a beam at the hundreds of purple flashing dots, "Tripp, these unidentified *things* everywhere. Observe, Primary Air Lock, Level One."

The vector contours of the airlock image enlarged, offering a more detailed view. A torrent of purple dots bundled up at the line pushing one of them through.

"We're *on* level one," Tripp gasped.

A thunderous crash rattled down the walkway followed by a cacophony of high pitch screeches.

"It's *them*. We're stuck," Baldron screamed, "We're all gonna die."

Jaycee lifted his K-SPARK to the windshield and yanked the trigger back with his index finger.

"You first."

The bullet charge bolted out of the barrel, tore through the vector image, and made its way to the dead center of the windshield.

KERR-RAASSH!

Baldron threw himself back. The plastic shield exploded, raining sharp fragments of plastic over the control deck. The giant creature smashed against the flight panel, accidentally knocking the yellow thruster level forward.

"Gaaah," Baldron swiped at the creature and missed.

Jaycee stepped back slowly as he led the retreat to the closed door, "Quick, behind me."

"What?" Tor yelled and pointed at Baldron, "You can't leave him there. That *thing* will kill him."

"Good riddance. He can keep that big, ugly bastard busy while we run."

The entire ship began to rumble to life. Manuel spun around on the spot, "Engines initiated. Prepare for launch."

"We're going!" Tripp backed up with Jaycee. Both held their K-SPARKs up at the enormous monstrosity.

"Holy hell, look. It's killing him."

"No, no," Baldron slapped the creature's bulbous mid-section with the glove. His Decapidisc kept his neck and head inches from the floor, rolling side to side. It also protected his neck from the sharp talons as they jabbed away at his face and neck, "Help me, p-please."

The creature roared into his face, rippling his skin up the front of his face.

"Gah, gah, please," Baldron rolled his neck along the rim of his disc and looked at Jaycee, "P-Please, shoot it."

"I will," Jaycee looked up from the sight on his gun, "Just as soon as it kills you."

Tripp looked away, somewhat resigned to the execution that was about to take place.

"Gimme that gun," Tor gripped the barrel of Jaycee's K-SPARK and tried to pull it away from his hands, "Shoot that thing. It's going to kill him."

Jaycee winced and booted Tor in his gut. The man tumbled bounced against the door, "Get off me." Jaycee swung the gun back at the creature. It lifted the first two of its mangled, black limbs and fanned out its talons.

STAB-SHUNT-CLAMP!

The sharp ends pinned Baldron to the ground on his back. It lowered its razor sharp teeth-filled slit down to his face and roared once again.

"Okay," Baldron convulsed with fear, "I-If I'm g-going, you're coming with me."

He gripped Jaycee's glove in his right hand and punched the creature in the throat, releasing it deep inside its throat.

The beast shunted back on its limbs as the ship tilted forward and pulled itself away from Pink Symphony's sandy surface.

The horizon shuddered in the background, wading around, suggesting the ship was struggling to take off.

Tripp, Jaycee, and Tor stumbled away from the door and hit the wall. "*Damn* it."

The creature munched away on Baldron's glove. The ship tilted back, rolling Baldron out from under the creature and sliding along the control deck floor.

"Comrade," Tor flung himself up the raised length of the ground and caught Baldron in his arms.

"Hey, you two," Tripp shouted at them as he clung to the door. His feet drifted into the air as the ship tried to launch, "Enough lessense, get over here."

Jaycee peered through the window in the door. The corridor seemed clear enough, "We gotta get to Medix and protect the others."

"Jaycee, open the door," Tripp shouted over the combined deafening sound of the creature's squeals and the ship's thrusters, "Now."

Jaycee waved Tripp through as the door slid open. He swung his gun back at the creature and prepared to blast it to pieces, "Come on, you ugly spider-looking bag of puke. Let's do it."

CRUNCH!

The creature's mouth crunched Jaycee's glove, spitting out strips of fabric. It nestled against the flight deck and roared again.

"Thank God," Tor said to Baldron, "Let's get out of here—"

Biddip-biddip-beeep…

Three white lights lit up on Baldron's Decapidisc. He gasped and tried to pull it away from his neck, "No, no, no."

Tor looked at the creature, "Oh *no*."

GULP! The creature swallowed the glove and spat the plastic activation button to the ground. It spun around on its axis and fell on its side.

"Help me," Baldron screamed and pushed away from Tor. He ran through the vector image of Opera Beta, toward the beast, tugging at the metal disc, "I'm going to die,"

The creature spread all twelve limbs across the floor, ceiling, and walls, looking for all the world like a fleshy spider-cobweb.

Beep-beep-beep...

The three white lights flashed on Baldron's Decapidisc. The creature widened its mouth behind Baldron as he squealed for the last time.

"Comrade, p-please," he begged Tor slumped to his knees.

"I c-can't," Tor squealed, utterly helpless.

Biddip, biddip, beeeeeeeeeep. The three indicators flashed faster and faster.

The Decapidisc vibrated around Baldron's neck. The blades within the metal housing spun to life and produced a whirring sound.

Baldron accepted his fate and closed his eyes.

SCHWIIRRR-SCHUNT.

The disc rocked gently around Baldron's neck. He lifted his head and looked at Jaycee with sadness, "I'm sorry."

"Yeah, you keep saying that."

Jaycee thumped his thigh compartment open with his fist. A red dumb bomb fell into his palm just in time for him to scowl at Baldron in his last seconds.

A comforting smile stretched across Baldron's mouth. His eyes, nostrils and mouth released a fountain of pink liquid. His head wobbled atop his shoulders for a couple of seconds.

The ship adjusted itself, throwing Jaycee and Tor to the left - and Baldron's freshly severed head from his shoulders. The opened Decapidisc clanged to the floor - mission accomplished.

"Go to Hell, you *sonofabitch*."

"Who are you talking to?" Tor asked.

"Both of them."

Jaycee hurled the dumb bomb at the creature. It unlatched its limbs from the wall and made for Jaycee and Tor. It screeched at the top of its vocal chords.

The bomb flew into its open, wailing mouth.

"Run," Jaycee grabbed Tor's sleeve, "C'mon, let's go."

Tor trained his eyes on Baldron's severed head rolling towards the flight deck like a lit sparkler. It bounced to a stop between the creature's limbs.

"What—? He's… he's not—"

"—Yeah, another Androgyne Series Three unit. Sucks doesn't it?" Jaycee pushed Tor through the door and jumped after him, "It's becoming something of a bad habit around here, lately. Finding out you're one of them can really screw up your day."

The creature pushed itself forward just as Jaycee slammed the door shut on one of its limbs. Its muffled squeals bounced behind the sound-proof window.

Jaycee took the opportunity to watch the impending execution, "Look at it, Tor."

"Wh-what?"

"That's *one* angry mother—"

KA-SCHPLATTT-TT!

The beast exploded, painting the entire control deck with pink gore and charred remains.

"We gotta get out of here," Tor held his hand to his

mouth like a frightened child.

"Damn straight," Jaycee bounded up the corridor and turned the corner.

Tor double-took and followed after him, "I need a gun."

"Ha. Very funny," Jaycee bopped him on the back of the head, "The only way you're getting a weapon is if you use it on yourself."

"Jaycee?" Tripp's voice shot through Jaycee's headset, "I'm at the Primary airlock. They're *everywhere*, man."

"Tripp?" Jaycee ran across the corridor, "Everywhere?"

"Those creatures. Listen, do *not* come here. Get to Medix. Bonnie and Wool are there with Jelly. I can't hold them off. Both airlock doors are damaged."

"But, we're taking off?" Tor muttered, "If we hit orbit— hell, if we leave its atmosphere, all the air will get sucked out—"

"—Understood." Jaycee turned left and made for the bank of descending stairs, "Come on, *Viktor*. We're going to Medix."

Chapter 17

Medix

Space Opera Beta - Level Three

A holographic scan of Jelly's brain projected from Wool's thumbnail on the central desk. The left and right hemisphere glowed red and blue, respectively.

"Head?" Jelly pressed her fingers to a digipad secured on her scalp, "What is?"

"No, honey. What… is… *this*?"

"What… is… *this*?" Jelly repeated verbatim, understand very little of what she'd just learned.

"It's a tracer," Wool walked around the image and analyzed it, "It shows us what's inside your head. We're just making sure you're okay. It'll take a few minutes for the report to return."

Jelly shifted her buttocks across the mattress still not fully accustomed to the new position. Her tail got in the way much of the time which went some way to distract her from the pain in her stomach.

"Tummy hurts."

"That's normal, Jelly. Probably adjusting to your new posture and diet."

"Ad… just… ing," Jelly repeated.

"Well, when you like things a certain way but something makes you change it. Adjusting."

"Oh," Jelly wiggled her nose and pricked up her ears. The bed began to vibrate, "Why bed move?"

"Why is the bed *moving*, honey."

"Not knowing," she purred and gripped the sides of the mattress for safety.

"No, I wasn't asking you, honey. I was correcting you."

"Correcting?"

Wool turned to the ceiling and stepped away from the image scan. The largest of the three sun's rings revolved in all directions around its body. The pink horizon slid down the window. Opera Beta was in motion.

"Thank God," She breathed a sigh of relief and smiled at Jelly, "Looks like we're going home."

"Like house," Jelly returned the smile, "Want Jamie."

"*Home*, sweetie. Not house. You *like* home. We all like home," Wool walked over to the bed and sat into the chair. She was on the verge of crying for joy, "I have to tell you something."

Jelly lifted her jaw, "Do chin."

Wool ran her knuckle under Jelly's chin, "Feeling better?"

A gleeful purr came from her throat as she spotted Bonnie napping on the chair.

"I guess you are," Wool enjoyed Jelly's relaxed nature.

Jelly turned toward the sleeping woman on the chair, "Bonnie. Dead?"

"Bonnie isn't dead, honey. She's recharging her batteries," Wool pretended to rub her eye with her fist, "Tired."

Jelly slid the side of her face along the back of Wool's hand, purring twice as hard.

"When we return home I don't know if Jamie will recognize you. He might be a bit scared."

"Scared?" Jelly's head bolted upright, confused. She pointed at the picture of Jamie on the wall, "Friend."

"No, I know that," Wool rose out of the chair and lifted Jelly's blanket over her shoulders, "It's just that you've grown up a bit and you look different. So he might not know who you are."

Jelly wiggled her nose along the top of the blanket,

"Smell? Know me?"

Wool removed the scan pad from Jelly's head and placed it on her stomach, "Hold still, honey."

"You *hold*. Picture," Jelly nosed around the device in her master's hand.

"No, *you* hold yourself still. Don't move," Wool strapped the pad in place and lifted the wires over her right leg, "We'll do your body next."

The brain scan image rippled wildly and replaces Jelly's body shape and the outline of her organs.

"PET scan report," the machine advised. "Two minutes."

"You know, a hundred years ago, they'd have had to put you in a big tube to do this."

"Big tube. Water?" Jelly extended her claws and touched her teeth, "Thirsty."

"Yeah, *kinda*," Wool looked at the machine and held the pad in place against Jelly's chest, "Commence enhanced magnetic resonance imaging, please."

"E-MRI activated."

"Now, don't worry, honey. This might tingle a little bit."

The pad sucked in and absorbed itself onto Jelly's abdomen.

"Miew," she whimpered. "Tummy. Hurts."

"I know. It won't hurt much longer," Wool flicked a switch on the front of the machine, "Administer tracer."

The door to Medix slid open.

A giant killing machine decked out in an exo-suit and K-SPARK shotgun was the first person in.

"Jaycee?" Wool held Jelly's head in her hands at once, realizing the two hadn't been formally acquainted, "What are you doing here?"

"You got time for a long, drawn-out story?"

"No, I don't. But I've been left alone here with jelly all this time. She's scared."

Without so much as a courtesy greeting, he yanked Tor by his collar and threw him into the room, "Get in."

The man staggered forward and crashed against an empty bed. The medician tools spilled from the attached tray. Jaycee rolled his eyes and lunged after him, "Get off the floor, you self-absorbed, Soviet ass-clown."

"No, p-please, no m-more—"

Jaycee bent over and grabbed Tor's collar, lifting the top half of his body into the air. "We've only just begun—

"—Hey," Wool barked at the pair, "Behave yourselves. We have a guest."

"What the—" Jaycee spotted the strange half-cat girl sitting with his colleague on Jelly's bed, "I, uh—"

"—Is that *Anderson*?" Tor asked, confused.

Jaycee absentmindedly released Tor's collar and dropped him to the floor. "What happened to her?"

"We don't know yet and she won't tell me."

"Huh? Won't *tell* you?" Jaycee pressed his knee against his gun. "Want me to make her?"

"Are you out of your mind, Nayall?" Wool yelled at his face, "It's not that she doesn't want to tell me. It's that she's not able to."

"She can speak?"

"Yes. Speak," Jelly scowled at the large mercenary filling her periphery vision, "Jaycee. Bad man."

"Yes, that's right, honey. Don't pay any attention to the bad man," she finished in a mocking tone and gave her a cuddle.

Tor winced and staggered to his feet, "You're right, he *is* a bad man."

The remark snapped Jaycee back to reality - and the severity of their current situation.

"Well," he half-mocked and thumped his exo-suit, "This *bad man* just saved all your lives."

"Did you?" Wool asked.

"The ship is swarming with those creature things. Just killed a massive one out in the control deck."

Wool stood out of her seat in shock, "What?"

"They're everywhere," Tor confirmed. He spotted Bonnie fast asleep on the chair behind Jaycee, "We got Manuel operational. He's trying to get us out of here."

"Cannot leave," Jelly blurted matter-of-factly and patted her mattress like an excited child, "Stay, stay, stay."

Jaycee approached the bed and felt the urge to touch her face, "What did you say?" His gloved fingers made contact with her cheek.

"Miew," she cowered, only for his finger to brush against one her whiskers.

ZAAPP-PP!

Each whisker lit up and jolted Jaycee's hand away, "Oww. What the hell is wrong with you?"

Jelly exploded in tears and held the sides of her head with her paws, "Brain. Hurts."

"Look what you've done," Wool scooped the sobbing Jelly into her arms. It wasn't until she felt her weight that she fully acknowledged her growth, "Honey, are you okay?"

"Bad men," she wept, "In head."

"Bad men? What bad men?"

Jaycee turned to Tor and pointed at Bonnie. "You, wake Dr. Whitaker up. Now. We need her online."

"Fine."

Tor raced over to the chair as Jaycee turned back to Wool and Jelly, "What's wrong with her?"

"PET scan complete," the machine advised, "J. Anderson, configuration one, one, eight. Congratulations, you've a clean bill of health. Generating quantitative report. Please standby."

The image displayed a 3D rendition of Jelly's brain. All four quadrants flashed green.

"What does that mean?"

Wool hugged Jelly and exhaled, "Like the machine said, a clean bill of health. Nothing wrong."

"Hey, wake up," Tor bopped Bonnie on the shoulder.

"Huh?" she licked her lips and opened her eyes, "Where am I?"

"Very funny. Get up. We're at war."

"War?"

"Apparently so."

Bonnie jumped to her feet and sprang into action. She reached for her Rez-9 and clasped the holster, "Who are we fighting?"

"You remember those ugly monster things?"

"Yes."

"Them."

"Where are they?"

"We're waiting here for Tripp. Just get ready," Tor immediately thought of a question, "Don't get angry, but… are you human?"

"Of course I'm human, you idiot," Bonnie spat and saw Jelly in Wool's arms, "Oh, there she is."

"Hey."

Bonnie lifted her boot at the end of her mechanical leg and wondered why it was vibrating, "Oh, it's not me. Are we *traveling*?"

"We're trying to," Tripp entered Medix. Covered in pink slime, his face and inner-suit had seen happier, cleaner days.

He slung the K-SPARK over his shoulders and held out his arms, acknowledging his gory state, "You're welcome." He turned to Jaycee and held out his hand, "Fresh mag, please."

"You got it," Jaycee released the magazine from his gun, "Here," he threw it at Tripp, who caught it and slotted it into his shotgun.

"Thanks," Tripp wiped a slew of pink gloop from his face and pulled the door shut.

"What's the situation, Tripp?' Wool asked. 'I'm hearing those *things* got into the ship."

"Yes, I've just killed about twenty of them."

"So, they're all dead?"

"Nope," Tripp cleared his throat and wiped his pink sludge-splattered face, "That was just the start. We'll be out of here soon. We need to kill however many of them are left. Where's Baldron?"

"He, uh, didn't make it," Jaycee said.

Tripp hawked up a pink wad of phlegm and spat it at Tor's face. He recoiled with apology when it splatted against the man's forehead.

"Eww."

"Sorry, I meant to miss you."

Tripp barged the man out of his path and looked at the E-MRI holograph hanging in the middle of the room, "This is Jelly, right?"

"Yes," Wool explained, carrying Jelly over to Tripp, "The brain scan came back all clear. Just a routine health check, really."

"You okay, Jelly?"

Tripp smiled at her, hoping for a positive reception. No such luck. She pressed the side of her head against Wool's shoulder and avoided him.

"Charming."

He turned around and addressed Wool, Jaycee, Tor, and Bonnie, "Okay, here's the lowdown. We're screwed. Manuel's trying his best to get us out of this godforsaken place, but the thrusters are playing up and we might not have enough throttle to reach the sky, let alone orbit," he shot Tor a look of utter disgust, "Ain't that right, comrade?

"I'm sorry."

"I swear on my wife and son, Tor," Tripp grunted, about ready to execute the man with his own bare hands, "If you say you're sorry just one more damn time, I'll tear off your head and thread it on a skewer along with Baldron's. Do you understand what I've just said?"

Tor pressed his hands together and decided it was best not to call his captain's bluff, "Yes, Captain."

"Good," Tripp reached into his belt, retrieved his Rez-9

and push it into Wool's hands, "Bonnie, are you carrying?"

"Yeah, just the one piece," Bonnie gripped her firearm and thumped her metal leg, "Got the K-12 on as a backup."

"Stay behind Jaycee, then. He and I are locked and ready to blast."

"I don't have a gun," Tor tried, temporarily forgetting that he was the bad guy.

"Why don't you try punching them in the face? See how far that gets you?" Tripp winked at Wool but she hadn't the heart to smirk back.

"This isn't funny, Tripp," Tor said.

"Yes it is. You're good at hitting things, aren't you?' Tripp pointed at Wool, 'Especially women."

"That's irrelevant. If we go out there unarmed I'll get killed."

"Want me to tear your arms off, then?" Jaycee joked, enjoying the man's distress, 'I'll rip them off and batter you to death with them."

"No, *armed*, you dummy. Give me a weapon *at least*."

"No guns for you, ass hat,' Tripp spat. 'If you die, you die. We'll be sure to send N-Gage your loved ones and tell them how awesome you are, or, hopefully, soon to be *were*."

Jelly's whiskers sparked up. "Miewww," She clawed at Wool's arm, wanting to be set down on the bed.

"Okay, honey."

Everyone watched as she dropped Jelly to her mattress, "Voice in brain," she shuddered and held her claws to her face, "Pink… *Pink Symphony*."

"What's she talking about now?" Jaycee asked, ready to storm out and do battle. The bizarre interlude was preventing him from doing his job, "We'd better go."

"No, wait," Wool leaned over Jelly and looked at her face, "What's wrong, honey?"

Jelly yelped and swiped her infinity claws at Wool, tearing three slits across her cheek, "ROOWAAR."

"Gah," Wool cupped her face and stepped back against the wall, "She scratched me!"

Tripp ran over and held her arm, "Wool."

Jelly snatched the radio on her bedside desk and slammed it against her thighs. The bone in her leg cracked pushing her feet out a further two inches, "Pink..."

She dropped the radio to the floor and writhed around in pain, "Waaaah."

The black device hit the floor, cracking apart. Beethoven's 5th Symphony piped up.

Da-da-da-dummm...

The crew backed up as Jelly's chest hulked into the air and carried the rest of her flailing body ten inches above the bed.

"Shaaah..." Her childlike voice deepened, mid-cry, "Shaaantaa..."

Wool caught sight of a commotion coming from outside the window, "Look, out there."

The two smaller suns in the sky converged into the biggest. Its rings whizzed around at speed, vacuuming the grains of sand off the floor like a reverse waterfall.

The ship shuddered and rocked around forcing the horizon to creep back into view.

"I don't like this," Tripp said. "What the hell is—"

THUD!

Jelly crashed back to the bed and wailed, "Ugghhh..."

Bonnie widened her eyes at Jelly. Her body had lengthened by five inches. Still covered by the blanket, she shook her head and flicked her ears, "They come."

"What?" Jaycee lost his temper. "*Who* come?"

"We stay," she said in her huskier voice, barely registering any pain, "We fight."

"Fight what?" Tripp asked, about to explode with frustration.

Jelly's blinks turned her orange eyes pink. Her whiskers lit up. Her voice husky and gravelly, as if possessed, "Do you know why you are here?"

Magnetized by Jelly's transformation, Tripp cleared his throat and calmed down, "No, we don't. Tell us."

"Look outside and see," she said, attracting the undivided attention of everyone in the room.

All sets of eyes averted to the window.

Hundreds of thousands of creatures scurried across the sand away from the ocean. Many crammed into each other as they funneled to the ship like a virus.

"God, look at that."

"We gave Jelly *The Gift*," the girl's voice slowed down, near unrecognizable, "We need your help."

"That's not Jelly talking," Wool said.

"Who are you?"

"Pink Symphony. Evolve."

"*Lessense*," Jaycee prepared to hop through the window and go down in a blaze of glory, "That's a stupid name for—"

"—It is the closest name we have. Beings from your universe cannot comprehend our true name," Jelly swung her legs over the side of the bed and stood to her feet. She pulled the E-MRI pad from her chest and clutched the blanket around her neck. "To you, we are Pink Symphony. Pink, because that's as close as your eyes can process…"

Jelly looked at the radio on the floor and sighed. A battered, tinny version of Beethoven's classic whimpered across the ground.

"Symphony. Because of the language your radio speaks. Your friends on the other ship came to help us, but they did not have the right species."

Tor put two and two together, hoping he hadn't arrived at five, "Wait. That makes sense."

"What makes sense?" Tripp asked. "It makes no sense at all."

Tor went for the radio. "No, hang on. Wait." He picked up the broken piece of plastic and tore out the wiring, "When Alpha went through Enceladus, it must have come here. To Pink Symphony. Right?"

"Can't say I disagree."

"Don't you understand?" The puzzle slotted together in Tor's mind, "Saturn Cry, the message it sent. It wasn't coming from Enceladus. It came from *here*."

"Why didn't Alpha crack the code?" Wool asked, still failing to get to grips with the idea.

"Because they didn't have a cat on board," Bonnie said, "They were useless to *whoever* this is we're speaking to through Jelly."

"*The Gift*," Jelly made her way over to the wardrobe and sifted through the hanging medician gowns, "Blind as the day you were born."

"She cracked the code when she was in Pure Genius," Tor continued. "She sent us through Enceladus and brought us here."

"Yes, but it was either that or run out of oxygen," Tripp tried his best to question the bizarre logic.

"No, this was no accident. Jelly had no choice."

"Pink Symphony is oxygen. We breathe, we live," Jelly slipped her arms through the sleeves of the medician gown and pushed the door shut, "The girl is cold."

"Whatever brought us here needed Jelly," Tripp asked. "Or, a *cat*?"

"The cat went into the water. She returned with The Gift we gave her," Jelly flicked her shoulder length hair over her shoulders. She stood an impressive three foot five and looked more human, "War is coming. You need to protect her."

"What are you talking about?"

"Not Jelly," Jelly held out her arms, encouraging Wool to go and hug her, "Pink Symphony."

"Are we… *talking*… to Pink Symphony right now?" Tor asked.

"Yes."

"Wow," Tor cackled wildly, "That's messed up."

Tripp shrugged his shoulders and waved Tor across the room, "Well, you're the communications expert. Go and talk to her."

"This is incredible. Let me look at her."

"Just don't touch her," Wool squeezed Jelly's shoulders from behind.

Tor lowered himself and looked into Jelly's possessed eyes, "Jelly?"

She blinked, shyly, and clung to Wool's leg as she awaited Tor's questions.

"Why did you bring us here?"

"To save us."

"Who is *us*?"

"Pink Symphony—"

"—Yes, I know. But, *who* are you?"

"Virus."

"That explains the pink gas," Tor looked up at Tripp for a response. He didn't get one and so returned to Jelly, "A virus?"

"You carry us," Jelly's face remained utterly still, "We cure humans, we kill humans."

"It hasn't killed me, yet. Or any of my crew."

Jelly shook her head, "Only kills *humans*."

"Right. So why aren't we dead, yet?"

Jelly twitched her nose as the voice radiated through the skin on her face, "No one heard Saturn Cry for the equivalent of an Earth millennium. Humans responded to the message. We didn't mean to kill your people."

"Is that what happened to Alpha?"

"We learned much from Alpha. They came, we heard noises we liked. We sent Alpha back, they helped to transmit our call for rescue. To save us."

"Save you from what?" Tor asked, carefully.

"Shanta."

"*Shanta*?"

Jelly scowled and roared in Tor's face, "Pink Symphony *is* evolution."

Wool turned to the E-MRI scan and noticed spotted a glowing pink orb in her belly, "What's that?"

"The gift," Jelly approached her and pointed to the stomach organ, "You protect cat."

"We can never go home," Jaycee said. "We've been infected by the virus. It'll kill everyone."

Jelly's eyes tilted up into her skull. "Protect. *Please*," She closed her eyelids and slumped to the floor in a crazy heap.

"Jelly," Wool crouched down and scooped her into her arms and lifted her up, "God, she's gotten heavier, Tripp. Help me carry her to the bed."

"Okay," He grabbed Jelly's calves in his hands. Wool pulled her over to the bed by her arms.

"Be careful with her tail," Wool set her top half onto the mattress, "I'm not sure what's going on here, Tripp."

"Join the club."

"The E-MRI is nearly complete. It's not my place to bark orders at people, but I think you guys should go and do whatever it is you need to do and help us get out of here."

"You're right," Tripp looked at Jelly and ran his thumb across her forehead, "Is she okay?"

"Yeah, BPM is one over fifty. She's sleeping. Probably a bit exhausted."

"I'm not going to let anything happen to her," Tripp absorbed the girl's beauty, "If we have to *protect* her, then that's what we'll do."

"Tripp?" Tor was eager to get a word in edgewise, "I, uh, I think we're—
oh, God."

"Not now, Tor."

Tripp nodded at Jaycee and Bonnie. The primary airlock is damaged, but we're off-ground, at least. Those creature things won't be coming in—"

Jelly's eyes flew open. "Shaaaanta."

"Shanta, yes," Tripp agreed before double-taking and realized what he'd just said, "Shanta?"

"Shanta," Jelly fumed and blinked.

"Okay, I guess they're called *The Shanta*," Tripp said.

"Botanix is vulnerable, so I suggest we go there and make sure it's sealed."

"There were enough of them trying to get in there," Bonnie said. "Good idea."

A bead of sweat ran down Tor's anxiety-ridden face. "Oh, God. She said it only kills *humans*," he muttered.

"Tor, not now. You can think about sabotaging all our future missions another time."

He grabbed at Tripp's hand in profound desperation.

"Get off me, numb nuts."

"Pink Symphony. It only kills humans. Why am I not dead?" Tor turned his back to Tripp and grabbed his left ear, "There's only one explanation. Please, look behind my ear. Do you see anything?"

Tripp sighed, "If it shuts you up, then fine. Show me."

Sure enough, the Manning/Synapse imprint was visible behind his earlobe now that Tripp held it up.

"Huh?"

"I *knew it*. I'm a damn Androgyne," Tor burst into tears and slumped against the bed on the adjacent wall, "You call me a conspirator? I just *knew* something was up. Baldron was Series Three, and now… now…" he started to hyperventilate, "Now you're keeping this from me?"

"Hey, calm down. No one knew," Tripp spat. "How did *you* know?"

Tor wiped his nose and stammered as he spoke, "Jelly, Pink Symphony. Whatever it's c-called. It's a virus. Some evolutionary virus *thing*."

"Yes."

"And it only *kills* humans?"

"Yeah, I heard her," Tripp tried to scramble for the answer before Tor had to spell it out, "Why?"

"Who died after we left Alpha?" Tor cried.

"Daryl, Androgyne—"

"—No. *Not* during the explosion. Anyone would have been killed in that. I mean, who died because they had the virus?"

"Haloo."

"Right."

"Right."

Bonnie and Jaycee knew what Tripp had failed to grasp. Wool knew it, too, and clocked on instantly.

"Oh, n-no, no," Wool's hand shook intensely as she reached up to her left ear, "No, I c-can't be."

Tripp dashed over to her and grabbed her shoulders, "Quick, show me."

"If… if I am, then I d-don't want to know," Wool treated the proposed diagnosis as terminal, "Tripp, p-please. Promise me you'll lie if I am, or tell me the truth if I'm not."

"Turn around."

Her eyes peeled away from his face as she turned around. Faced with her shoulders, he carefully lifted her earlobe up with his knuckle.

Jaycee scrunched his face and felt a lump form in his throat. He *knew* what it felt like it. Everyone else fell silent in anticipation.

"Tripp?" Wool whispered. "Is it there?"

He opened his eyes but couldn't squeeze the words out.

"Tripp? *Say something*!" Wool squealed as he turned her around to face him.

"I'm so sorry, Wool."

Jelly let out a cat-like whine in reverence for Wool's torment. "Not sad, mommy."

A stream of pink tears ran down Wool's face, "I c-can't…"

"I, uh, don't know what to say."

"Kill me, *please*," Wool grabbed his wrists like a woman possessed and threatened to lash out at everyone, "I *can't* be an Androgyne. It's not true. It's some sort of sick trick. Someone must have put it there—"

THWOCK.

Tripp punched her across the face, knocking her out. She crashed shoulders-first to the floor. Pink saliva shot across the tiles from her lips.

Tripp wiggled his fingers around and ironed out the kinks in his neck, showing little remorse for his actions.

Bonnie, Jaycee and Tor watched Tripp turn to face them and crack his knuckles.

"I'm not proud of what I just did but it was necessary. No one say a damn word."

No one dared say a damn word until Tripp gave his permission. He calmed his breathing and opened his eyes on Wool's snoring face, "When she wakes up, she'll be back to normal. She'll have forgotten this."

"Not stop Shanta. They come," Jelly jumped from the bed and landed on all fours. "I go." One by one, the pads and wires pinged away from her body.

"Who come, honey?" Bonnie squeezed the Rez-9 in her hand.

"Shanta," she swiped the panel on the wall and pressed the end of one of her infinity claws to her chest, "Jelly. Help humans fight. War mage."

The door whizzed open, letting Jelly disappear into the corridor.

"For heaven's sake," Bonnie bolted after her, "Come back, girl."

Jaycee nodded at Tor to follow Bonnie, "Protect the young lady, trooper."

"What with?" Tor held up his bare, decidedly weapon-free hands.

"Your sense of humor?" Jaycee punched him on the back with his broken wrist, "Get out of my sight."

"Oww. Okay, okay," Tor darted out of the room, "Bonnie, I'm coming."

"Are you staying here with Wool? I think we should—" Jaycee turned to Tripp in shock, "What the hell are you doing?"

Tripp inserted the business end of his Rez-9 into his mouth. He hooked his finger around the trigger.

"No."

Jaycee jumped forward and punched the gun out of Tripp's hand.

BLAM!

Jaycee got there in the nick of time. The barrel slid away from Tripp's mouth as the bullet tore through the inside of his cheek. The contents of the left hand side of his face splattered against the wall.

"Are you crazy?" Jaycee kicked the Rez-9 across the tiles and held Tripp's left cheek. "What's gotten into you?"

The right side of Tripp's face convulsed, spitting electrical sparks over his busted titanium cheekbone. The top and bottom rows of his teeth chattered together through the singed synthetic skin.

"I c-c-c-c-cannot-t," the rotors in his eyelids whirred as they windscreen-wiped over his pupils, "J-Jay-Jay-Jay…"

"—Hey," Jaycee screamed into his face. "Knock it off."

THWUNK!

Jaycee thumped Tripp's neck connector back into place. "Don't *ever* do that again."

The two rods in Tripp's throat whirred and lifted his head back into position. His retinas spun around and focused on Jaycee's face.

"Who's ugly now?" Jaycee said.

Tripp felt the cavity on the right side of his face with his fingers, "You bastard."

"Me? I saved you."

"Saved me? Saved me from what?" Tripp's voice flew out of his half-singed lips and the hole in his cheek, "Saved me from an eternity of rest and peace? Screw you."

Tripp planted his palms on Jaycee's chest plates and pushed him back with all his might - enough time for him to dive for the discarded Rez-9 and finish himself off for good.

"Oh, no. No, you don't get to take the easy way out you selfish—" Jaycee kicked himself away from the wall and slid onto his ass, feet-first, priming himself to boot

Tripp up the backside before he reached the gun.

"No, no, no—" Jaycee bent his knees as he barreled toward his friend, "Don't so that—"

Tripp grabbed the grip of the Rez-9 in his hand and rolled onto his back. He jammed the barrel under his jaw and buried it deep into his chin.

THWOCK-BLAM!

Jaycee's boot smashed into Tripp's hand, crunching his mechanical fourth and fifth fingers up and out. They splintered and fizzed away at the knuckle as Rex-9 sprung from his hand.

"Ngggggg," Tripp hopped to his feet and grabbed the K-SPARK strap secured around his chest, "Leave me alone, leave me alone—"

"—Hey," Jaycee bent his elbow, ready to punch Tripp through the window, "You move one damn motor and I'll kill you myself."

"You wanna do me a favor?" Tripp lifted the strap, hoping Jaycee would kill him, "I consider it externally assisted suicide. Come and kill me."

Jaycee clenched his fist, "Don't do this, Tripp."

Tripp lifted the K-SPARK strap over his fizzing, brutalized face. Jaycee jumped forward and pushed him against the wall by his shoulders, 'Stop doing that."

Tile dust coughed down around them as Jaycee slammed Tripp against the wall.

"Damn it, *listen* to me," Jaycee whispered. "You're an Androgyne, right?"

"Yes," Tripp's voice developed a jarring and somewhat inhuman tone since the blast to his head, "I am."

"No one cares, my friend. And why should they? What was it you told me when I found out I was, too?"

"No, don't—"

"—You're a *man*, aren't you?" Jaycee thumped him against the wall, shattering the cracks apart.

"Yes," Tripp muttered through his tears, "I am a man."

Jaycee slapped the good side of Tripp's face, "Don't

you *dare* cry in front of me, Captain."

"I d-don't know what to—

"—You have memories? A loving family, right?"

"Yes. I do."

"What's your son's name?"

"Ryan," Tripp's pink tears sluiced through his shiny, synthetic skeleton. It trickled down his exposed row of teeth, "At least, I th-think he's my son. I'm not so sure, now."

Jaycee screwed his face at the lump of emotional technology he kept pinned against the wall.

"Then as far as everyone's concerned, you're a human being. What's the difference?"

Tripp's broken face revealed he was far from human. Both men knew that the reality of their situation was merely - literally, even - skin deep.

"You may be made of reinforced titanium, but you have a healthy set of organs like any other human. And a fully-functioning brain. You have memories."

"I remember *everything*."

"All that anger deep in your gut? Put it to good use. Focus it at those bastards in *there*." Jaycee pointed at the door with his wiry stump and chucked Tripp forwards.

Wool's eyes fluttered. She pressed her elbows to the ground and groaned. "Oh, oh, my head. I must have fallen asleep."

Tripp moved away from the window and offered his hand to Wool, "Get up."

None of them saw the view of the ocean through the window. If they had, they'd have seen the tree slowly re-emerging in the center. This time, the branches resembled limbs rather than branches.

The spinning sun above it ravaged the sky, creating a soft vortex-like shape amongst the silky white clouds.

"What happened?" Wool groaned and held her forehead. The scratches on her face were still fresh, not that she'd noticed.

"We're going to fight the bad guys—" Tripp threw Jaycee off him and grabbed his K-SPARK in both hands.

"—Wh-where's Jelly?"

"We're going to protect her," Tripp pulled the creases out from Wool's crumpled inner-suit, "Stay here and keep an eye on the E-MRI report. It's the safest place for you."

Wool saw half of Tripp's face was missing, "My God, what happened to your face?"

"I fell."

Jaycee burst with laughter at Tripp's crap retort. At least his friend had finally snapped out his depression.

"That's one hell of a staircase," Wool attempted to touch the broken half of his skull, "It's okay, Tripp. You're human to me. I can't imagine what it must be like discovering you're an Androgyne."

Jaycee shook his head at Wool's fresh naivety, "Better the devil you know, eh?"

"Jaycee, let's go," Tripp walked backwards toward the door and threw Wool a wink with his right eye. A partial success, given his eyebrow had ceased operation, "And I'm sorry for hitting you."

"You hit me?"

"Never mind," Jaycee bounded after Tripp as he walked through the door.

Wool felt the scratch on her cheek, "That explains *that*, then," She turned to the E-MRI image and clicked her finger, "Commence diagnostic report, please."

The abdomen contour glowed a bright pink. "What's *that*?" she whispered, surprised by the image.

"ETA three minutes," advised the machine.

***

Jelly bounded on all fours through the sliding door to Botanix. She slowed down to a cautious crawl, splashing along the three-inch pool of water that had formed from the broken H2O unit.

She lowered her head and lapped away at the water with her tongue.

CRASH-BAM-BAM-SCREECH!

The force field blanketing the broken end of Botanix prevented thousands of Shanta from entering the ship.

Jelly had yet to clock the apocalyptic commotion from outside. She was thirsty, and feeding time came first. Her ears lifted, finally attuned to the chaos that lay fifty feet away.

Bonnie ran into Botanix and clocked the Shanta trying to get in. She slid behind a battered plant and held her Rez-9 at the force field, "Jesus, they're everywhere."

Tor ran in after her and froze solid. "Oh, jeez. *Forget* that." He turned around and made for the door.

"Hey, ass clown," Bonnie pointed her gun at him. He threw his hands up and gasped.

"Where do you think you're going?"

"Um, I thought I'd—"

BLAM!

She fired a warning shot across his shoulder, "You're not going anywhere. You're staying and fighting."

"I don't have a gun."

"I know. We might need you as a protective umbrella, so stick around. Get over by the H2O unit and quit your whining."

"Okay."

It was either get shot by Bonnie or torn apart by those things outside.

"Yeah, that's right," Bonnie smirked as she watched him run, "Our own little maggot bait to hook the fish."

Jelly lifted her head at the word *fish*. She clamped eyes on the Shanta jumping at the force field and growled.

"Jelly, sweetie?" Bonnie yelled, "What are you doing?"

She pushed herself back on her hind legs and squatted on her knees. "Miew," She lifted her behind, straightened her tail and stood up straight for the first time in her life.

"*Good God*," Tor's jaw dropped at the wondrous sight

of Jelly standing up straight like a proper, regular human.

She arched her back and pushed her chest forward. Her arms stretched out sideways. The infinity claws on each hand sprung out like a bladed star.

"Nggggg," she winced and threw her head back, feeling spine adjust and straighten to that of a human. "Uh, uh, uh…"

Tripp and Jaycee stormed into Botanix, ready for war.

"Shhh," Bonnie turned to them and waved them over, "Something's happening to her."

Jaycee clomped over to the opposite wall and sneered at the Shanta. He lifted the mount lever down on the side of his K-SPARK and lowered it to the ground.

"Stand back, people."

The gun's grip folded out in three directions and attached itself to the floor, propping the bulk of the weapon on a tripod. A devastating-looking turret waved its barrel left and right ready to open fire.

"It's armed."

Jelly's hair dropped down the back of her neck. Standing a clear four feet tall, the back of her neck and shoulders suggested she'd formed into a healthy adolescent.

She turned around and faced Tripp, Bonnie, and Jaycee.

"Jelly," Bonnie said, softly. "You're—"

"—I am," she said in her new sultry and husky voice. Only a small semblance of cat remained as the ship hovered a few feet from the grounds, "They like war. Let's give them war."

"Okay, Jelly," Tripp said.

"Then, we go," she finished in her six-year-old girl's voice.

He lifted his K-SPARK in both arms, "Do it."

Gracefully, Jelly twisted around and held her palm out. The pain in her stomach bulged a glowing, bright pink color.

She spread her infinity claws out and held her palm to the force field, humming to herself, "Da-da-da-dumm..."

"Wh-what's she doing?" Tor peered out from behind the water unit.

"Shut up," Bonnie snapped.

The ship's thrusters double-powered, lifting the lip of Botanix up from the sandy surface by a few meters.

A pink beam of light waded through the air from Jelly's stomach and sucked into the padding in her palm.

The infinity claws lit up like a sparkler, surrounding a beautiful pink orb of light between her fingers.

"War... *Mage,*" she whispered softly to herself.

WHOOSH!

She threw the ball of light against the force field and cowered, slapping her tail against the ground, "Quack-quack."

"What?" Tripp blurted.

"Ah. Uh, *duck,*" Jelly giggled, correcting herself.

Bonnie, Tripp and Jaycee turned away and crouched as the ball shattered the force field into a thousand sharp pieces.

The stalactite remains stabbed through the first row of Shanta, severing their limbs and impaling their opened, central mouth-slits.

The badly injured Shanta collapsed to the floor, trampled by the onslaught of hundreds - if not thousands - more.

"Open fire," Tripp began blasting at the swarm of Shanta bouncing across the walls and swinging from the ceiling by their limbs.

BLAM-BLAM-BLAM-BLAMM!

"Get some of that you ugly bastards!

The floor-mounted K-SPARK rotated left and right, firing off sixty rounds per second. The bullets tore through the nearest flurry of Shanta, separating their limbs in a gory torrent of pink liquid.

FLUMP-THRASH!

Tripp sprayed a round of bullets at the Shanta, killing off the Tetris-like build-up of creatures flooding around the planets and walls.

"Tripp, this is Wool," her voice came through his wrist, "Can you read me? Christ, this is urgent."

"What is it Wool? I'm in the middle of a gun-fight."

"Switch to personal headset. This is *amaziant*."

The side of Tripp's burnt ear lit up, transmitting Wool's voice into his head as he fired shots at the oncoming beasts.

Jelly sprinted on all fours over to the H2O unit with Tor and took cover from the battle.

"Hey, Jelly."

She scowled and flipped him her middle infinity claw, "*Hating you.*"

"Tor," Tripp shouted between blasts, "Protect Jelly, or I'll blast your head clean off your shoulders like Landaker."

"What?"

"Protect Anderson."

"Tripp?" Wool yelled into his head, "Personal comms, Tripp. Do you read me?"

"Yes, Wool. I read you. Can't it wait?"

"No. It can't."

Tripp joined Bonnie and blasted a Shanta beast away from the ceiling. Its limbs exploded as the inertia of the bullet pushed it back into the others like a bowling ball against a fresh stack of pins.

Bonnie emptied her magazine into the gory crowd. "I'm out," She flung her Rez-9 at the baying aliens and lifted her knee.

"Look at that," Jaycee booted a creature in the face and blasted its mid-section apart. He pointed at the horizon. The black tree had fully regrown to its enormous size - and developed twelve limb-like branches, "Tripp, man. You seeing this?"

"I'm talking to Wool—" he stopped mid-sentence and clapped eyes on the tree, "Oh, God, it's moving."

The ship jolted around and pushed the edge of Botanix against the sand. The hordes of Shanta crashed along the floor. They spilled over one another and tumbled out of the ship..

A few dozen remained inside and continued to attack.

"We're losing altitude. We've hit the ground," Bonnie held her mechanical leg in her arm and fired a burst of bullets from her toes. She raised her left arm to her face, "Manuel, get us out of here."

"Dr. Whitaker. I cannot engage the thrusters."

"What?" Bonnie backed up to the wall and shot an approaching creature in its mouth-slit. It detonated, contributing to the already-gore-soaked floor with its pink blood and liquefied organs.

"Ugh, this is insane," Bonnie looked at Tor, "You keep Jelly safe, you hear me?"

"Tripp?" Wool shouted over the deafening chaos, "Get Jelly out of there *right now*."

A Shanta jumped from the top of the H2O unit and made for Tripp.

"I can't hear you, hold on," Tripp removed the empty magazine from the K-SPARK grip and tossed it at the creature, "I'm out,' He retrieved his Rez-9 from his belt and aimed it at the monstrosity, "Come and get it, beautiful."

BLAM-BLAM-SCHPLATT!

Five of its limbs splattered in the haze of bullets, pushing what little remained of its body at Tor's feet.

He yelped and stomped on its slit in utter terror, "Ugh, get it away from me."

"Yes, Wool," Tripp said. "What's that? Oh, good."

Jaycee turned to Tripp and raised his eyebrows, "What's up?"

Tripp lowered his gun and turned to Jelly. The news he received was *very* important, "Are you sure?"

Jaycee hopped onto the back of the floor mounted K-

SPARK and aimed it at an influx of Shanta creeping over the dead plants, "Bonnie, reload. Get behind me."

"Thanks," she dived behind him and released her dead magazine to the ground. She kicked it away and palmed a fresh magazine into the grip, "Reloading!"

"I understand, Wool." Jelly's cowering reflected in Tripp's glazed eyes. "I'll… *God*… I'll send her back up."

"Tripp, what's going on?" Bonnie held her foot up and blasted three Shanta creatures to smithereens with her leg.

BLAM-BLAM-BLAM-KA-SCHPLATT!

She took out three Shanta in a row with three shots, "Tripp, what's—"

"—Hey, Tor," Tripp barked. "Take Jelly back up to Medix right now."

"What?"

"Do it," Tripp blasted another creature out of the ship.

SCHTAAAMMM! SCHTAAAM!

The one-hundred-foot tree in the middle of the ocean thumped its first limb to the sand, followed by the second. The pink sky swirled around like milk pouring into a freshly-stirred cup of coffee.

"Get her out of here, numbnuts," Tripp barked.

Tor offered Jelly his hand, more than happy to escape battle, "Come with me. Take my hand."

"Hisssss," she scowled at him and swiped her infinity claws at his face.

"Uh, Tripp?" Tor struggled, "I don't think she likes me. She doesn't want to go."

"Jelly, *bad* girl," Bonnie shouted at her, "Go with Tor. He'll take you to Wool. It's for your own safety."

Jelly bushed her tail out in a fit of rage, disobeying a direct order. She bolted out of Botanix, refusing Tor's offer to escort her.

"Damn it, Tor," Bonnie screamed at him, "Go and make sure she gets to Medix."

"Okay."

He ran through the door and into the corridor after

Jelly, "Come back, girl."

Bonnie held her fists up as the approaching Shanta. She roared at them to come closer, "Ever heard of Jitsaku, you ugly critters?"

She punched the first one in the mouth with such force, its bone-like frame cracked in two and released a jellied substance - possibly its brain - to the ground, "That's today's training over with," she said, butting her palms together.

The tree spider-climbed out of the ocean. The sheer size and weight of the monstrosity created a mini tidal wave, clearing some of the Shanta away in seemingly extreme slow motion.

"What did Wool say?" Bonnie asked Tripp.

Jaycee's turret cleared enough of the approaching creatures to enable everyone to reload.

Tripp replaced his Rez-9 with a full magazine and aimed it at the hoard of approaching Shanta.

"Answer me, Tripp," Bonnie took aim at the army of beasts with her K-12 Combat leg-firearm. The tree's ungodly stomps cracked the ground. It creaked the top of its body and squealed into the sky.

Certain death was on the way.

"I only have one mag left," Tripp said, avoiding the question. "Jaycee, you got any fresh?"

"Nah, I'm out. I got like two left, but they're for the turret. It's the only thing keeping these damn space invaders from smothering us."

"Tripp," Bonnie stomped her smoking, mechanical leg to the ground, catching his attention, "Are you gonna answer me?"

Space Opera Beta slammed to the ground. The thrusters died out. The vibrations in the ship came to a halt.

The trio were twenty seconds away from a stampede of Shanta and the unfathomably large God-like antagonist that stormed behind them, wanting to finish off the job once and for all.

"Tripp?"

The Shanta pummeled through the wall and flooded into Botanix in great quantity.

Tripp cocked his K-SPARK and aimed at the first of at least a thousand creatures.

"Get ready guys," Jaycee punched the back of the floor-mounted K-SPARK turret, "It's do or die time."

BLAM-BLAM-BLAMM-MM!

The turret swung left and right, unleashing its final magazine at the swathes of approaching Shanta.

Tripp squeezed his trigger and blasted the first of the creatures to messy, pink pieces.

"What did Wool say?" Bonnie asked. "What's up with Jelly?"

Tripp trained one eye on her and then immediately back to the approaching monsters. He hooked his finger around the trigger, prepared to take a shot at the next creature.

"She's pregnant."

Acknowledgements

For K

Also to:

My immediate family.
The CVB Gang Members / ARC Street Team.
Jolene Huber, the real captain of the ship.
Jennifer Long, the "Bonnie" of stalkers.
Adele Embrey, the "Androgyne" of proofing.
The members and admins of 20BooksTo50K.

Up next… Star Cat 3: War Mage.

The universe is one hell of a *mother*.

mybook.to/StarCat3

Get Your FREE ebook

Subscribe to the
Chrome Valley Books mailing list!

The prequel to the **Star Cat** series.

Just type the link below
in your internet browser!

bit.ly/CVBSubscribe

Join the **Chrome Valley Books Advanced Reader Group**

1: You'll get each hot, new release before launch.
2: Each release has a party and freebies and giveaways.
3: Exclusive material is *always* forthcoming.

All we ask for is an honest review at Amazon and Goodreads! Please email me for details

andrew@chromevalleybooks.com

Follow me at Amazon for all the latest releases
Amazon (US) - bit.ly/AndrewMackayAuthorUS
Amazon (UK) - bit.ly/AndrewMackayAuthorUK

About the author

Andrew Mackay is an author, screenwriter and film critic. A former teacher, Andrew writes in multiple genres: satire, crime, horror, romantic thrillers and sci-fi.

His passions include daydreaming, storytelling, smoking, caffeine, and writing about himself in the third person.

A word from the author

I hope you enjoyed this book. Please check out my other books at Amazon and remember to follow me there.

If you enjoyed the book, please leave a review online at Amazon US, UK and Goodreads. Reviews are integral for authors and I would dearly appreciate it.

I love to engage directly with my readers. Please get in touch with me - I look forward to hearing from you. ***Happy reading!***

Email: *andrew@chromevalleybooks.com*

NOTE: If you purchased this title at Amazon, then you can download the e-book version for **FREE** with Kindle Matchbook. The last pages of the e-book version contains exclusive author notes and behind-the-scenes material for each title. It's a real treat for fans, so *download it now*! ☺

CPSIA information can be obtained
at www.ICGtesting.com
Printed in the USA
LVHW04s1603021018
592154LV00001B/28/P